Inheritance

WELCOME TO SEA PORT
BOOK TWO

KATRINA JACKSON

Editor: A.K. Edits

Cover artist: Celia Moscote

Cover designer: Katrina Jackson

To Kai-
Thank you for your keen eye and all your tears.

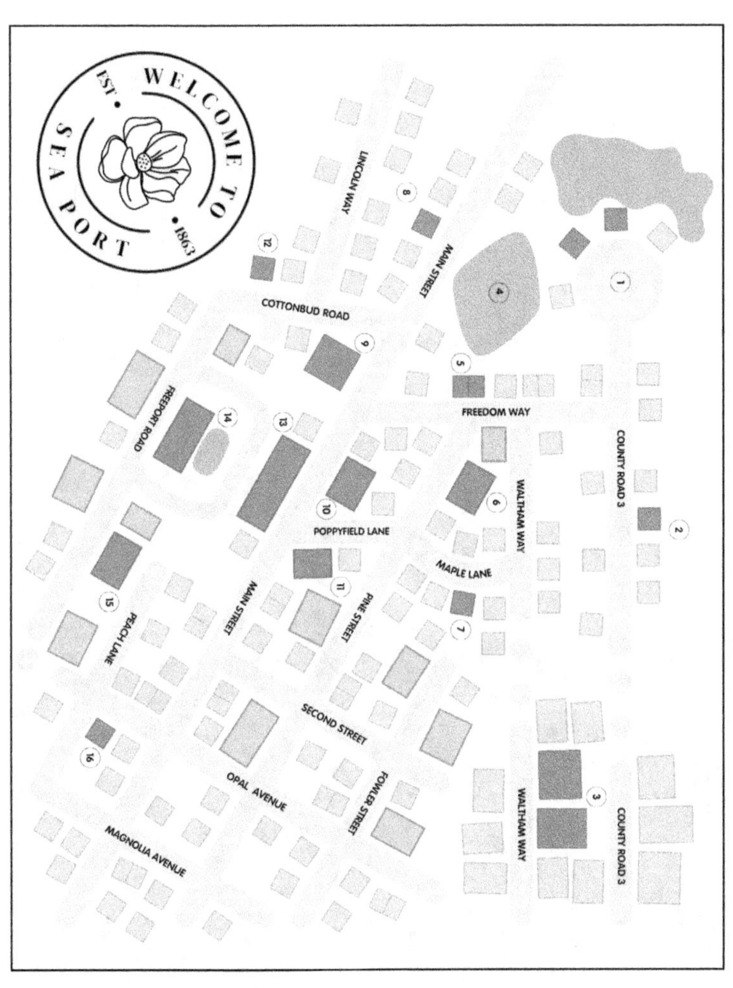

WELCOME TO
SEA PORT
EST. 1863
LINCOLN WAY
COTTONBUD ROAD
MAIN STREET
FREEDOM WAY
COUNTY ROAD 3
FREEPORT ROAD
WALTHAM WAY
POPPYFIELD LANE
MAPLE LANE
PINE STREET
MAIN STREET
PEACH LANE
SECOND STREET
FOWLER STREET
OPAL AVENUE
MAGNOLIA AVENUE
WALTHAM WAY
COUNTY ROAD 3
1
2
3
4
5
6
7
8
9
10
11
12
13
14
15
16

Map Legend

 1. Perv Place
 2. Santos's house
 3. Freedom and Waltham farms
 4. Douglass Park
 5. Sully and Willie's duplex
 6. Confections
 7. Mary/Lorraine's cottage
 8. The Grove
 9. Knox's apartment
10. Sully's
11. Sunnyside Diner
12. Jonah's house
13. Sea Port Administrative Building*
14. Orange Grove County Library
15. La Bella Rosa
16. Bria's house

　　*containing the Firehouse, Mayor's Office, Police Precinct, and Post Office

Content Warnings

Grief (parental death)
Allusions to abusive family dynamics
Allusions to racism

WELCOME TO SEA PORT

Mary

"Are we going to do this? Or are you two just fucking with me to make me late?"

Before she moved to Sea Port, Mary Woods hadn't been much of a morning person. She used to be an unhappy academic who slept in because facing her life — her students and her colleagues — made her physically ill. By the time she was denied tenure, her body was riddled with anxiety, and stress had her muscles so tight she had to stretch first thing in the morning and right before bed just to stand up straight in lecture. She used to crawl into bed long past midnight because it was just easier to face the mountain of work she hated in the dark with a large glass or two of wine.

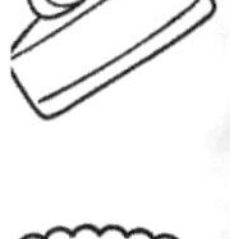

But that was her life before Sea Port.

Since she moved to this town so small she could hardly find it on a map, everything about her life had turned upside down. In Sea Port, she was living her entrepreneurial dreams as owner and head baker of her own bakery, Confections by

Mary, which meant she was in the kitchen before sunrise baking teacakes, brownies, and muffins.

Oh my.

And for the past few months, she'd been waking up a little bit earlier than normal to spend a little more time with her boyfriends.

Yep, that's right. Boyfriends. Plural.

Dating had never been Mary's strong suit. She'd done the apps and hated them, she'd met random men at even more random bars and blocked their numbers within weeks. No matter what she tried, she'd never been able to make a relationship work until she moved to Sea Port and two fine men, Knox and Santos, fell right into her...lap.

Knox had moved to Sea Port first, taking over as the town's fire chief. From what Mary could tell, most of his work consisted of applying for grants and being everyone's friend, two things he excelled at. He was so good at his job — and so universally liked, for a Transplant — that Mayor Waltham had bullied him into accepting a seat on the City Council — a role he grumbled about hating but clearly loved. Santos moved to Sea Port next, Knox's old friend from the Marines. He joined the tiny police department with a calculated plan to take over as soon as the only other officers retired. In just under a year, Santos had gently ushered his superiors into a comfortable retirement and now he was the new chief of Sea Port Police.

They'd each moved to this small town looking to start over but hadn't expected their lives to look quite like this. Well, Santos might have been pining for Knox, but Mary had been shocked to find two fine ass men in her new town and for them both to be interested in her. And each other. Her new life was better than she could've dreamed. She was in love and happy but running late.

Mary pressed her back against the headboard on their California King bed — the bed they'd had to ask Mr. Wright to build rather than drive four hours each way to order one at the closest furniture store. It took up nearly their entire master bedroom, but Mary sure wasn't complaining — not about the size of the bed, at least.

"Hurry up," she whined, her fingers circling her clit. Her eyes darted to the clock on the bedside table. "We're running out of time."

Santos and Knox weren't the only people with new roles in town. Mayor Waltham had recommended Mary to the Sea Port Welcome Committee almost as soon as her relationship with Knox and Santos went public. Sure, Mary could've turned her down, but no one turned Willie down — not Transplants or Porties — and everyone knew that recom-mendations from Willie Waltham were just shy of orders. So now, in between her busy schedule at the bakery and making up for years of celibacy, Mary was also working as a part-time property manager for Sea Port's new arrivals, whether she wanted to or not.

Mary worried Mayor Waltham was trying to maneuver her into becoming an official town representative, but she resolved to cross that bridge when they inevitably got to it. In the meantime, she had a meeting in less than an hour and a burning desire to get off one more time before she absolutely had to shower, make herself presentable, and meet the town's new librarian at Mary's old cottage.

Unfortunately, Santos and Knox were not cooperating. Well, not completely.

They were laid across the middle of the bed, arms wrapped around one another's torsos, legs entwined and kissing one another with a quiet passion. Mary was enjoying the view — little flashes of their tongues twisting together, blunt fingers moving over a hairy chest — all enough to make her shiver but not come. And Mary wanted to come.

 "Stop making out! I don't have time for this," she warned, not that they listened to her.

Knox kissed his way across Santos's jawline to his neck. 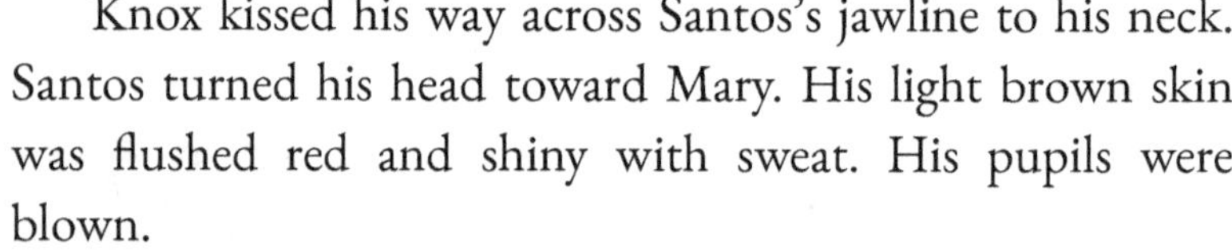 Santos turned his head toward Mary. His light brown skin was flushed red and shiny with sweat. His pupils were blown.

 Mary dipped two fingers into her pussy and he smiled, shifting his hips into Knox. "You said you could watch us kiss all day and be happy," Santos mumbled in a deep, horny voice that made her clit throb.

 "Believe me, I am *very* happy," she moaned, pushing her fingers deeper inside herself. The sound of her own wetness was obscenely loud in their otherwise quiet bedroom. "And horny," she added at the last minute.

 Knox laughed softly as he suckled on Santos's earlobe. The bed creaked slightly as their dry humping started to pick up momentum. Finally. Mary's fingers sped up with them.

"This isn't enough?" Santos asked with a playful grin on his face. But then he groaned loudly, his eyes dipped closed,  and he reached between their bodies. Knox moaned next. It was different when they were together, still gentle but also rough, as if they liked to push each other just a little bit further than they could with her. It was nice to be all in the mix, but Mary didn't mind stepping aside every now and then to enjoy the view with a few fingers shoved into her aching pussy.

Besides, Santos got off on teasing them, making every moment last as long as possible, and the orgasms were always worth the wait. But two could play that game. 

She pulled her fingers from her sex and shoved them into her mouth.

Santos's eyes lowered to hungry slits as he slid off Knox's  body, finally giving Mary an unobstructed view of his hand on Knox's shaft. He momentarily let go and licked his palm before grabbing Knox's dick again. 

"Fuck," Knox gasped, lifting his hips into Santos's hold.

"Satisfied?" Santos asked.

Mary smirked and pulled her knees wider, slipping her  fingers back inside. "No. You know what I want," she moaned, trying not to fuck herself over the edge too soon.

Knox moaned loudly, smiling up at the ceiling. "Are we  pieces of meat to you?" he gasped, hips bucking under Santos's rough stroke.

Mary pulled her fingers free and then crawled across the  bed to Knox. He turned toward her, a blissed-out smile on his face, his gorgeous dark eyelashes fluttering. She slipped her wet fingers into his mouth.

"That's rich coming from you," she whispered, watching  him lick the taste of her pussy from her skin.

Santos started kissing Knox's neck, then made a pathway down his chest. 

"Meaning?" Knox groaned.

Mary caressed his bottom lip. "Meaning the two of you literally used me all night long, throwing me around like a rag doll." Her pussy clenched remembering just how little sleep they'd gotten last night. She didn't feel an ounce of regret.

"You said you liked it." A thread of worry seeped into Knox's voice.

She kissed the tip of his nose. "I loved it."

He was about to respond, but out of the corner of her eye, Mary saw Santos lean down and suck Knox's shaft into his mouth down to the root. Knox moaned around her fingers, and Mary moved her free hand back to her pussy, pinching her clit.

"Is his throat tighter than my pussy, Sergeant?" she moaned.

"Fuck," Knox cried out. "Wait. Wait." But it was too late. Knox came and Santos swallowed it all before lifting to his knees.

He wiped at his smile. "Not fair," he panted, his voice rough. She blossomed under the proud look on his face.

"I learned from the best."

Knox panted out a laugh. "You sure did."

"Can we stop fucking around now?" she asked. "Please..."

It was a dirty trick, she knew, to say 'please' in just the way they liked, but she really was running out of time.

"Get on your back," Knox said. He was still panting, but his voice had that hard, commanding tone that made Santos's balls churn and Mary's pussy shiver.

"Yes, sir, Sergeant," she whispered, happy to ease them along.

They both glared at her as she scrambled into position. She started massaging her breasts, far too close to chance even touching her clit again. Santos helped Knox onto his knees and they kissed, but with a little more urgency this time. Mary was still impatient, but she knew what was coming and that eased her frantic desire. Well, that and rolling her nipples between her fingers.

They didn't need to talk now. They'd been together for just long enough, had learned so much about one another's bodies, desires, and needs that when they got into a groove, they could get one another off with surprising ease and intensity. Mary had never experienced anything like this before.

Knox whispered something to Santos, and the two laughed quietly before Santos crawled up her body. He kissed her toes until she giggled, charting a path up her shins to her knees, an unexpected erogenous zone they'd discov-ered together. He pushed her knees to the bed and kissed his way up her left thigh. She hissed when he licked her slit. She was still sore from last night so Santos didn't linger at her opening, licking his way up to her clit, circling the hard nub of her arousal with the tip of his tongue.

"Keep going, Marine," Knox said.

Santos looked up Mary's body with a grin and nipped at the softest, roundest part of her stomach.

"God, yes," she moaned.

Santos placed soft kisses over her stomach and up to her left breast to lick at her nipple and set some of his weight on top of her. This had become one of their favorite positions, even if the first time they'd tried it had been a mess of tangled legs and trapped arms. They'd been forced to abandon it at the time out of fear they'd sprain an ankle or worse, but they weren't quitters. Once they got the hang of it... Mary moaned when Santos slipped his tongue into her mouth,

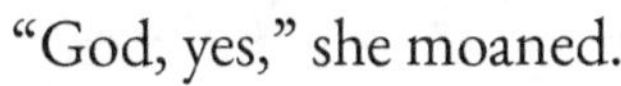

giving her a taste of Knox's release. His hips settled perfectly between her legs and his long, hard shaft put just enough pressure on her clit to keep her wet and get her off. Eventually.

Santos wrapped his arms around her back, holding her close and tight, while Knox got his dick slick and ready.

Mary closed her eyes and held on tight to Santos's body, waiting for the telltale signs of Knox entering him slow and gentle. Santos grunted onto her tongue in desperate pleasure as Knox rocked him right onto Mary's clit. She kissed and sucked and licked at him, running her hands up and down his spine, reaching for Knox over the arch of Santos's lower back and butt.

Mary and Santos held onto one another as Knox picked up the pace, pressing his hips forward in one short, sharp slap and then pulling back for more, faster and faster each time. At some point, Santos couldn't kiss her anymore. All he could do was pant and moan into her mouth, and Mary was happy to receive it.

None of them would last much longer; Knox made sure of that. He leaned over Santos's back, putting more of his weight onto them as he fucked his way into Santos's ass. Mary reached for Knox and pulled him into a kiss while Santos groaned into the crook of her neck. She was so fucking close.

If they angled it perfectly, she'd come just like this. If the angle was right but not perfect, she'd be dripping wet by the time they came and someone, anyone, would happily suck her pussy until she did. The exact kind of loving care that made the life they'd built together so amazing.

"You alright?" Knox panted against her mouth.

Knox was so beautiful like this, sweaty, happy, horny, and loved.

"Harder," she moaned.

"We aren't hurting you?" he panted back, the question punctuated by the sharp sound of his skin slapping into Santos's ass. 

"No, baby, I promise."

Santos cried out in a voice so deep it made Mary shudder. He was closer than either of them, falling apart between them where he was safe. 

"Where's he gonna come?" she moaned.

Knox's eyebrows knit together for a minute. There were so many options, but when that toothy grin spread across his mouth, she knew he had an idea. 

It took a bit of repositioning but soon enough, Santos came in Mary's mouth, Knox came in Santos's ass, Mary rubbed her clit to her own release, and now she could really start the day. 

She would've loved to enjoy the afterglow but— "Fuck, I'm gonna be late!" She wiped her chin and pushed Santos out of the way, scrambling to her feet. 

Mary rushed into their en suite bathroom and took the hottest, quickest shower she could stand. She brushed her teeth and washed her face in record time, all while Knox and Santos crawled back under the sheets. They watched Mary rush around the room like she was their favorite TV show. And when she almost killed herself stepping into her panties,  Knox had the nerve to laugh. Santos suggested she go without them. Neither seemed fazed when she glared in their direction.

"Who are you meeting again?" Santos asked.

Mary was putting on her bra, a task that always seemed exponentially harder when she was in a rush. "The new librarian," she huffed.

"Oh, she's got your old place, right?" Knox added.

"Yeah. And then I'm taking her to the library."

"You mean the construction site," Santos said, joining Knox in laughter.

She threw a sundress over her head and pulled the satin ponytail holder from her hair. Her big, soft curls fell around her ears. "How do I look?"

Mary normally knew better than to ask them this question because they couldn't be trusted, but she wanted to make a good impression. Mayor Waltham was a little intense on a good day, but even more so when it came to Transplant greetings. Sea Port was an acquired taste and the goal of the Welcome Committee was to put the town's best foot forward.

The small group of funny, flighty older women who'd welcomed Mary to town and fussed over her had made her feel welcome, even if her cat, Cat-leen Cleaver, had hissed at them during their visit.

In Cat-leen's defense, she'd been drugged and caged for the drive down south.

In any case, Mary wanted to pay that good will forward and provide the new librarian with a stellar welcome, even if she was a minute or two later than planned.

"You look like you should be naked," Santos said.

Mary rolled her eyes and switched her attention to Knox.

"You look beautiful," he said with a smile. "Also, I can see your nipples."

She was about to gently cuss them out when an alarm on

her phone started blaring, announcing that she needed to leave now or else. "Shit," she said, running from the bedroom to the sound of Santos's and Knox's laughter.

Thankfully, Sea Port was tiny. She'd have to power walk there, but she wouldn't be more than a few seconds late. If that! 

Hers might not be the most put-together welcome wagon, but she was a walking billboard for the Sea Port  Relocation Initiative. Where she was once an unhappy academic, she was now a successful small-town baker, happy and  well-fucked.

Amen.

WELCOME TO SEA PORT

TWO

Lorraine

"Please don't do this."

"I'm gonna."

"Okay, but I'm asking you to consider *not* doing this."

Lorraine had been standing in the middle of her living room, half-packed boxes littered around the floor and her favorite smooth jazz radio station playing in the background.  Her arms were stuffed with books from the shelves that weren't emptying fast enough for her liking.

She surveyed the boxes at her feet, looking for places to slip a few more books but coming up empty.

"Lorraine. Lorraine Freeman, do you hear me?" her best  friend, DeJuan, asked.

She glared over her shoulder in DeJuan's direction. He  was lounging on her emerald velvet couch, elegantly holding a glass of rosé in his hand, not helping her pack. Technically, he was here to help her get through some of the wine she'd been meaning to drink for ages, but it wouldn't have killed him to pack a box or five.

"I heard you, Juan. I just haven't changed my mind. I'm gonna do it."

"Why are you so hardheaded?"

She exhaled with a shrug. "Unfortunately, it's in my DNA."

"Okay, but nature versus nurture," he cried dramatically.

"I got screwed both ways," she said.

"Well," he laughed, taking another sip of his wine. "But you're gonna be so far away. How will I get to you when you inevitably implode your life again?"

"You'll put the plane ticket on your credit card like always. Also...implode? Really? That's a little harsh."

"Things can be harsh and true," he said, tipping his glass in her direction.

Lorraine rolled her eyes and went back to her boxes, finding a spot for a slim volume of *Rachel* by Angelina Weld Grimké. One book down, far too many still to count.

"Juan, you're my best friend. I trust you with my life, my heart, and the spare keys to my apartment. If I go on vacation to the Caribbean and call you with the ludicrous news that I'm engaged to a Jamaican man twenty years younger than me, *you* are the person I expect to max out your credit card, hop on a plane, and come smack some sense into me."

"Natch," DeJuan breathed with an elegant tip of his head and a demure sip of his drink.

"And because we are the only two peas in this pod, I also expect you to find your own Jamaican man for us to foolishly marry together."

"Spring Break 2030," he laughed, even as he nodded seriously.

"Absolutely. But I'm still taking this job. And nothing you say will change my mind."

DeJuan inhaled loudly in annoyance, glaring at her across the room. When he exhaled, he leaned back onto her couch and took another deeper sip of wine. "Fine. I just had to do my due diligence." 

"I appreciate you."

"But if this turns out to have been the worst decision of your life, remember that I tried to stop you." 

"Deal," she said, right as she spotted an empty box across the room. Lorraine wound her way through the maze of packing materials and carefully placed the books in her arms into the box, arranging them neatly to maximize the space. "Perfect." 

Lorraine grabbed her own wine glass from the side table next to DeJuan and took a large gulp of a Spanish red her ex — not her last ex, the one before that — bought her to celebrate three months together. She broke up with him two days later, but his exceptional taste in wine endured. 

"So where the hell are you moving again?"

Lorraine took another sip and racked her brain.

"Dear Lord," DeJuan groaned.

"I remember," she cried, and it came to her by the time she opened her mouth again. "It's a town called Sea Port." 

"Never heard of it."

"Me neither. Don't bother trying to find it on Google Maps. I literally had to put in actual coordinates to find the town *next* to it." 

"Oh, I don't have time for all that," DeJuan said, shaking

his head in disgust. "Also, this sounds like the start of a horror movie. Girl, why are you trying to star in a horror movie?"

"I need a little thrill," she said with a wink.

"Girl, if you wanna get your heart racing, you can come to a circuit party with me. You ain't gotta move to the middle of nowhere."

Lorraine coughed on her wine. "No. Risky sex is not for me. I'd rather play games with my credit score," she said, wading back into the mess of packing.

"Your priorities are wild," he whispered.

"The feeling's mutual. Throw me that roll of packing tape."

DeJuan tossed her a new roll of tape and she loaded it onto the industrial-sized dispenser. She took a deep breath and started the long process of closing all these boxes of books she'd decided to ship to Sea Port. She'd already dropped a few boxes off at her old job for their next book sale event and given away some special copies to some of her favorite patrons, but she still had so many more books to sort through.

And because he knew her so well, DeJuan said the exact thing she'd been thinking all day. "Do you need to take *all* these books with you? Can't you sell some?"

Lorraine chewed on her bottom lip, refusing to meet her friend's eyes. "I already sold almost a hundred books when I got the job offer. I gave away another hundred and fifty at least."

"Oh, girl, you have a problem."

"I'm a librarian."

"Which is even worse. You work in a library. You don't

need to live in one as well." He stood from the couch and gingerly stepped over extra packing tape and boxes, as if he was worried even touching one of the boxes would obligate him to tape it shut.

Lorraine knew DeJuan was right; she didn't *need* all these books, but she wanted to keep as many as she could.  They were cherished possessions — books she'd lugged with her from her college dorms to every apartment since, books  that had changed her life when she needed it — and she wanted them at her fingertips at a given notice. She wanted her copy of *Wuthering Heights* for when her seasonal depres-  sion ran amok and the copy of *Their Eyes Were Watching God* with all her notes in the margins. Some of the books she probably could have let go, but she wasn't ready to make  those decisions just yet. She might never be ready. Besides, she was upending her life to take a job in a small town in the middle of nowhere that no one could find on a map; she  didn't have time to think through why.

"You gonna help?" she asked DeJuan.

He was pouring an extra-large glass of a Sauvignon Blanc  now. "I am helping."

She rolled her eyes. "With the books," she corrected, knowing full well he knew what she meant.

"You invited me here to get giggly drunk and that's what  I'm doing," he said, taking a long sip of his drink.

"You gon' miss me when I'm gone," she said.

He glanced at the mostly full bar cart which would be going to his apartment when she left. "I'll remember you every time I make a cocktail," he said, breaking into a little tipsy giggle while Lorraine started taping the first heavy ass box of books closed.

A week later, Lorraine's apartment was empty, most of her belongings were already on their way to Sea Port, and she had her essentials, including satin sheets and a well-loved copy of *Sula,* in her car. She was officially ready to go. She dropped her keys into the rent slot in the lobby of her apartment and slipped out of town in the middle of the night.

The first few hours of her road trip were lovely. Just her, empty dark roads, and a perfectly curated road trip playlist, but after a few hours on dark interstate high-ways, the excitement started to wear off and the doubts began to settle in. DeJuan wasn't the only person who thought Lorraine was making a rash decision, he was just the only one in her life to say it to her face, and the truth was that there was a small part of Lorraine's brain that agreed with him. She'd put on a good show of pretending she didn't have any doubts, but once she was all alone and the gas station coffee had her brain wired, she was prepared for those doubts to intensify. It never happened.

On that first night of her road trip, Lorraine drove over the metaphorical cliff of good sense and it felt fucking amaz-ing. Two days later, however, Lorraine finally pulled into Sea Port butt ass early in the morning, tired and feeling anything but amazing. Her back hurt, her ass had gone numb fifty miles ago, her eyes were bloodshot, and she really needed a hot shower and a week spent entirely unconscious on a pillow-top mattress.

Her stomach grumbled as she turned immediately off Main Street onto Poppyfield Lane. "Food," she mumbled to herself. "Lord, I need food." 

She drove down a quiet, almost rural street, passing wide, neat lawns. She stopped at the next corner even though there was no stop sign in sight. But there weren't any  other cars on the street either, so she unlocked her phone to go over her welcome email again. She was renting a small house for half what her compact one-bedroom luxury apart-  ment had cost. When she'd told DeJuan how much they were charging in rent, he'd briefly considered moving with her before reality hit, which was for the best since the email contained directions to her new place because they figured  her GPS wouldn't work in town. And it hadn't.

She read over the directions again and then eased her foot onto the gas. Her head swiveled left and right as she  took stock of her new town and all it had to offer. Mostly she saw houses that had seen better days but were still  lovingly preserved. That, if nothing else, was a good sign.

Lorraine's contract with the Orange Grove County Public Library was for one year with the option to extend indefinitely if she wanted. Considering how far this town was from anything even resembling a big city, she highly  doubted she'd be taking them up on that offer, but she resolved to give this job her best for as long as she was here. 

At Maple Lane, she turned right and started looking out for the member of the town's Welcome Committee. Because of course, Sea Port had a welcome committee.

"Eight twenty-four Maple Lane," she repeated to

herself, squinting across the sprawling lawns, trying to decipher the house numbers from afar. She couldn't see them, so she turned back to the email, noticing the description of the house at the end of the email for the first time.

"Yellow with a dark gray roof," she read.

Lorraine lifted her gaze back to the street and spotted someone on the sidewalk walking in her direction. The woman's dark brown skin was gleaming in the early morning sun, contrasting perfectly with her palm tree print sundress. Her big, curly afro bounced with her little steps. It had been an hour since Lorraine had seen another person and her mood brightened instantly.

The woman stopped in front of a house that just about fit the description in her email and raised her arm in the air, waving at Lorraine. If this was her welcome to Sea Port, it was the cutest welcome she could've imagined. The woman pointed at a spot along the curb and Lorraine followed her directions.

She gratefully turned the car off, took a deep breath, and then finished the last of the bottle of water in the center console. She had to ease her stiff body from the car and stretch before she could greet the woman. "Oh god," she groaned at her tight back. "Never road tripping again."

"Um, are you Lorraine?" the woman asked.

"I am," she said. "Are you the welcome committee?" she asked, stepping carefully onto the sidewalk.

"I am. My name's Mary," she trilled, sticking her hand out. "Welcome to Sea Port!"

Lorraine offered her hand with a skeptical squint. "Are you a morning person?"

"Absolutely," she said. "What time did you leave Port Graham?"

Lorraine had considered driving through the night to take a few hours off her trip but decided to stop at Port Graham, one of the bigger towns nearby, to get a few hours' sleep. "Three in the morning," she croaked. 

Mary's face fell. "Why?"

"I wanted to beat the morning rush," Lorraine said, real- izing how foolish that sounded now that she was here and hadn't passed more than five cars on this last lonely stretch of her trip.

"What rush?" Mary laughed.

"Yeah, I get that now," Lorraine laughed. "Sorry you had to meet me this early."

Mary's smile brightened and she shook her head, dark curls bouncing happily. "No worries, I was up. You look exhausted."

Lorraine yawned. "I am. It took me two days to get here. I might not look like it, but I am really happy to be here and I'm really thankful you agreed to meet me. I'm not sure what I would've done until things opened," she said, looking around at the sleepy street. "What time do things open?"

Mary swatted away her gratitude. "Now," she said brightly. "And you don't have to thank me, I swear I was in your shoes what feels like yesterday. I'm happy to pay this forward."

"You're not a Sea Port native?"

"They call themselves Porties, and no, I'm not. I moved here from back East. I used to teach literature in a university ten times the size of this place. I'm originally from California, though."

Lorraine's attention snapped to Mary. In all her time preparing to move to Sea Port, she'd held her reservations close to her chest. Sure, she'd spent the last three months assuring DeJuan this was a good decision, but that was because he could be overbearing when he wanted. At the end of the day, Lorraine knew this was a professionally risky move, but it was a move she wanted to make.

Her last job had been nice, but not quite right. She liked the city, her coworkers, and her patrons, but the job had no growth potential. Her boss had promised her raises and new positions eventually, but they both knew eventually could be next month or never. Lorraine couldn't wait for either.

In Sea Port, she'd be the head librarian. It paid a fraction of what she'd been making at her last job, but she balanced the salary cut with the cost of living and hoped for the best. Besides, money wasn't the reason she took this job. Lorraine had loved books her entire life. When she was six or seven, she'd read a book about a library in a small town full of people who looked like her. She couldn't remember the name anymore, but she could remember the exact moment she realized that was the life she wanted. When she stumbled on the Sea Port job ad, the town's history made her think of that book and the way it made her feel.

Nostalgia was a ridiculous reason to derail her career, but Lorraine believed in living every day like it was her first. She uploaded her résumé to the Sea Port Relocation Initiative's website and the rest was history.

But now she was standing in front of someone who'd made the same gamble and all those doubts resurfaced again. "Did you have to adjust to living here?" Lorraine whispered.

Mary let out a big, booming, pretty laugh. She laughed

so hard and long, Lorraine became convinced that either Mary hated Sea Port or she was the happiest person she'd ever met. There was a dark bruise on Mary's neck just under her left ear that looked like a fading hickey and it made Lorraine look at Mary in a new way. She knew what a well-fucked woman looked like, which maybe explained something. 

When her laughter finally petered out, Mary wiped at her wet eyes. "I definitely had to adjust. I went from a medium-sized city with people everywhere to...this," she said, looking around. "Like where even are we?" 

"Oh my god, right?" Lorraine gasped.

Mary nodded. "But honestly, as soon as I got here, I felt..." Her voice trailed off as she closed her eyes and exhaled. "I felt free. I think this place has a lot to offer. That's why I'm here." 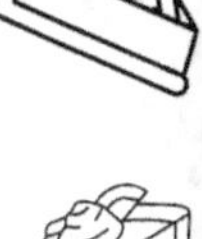

Lorraine tried not to be envious of anyone, but she tasted a dollop of envy on her tongue, but it dissipated quickly. And then she decided that she liked Mary. She was a bit too cheery for first thing in the morning, but she seemed sweet and kind and she smelled faintly of vanilla. 

How could she *not* like her?

"But hey, we can talk about Sea Port's virtues some other time. You probably want to shower and sleep, right?" 

"Oh my god, yes," Lorraine breathed. "I know the Mayor said there's a tour, and I want to see the library, of course, but—" 

Mary shook her head firmly. "I don't have to do any of that right now. How about I help you bring your bags inside, and whenever you wake up, you can meet me at my shop? I'll give you the walking tour of downtown Sea Port, 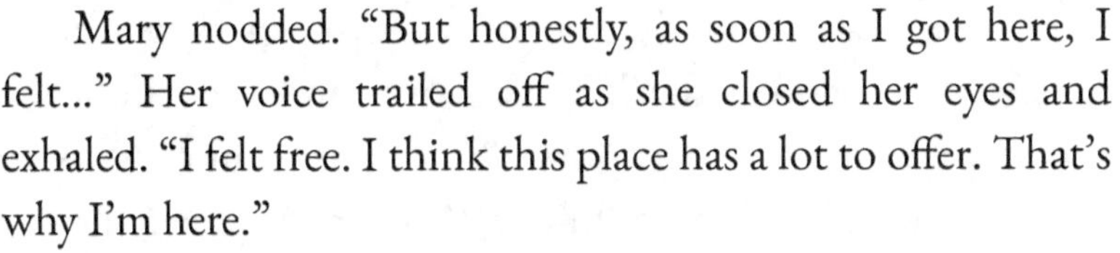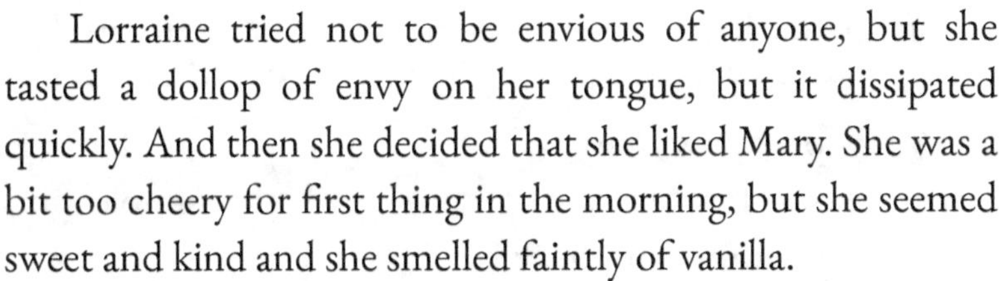

including the soon-to-be newly renovated, state-of-the-art Orange Grove County Library." Mary said the last words while raising her hands in the air as if unveiling a banner, a mischievous smile on her face.

"That sounds perfect," Lorraine replied, stifling another yawn.

It only took two trips each for Lorraine and Mary to unload her car.

At the door, Mary lifted a leather keychain shaped like a cotton flower with two keys hanging from the ring. "Front door," she said, holding up one key. She pointed at the other. "Shed door. I lived here when I first moved here too. This place was wonderful to me. I hope you'll be happy here." Mary handed the keychain over and then pulled a brown paper bag from her purse. "Also, I brought muffins."

"Oh my god, I'm so hungry!" Lorraine cried, nearly dropping the keys in her excitement. She pulled the bag open and shoved her face inside. "These smell amazing."

Mary practically beamed at her, pointing at the bag. "Confections by Mary," Lorraine read the simple and tasteful logo printed on the front.

"I'm Mary," she laughed. "And Confections is just down the block." She pointed to her left. "Turn right at the corner onto Pine Street. You can't miss it. Just follow the smell of sugar and vanilla.'

"I can do that," Lorraine said distractedly. She heard Mary's instructions, but most of her attention was on the top she was breaking off the chocolate muffin. She popped the piece of goodness into her mouth, nodded, and then closed her mouth on a pleased moan.

"That's what I love to hear. Alright, I'll leave you to

yourself. See you later," Mary said, jogging down the porch steps. She waved at Lorraine and then strolled back the way she came.

Lorraine closed and locked the door, kicked off her shoes, and then walked to the kitchen to polish off the entire chocolate muffin and half the blueberry. She couldn't eat the other half of the muffin but saved it for her post-nap snack. 

Lorraine rolled the suitcase with all her toiletries into the bathroom and took the hottest shower she could stand. She walked naked back to the kitchen for the rest of the blue-berry muffin and ate it before crawling into a bed mercifully made with clean, fresh sheets. 

For a split second between consciousness and sleep, Lorraine soothed herself with a quiet whisper. 

"I'm right where I need to be," she sighed to herself.

That she was in the middle of nowhere was beside the point.

WELCOME TO SEA PORT

THREE

Jonah

J onah Brown was an early riser. Always had been. Always would be.

Whenever he thought about sleeping in, he'd hear his father's rough voice in his head.

"That extra hour of sleep'll cost you more than time."

Jonah's father didn't yell or threaten him, he just guilt tripped the hell out of him one sage bit of advice at a time, and it worked. By the time Jonah was a moody preteen, Jonah's father didn't need to guilt him into waking up early to get his chores done, Jonah just did it. Even when he left Sea Port to attend college in Atlanta, Jonah took his father's habits with him.

A little slice of home in the big city.

But now he was home.

Jonah's eyes opened when it was still dark out. It took a few seconds for his brain to make sense of his surroundings, but his old, lumpy twin mattress reminded him the second he moved. Jonah's dad left his room largely untouched after

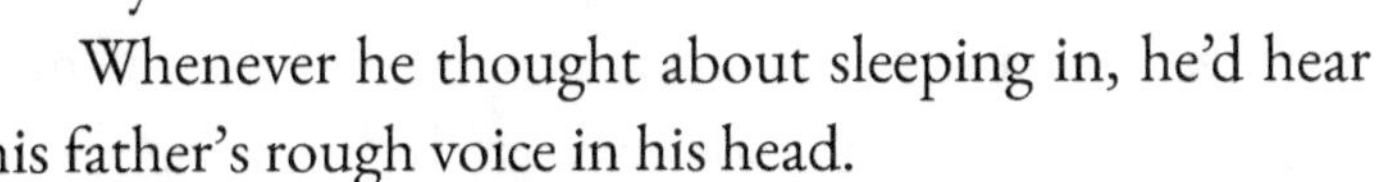
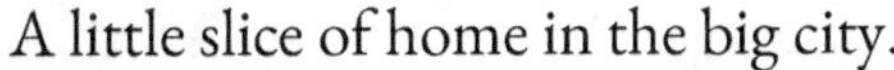

he left for college. The most he'd do was vacuum or dust when he was cleaning the rest of the house anyway and change Jonah's sheets before a visit. Otherwise, even in the dark, everything in his childhood bedroom was just about as Jonah had left it when he moved to Atlanta.

He threw the sheet from his body and crawled from the bed that was too small before he ever left home. He didn't turn on any lights until he made it to the bathroom, and even then, he averted his eyes from the L-shaped mirror over the sink while he took a piss and washed his hands.

If it had been up to Jonah, he probably wouldn't have ever moved back to Sea Port. He would have come back for all the major holidays, sure, but move back here? Never. Even as a child, Jonah had found Sea Port suffocating, too small for him and all his dreams. There also wasn't an ounce of privacy in a town as small as Sea Port. Even if his father was clear across town, there was always someone around who'd known him since birth or before. Someone who remembered when his mom was pregnant with him or who could recognize him 'cause he had his granddaddy's nose. Or, even more than anyone else, the people who knew him first, foremost, and maybe even only as an extension of his father.

Everyone in town knew Wesley Brown. He was the person they called when a floorboard was loose or they needed a new window fitted or a back porch screened in and everything in between. But he was also a widower, and that, Jonah realized over time, was the specter hanging over his entire life — the other thing people saw when they looked at Jonah and recognized him as Wesley and Sarah's son.

Jonah's mother died before he ever got the chance to

form his own memories of her. Wesley had remembered enough for both of them. His father never missed the chance to remind Jonah of the woman they'd lost or how much she'd loved being a mother to him — for the little time she got. Jonah was raised in the shade of his father's grief, the house a testament to the life they were supposed to have — father, son, and mother.

But outside the mausoleum of their home, things were different.

"Now, how is your father?"

"What's your father getting up to these days? My floor-boards are squeaking up a storm lately."

No matter where he was or what he was doing, there was always some single woman — or sometimes a very-much-married woman — who was happy to use Jonah as an entrée into his father's romantic life. But the joke was on them because even before he understood why, Jonah knew his father didn't want to date. He wasn't interested in anyone who wasn't his late wife and Jonah wasn't interested in running interference between his father and the women vying to be his stepmother.

Leaving Sea Port had given Jonah an identity of his own. For the first time in his life, he wasn't Wesley Brown's son; he was just Jonah, and he hadn't wanted to give that up.

"Some decisions aren't ours to make," his father used to say, and apparently, he was right because here he was, back in his little hometown. Back to being Wesley Brown's son above all else.

Jonah walked from the bathroom down the short hallway to the center of the house. The living and dining rooms on his left opened up to the kitchen on his right. This house had been in the Brown family for four generations. From old pictures he'd seen, it had just been two rooms that grew to fit the family over the years. By the time Jonah was old enough to read, his dad filled what little free time he had fixing up the house, one building code violation at a time. Everywhere he looked, Jonah was surrounded by his father's woodwork. And love.

Jonah flipped the light switch, flooding the kitchen with dim, warm light. This kitchen hadn't been updated since the late Eighties. Jonah used to hate how dated it was, but the nostalgia was comforting now when he needed it the most. He grabbed the carafe from the drip coffee machine he bought for his dad's birthday nearly a decade ago. When he asked his dad why he didn't get a new one — or let Jonah get him a new one — the answer was as expected for a man as set in his ways as Wesley.

"If it ain't broke, don't try to fix it," he'd said, which described his relationship with everything in the house.

Jonah waited for his coffee to brew, looking around the dated room. The old countertops were chipped Formica, but still functional. The laminate flooring was old and peeling up at the edges, but not too much — not enough for his dad to invest in pulling it up and laying down something new. His dad built the cabinets years ago and they were made of hardwood; they weren't going anywhere. Jonah had pestered his father to renovate this kitchen for years, but now he couldn't imagine changing a thing.

He'd been doing just fine in Atlanta. He had a condo, a girlfriend he was seriously considering marrying, a good job as an architect for a successful design firm, and a life that was his alone.

But seven months ago, he got a call from his father's best friend and the owner of the Sunnyside Diner, Mr. Wright, a man who was as close to an uncle as Jonah had ever known.  Moses Wright was just as allergic to phone calls as Jonah's father, so when he saw the Sunnyside's phone number on his caller ID, he knew something was wrong. 

He got the news of his father's heart attack after a long, tiring day in a long, tiring week, but Jonah didn't skip a beat. It took him one short flight and a three-hour drive from the  closest small- to medium-sized airport, counting every minute.

Your mama's watching over you. And me.

Jonah made it home in just enough time to say goodbye,  proving Wesley Brown right again.

One morning, Jonah woke up knowing exactly where he  could find his father, and the next morning he woke on that old, lumpy twin mattress an orphan. There was something about losing both parents before thirty that forced Jonah to  see his life with new eyes, and once he did, the life he built in Atlanta crumbled in an instant.

Was his condo in an "up-and-coming" Atlanta suburb really that great if he had to travel an hour away to get good  barbecue? The equity on his property had risen since he bought it, but so had his taxes. And still, his favorite barbecue joint was an hour away if traffic was light. Atlanta  traffic was never light.

He'd been on the verge of ring shopping, ready to propose to his girlfriend, Angie. They'd been together for two years, she was gorgeous and funny, and the sex was great. She was materialistic, but Jonah didn't mind spending his money on her. What more could he ask of the life he'd built?

But then his father died and all Jonah could think about was that he never brought her home to meet his father. He'd been so worried what she'd think of Sea Port and his dad's small but cluttered home, of him if she knew his roots, that he'd never asked himself what his dad would think of Angie and the life Jonah was living in Atlanta.

He'd robbed himself of something — so many things — he could never get back and it was hard to move forward in the wake of such a monumental loss.

Jonah would never have pictures of his dad at his wedding, he'd never get to see his father holding his child, and hovering over all of that was an overwhelming sense of guilt.

He'd planned to go back to Atlanta eventually, but there was a funeral to plan, affairs to settle, and days to spend crying alone in his childhood bedroom, so he stayed. And the thing about being in Wesley Brown's house too long was that there was always work to do.

Idle hands and all that.

He started close to home. When the Wrights stopped by to drop off Jonah's favorite peach pie, they mentioned a booth at the diner his dad was going to fix. Jonah finished his lunch and a piece of pie and then followed them to the diner in his dad's work truck. When he grabbed his dad's toolbox from the back of the truck, he was surprised it didn't seem as heavy as he remembered. It took twenty minutes to tighten the booth to the wall, another five to check the wiring on their main fryer, and then another few minutes to eat a slice of apple pie.

Work cleared a pathway through Jonah's grief. It gave him a reason to get out of bed in the morning and leave the house. Tackling his father's projects brought Jonah closer to the man he missed more than words could express.

Next to Jonah, Brown & Son Construction had been Wesley's pride and joy. He'd been preparing Jonah to take over the family business practically from birth only for Jonah to run away to Atlanta. But now he was back home and the thought of returning to his life in Atlanta slipped further and further away.

Now, he had to consider if his hesitation at proposing to Angie, painting his condo, or even applying for a promotion at his job weren't signs that Atlanta would never be his home. Home would always be Sea Port. Home would always be this dated kitchen in this old house and that lumpy mattress.

But coming home didn't solve his problems because without his father, Jonah didn't think he was living. Sure, he knew Sea Port in ways he'd never know metro Atlanta, but things had changed. His father was dead and buried next to Jonah's mother. There was a fancy coffee shop downtown. Sea Port *had* a downtown. All the things that had moored Jonah to this place were gone or slipping away and he didn't know if he fit here either anymore.

He drank his first cup of coffee from his father's favorite mug, ate his dinner on his father's old, chipped plates, and  slept in his old bedroom wishing he could be a child again.

But that wasn't quite living.

So he worked because his father had been right about

that too — doing the work you loved *was* better when you worked for yourself.

He opened his laptop and pulled up his calendar. When he left Sea Port, his dad worked alone, waiting for Jonah to join the family business, but in his son's absence, Wesley had become a bit of an entrepreneur. According to his father's messy books, Brown & Son had grown exponentially through Willie's new Sea Port Relocation Initiative. Instead of leaving his son with a small family business struggling to survive, Wesley had left Jonah with a business so well-run there hadn't been a dip in productivity after his death.

A legacy indeed.

Right now, Jonah had two crews working. About a quarter of the workforce was finishing a basement in one of the mayor's properties — a house she was hoping to sell to a doctor she was courting as a Transplant, even though their local hospital was barely better than a clinic in Atlanta and half the town thought you could cure most things with Vicks, ginger ale, and witch hazel.

The rest of his crew were hard at work on the new library. They'd spent a month pulling the building back to the studs. Mayor Waltham had been looking to hire an architect from out of town, but then Jonah inherited the job. He and Willie had known one another since they were children. She left Sea Port a couple years before him, but now they were back. She showed up on his doorstep with a pot roast in one hand and a contract in the other. Jonah rolled his eyes and accepted both. It was pointless to fight Willie, so he just got to work.

Jonah went over the construction plan as he did every morning, portioning out weekly and daily tasks for his crew members. He typed up to-do lists and printed them out on his father's ancient printer. He checked the budgets and input any new receipts in his bookkeeping software.

Each morning, Jonah tended to his father's business as a tribute to the man himself.

It was the least he could do.

WELCOME TO SEA PORT

FOUR

Jonah

Jonah drove to the library site in his father's old tan Ford. It still smelled like him — leather and peppermints. Sometimes, he wondered if the scent would fade with time and start to smell like Jonah or if he'd just start to smell like his father after a while. The latter was a distinct possibility since the peppermints in the center console were a brand-new bag he'd bought himself, and he popped one into his mouth halfway through his quick journey.

He used to ride his bike down these same streets with reckless abandon. Now he passed kids he didn't recognize with a similar disdain for traffic on their bikes and it made him nostalgic and homesick at the same time.

Homesick for a world where his father was just a phone call away.

Jonah turned left on Freeport Road, blinking back the pressure of tears.

Years ago, maybe when his dad was a boy, this small

valley had been fallow farmland waiting for the right farmer and the right crop, but Mayor Waltham — not the current one, but her grandmother — had a vision of developing this part of town and that field became the library instead.

It was Jonah's guess that the current Mayor Waltham put the library renovation high on her priority list as a way to honor her family's legacy, but that wasn't any of Jonah's business. He stayed out of town politics until it was time to build or fix something, just like his father had before him and *his* father before him.

If the Brown family had a motto, it was to keep their eyes on their own plate, so he did.

Still, he couldn't say Mayor Waltham's priorities were all wrong because the view of the library under construction was a sight to behold. It was hardly more than steel posts and concrete at the moment, but in a few months, it would be beautiful and brand new. He was only sad his father wouldn't get to see it.

Jonah pulled his father's truck into the parking lot under the shade of the old oak tree where Jonah had his first kiss. He would've liked to sit in his car for a few slow moments and gather his emotions, but the fire department's new pickup truck was parked in front of the building site.

Knox was an easygoing guy, but the county's building codes didn't play. Before his heart attack, Jonah's father had mentioned how the work to get buildings up to code was half the battle — and the budget — and now Jonah knew he wasn't exaggerating. Brown & Son had Knox running around town, checking the wiring and foundations on half the vacant structures in Sea Port. Jonah had a lot of work ahead of him, so there was no need to keep the man waiting.

The sound of his boots hitting the gravel sounded just like his dad's, but he pushed through that bit of painful nostalgia and slammed the door with a little more force than necessary.

He found Knox standing in the middle of what would  soon become the library's circulation area. He was staring up at the ceiling, or where a ceiling should be if not for the termites and the water damage. Jonah figured Knox was  admiring the clear blue sky as he had more than once himself.

"Morning, Knox," Jonah called. 

"Jonah. Good morning," the man replied, still staring upward. When he tilted his face down, his mouth was split into his ever-present smile. Jonah'd heard a lot about Knox  before they met, and everyone — man, woman, young, old, everyone — had great things to say about his smile. It set everyone at ease, even Jonah. 

"What can I do for you, Chief?"

"You can just call me Knox, no need to use official titles," he replied nonchalantly. Knox extended his arm and they  shook hands quickly. His father had had nothing but good things to say about Knox, including his handshake. His grip was strong and he made easy eye contact — two things Wesley Brown had believed was necessary to adequately  convey respect.

"Does that mean you're not here in your official capacity as fire chief? Or as a member of the City Council?"

Knox grimaced. "Don't even mention the City Council  to me. Biggest pain in my ass. I don't know why I let the Mayor talk me into that."

Jonah had a pretty good idea. A couple of them, actually.

No one said no to Mayor Waltham, and if Knox was on the City Council, the town gossips had something else to whisper about besides his unusual relationship with the police chief and the baker.

Jonah didn't care about any of that. So long as no one was getting hurt and everyone was a consenting adult, what happened behind closed doors was none of his business.

"I'm here to go over those coding issues you called me about last week. I know we're meeting on Friday, but I had a little bit of time this morning. I don't know what you have on deck, but if you got a few minutes, I'd love to cross something off my to-do list before somebody gets on my nerves."

Somewhere his father was nodding sagely because this was exactly why it paid to keep your nose out of other people's business. Knox was damn good at his job and moving their inspection up would shave at least three days off his schedule, and that was worth more than gold.

He gave Knox his best smile and gestured toward the steps that wound up to the top floor, one of the few things from the old library his crew had managed to salvage. "Right this way. Just be careful to step where I step."

Knox laughed. "Will do. I don't got a death wish, no matter what I say at the Council meetings."

Jonah laughed and led him upstairs, finding it easier to work down than up.

"You met the new librarian yet?" Knox called.

"Nope," Jonah said. "I suspect I won't need to until we've got a roof and walls, at least. Why?"

"No reason, I was just asking. Mary went by the Mayor's cottage to welcome her to town just this morning. I think she said something about bringing her by here today."

"For what?" Jonah asked, stepping onto the first-floor landing and looking up. The sky was perfectly blue, not even a small tuft of white cloud to mar the view. "Like I said, we don't even have a roof."

Jonah could hear the shrug in Knox's words. "Mayor  Waltham probably just wants her to get to know the town and see where she'll be working."

Jonah shrugged back, starting toward the next floor.  "Not much to see, in my opinion. But if we cross paths, I'll be on my best behavior."

Knox laughed. "We all will. You know how she feels about scaring away the new folk."

Jonah turned and smiled at Knox again. "You say that like you ain't one of the new folk."

Knox laughed louder. "Oh, believe me, I ain't forgot nothing. No matter how nice y'all are, you won't let any of us forget we're not from old Sea Port stock."

"Good," Jonah laughed, clapping Knox on the shoulder. "That old Portie blood is strong."

Knox laughed as Jonah turned back toward the second floor, stepping carefully onto the next landing to the plywood guiding their path.

He walked through the wreckage of the library pulled back to nothing but a shell as an intrusive image of his parents flooded Jonah's brain. Two old Sea Port bloodlines would probably end with him. He was all the legacy his parents left and he didn't feel worthy of that gift.

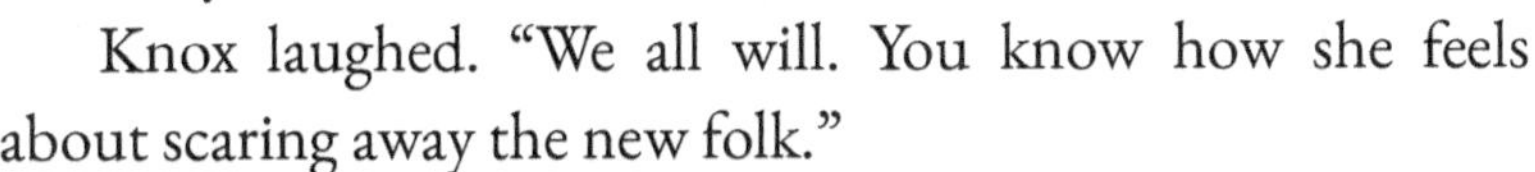

WELCOME TO SEA PORT

FIVE

Lorraine

Lorraine was raised by a mother who believed that a woman should never step outside without perfectly coiffed hair and lipstick at the very least. Inès Freeman was conceited but beautiful and charismatic, which meant most people endured her narcissism because she was easy on the eyes.

Lorraine spent years in therapy working through the indelible impression her mother left — how she viewed herself, the world, and men. But just because her mother was vain didn't mean her advice wasn't sometimes useful. Inès taught Lorraine that she'd never get a second chance at a first impression, so she woke from her three-hour nap and spent careful time pulling herself together through habit and sheer force of will. By the time she was showered, dressed, and had drawn the sharpest winged liner she could manage, she stepped back from the bathroom counter to look at her reflection, proud of herself, and not just because she was pretty.

Her mother had never been the kind of person to express pride in her daughter, but maybe — possibly — Inès would have approved of Lorraine hiding the exhaustion with concealer, a few coats of mascara, and the shiniest lip gloss she owned. It was only spring but humid already, so Lorraine skipped any more makeup and hoped for the best.

She pulled her thick curly hair into a bun on top of her head to get it off her neck. She shimmied into a black jersey dress with cap sleeves and slipped on a pair of strappy sandals. She looked approachable, casual, and cute — the perfect first impression.

She grabbed her keys and purse and stepped onto her cute new porch. "Goddamn," she whispered, already feeling beads of sweat forming at her hairline. She walked down Maple Lane and turned onto Pine, just as Mary had directed, but almost immediately realized she could've navigated her way on her own, Sea Port was so small. And Mary was right — following the smell of warm sugar was better than any directions, and she found herself at Confections by Mary in minutes.

Her forehead was sweaty and her stomach was grumbling, so she appreciated the air conditioning and the fresh donuts that welcomed her in the adorable little bakery. She needed real food, but damn if Mary's baked goods didn't smell amazing.

A young woman behind the display cases popped up at the sound of the bell. "Welcome to Confections! You the new librarian?" she asked cheerfully. Lorraine had thought Mary was chipper, but this girl was on another level.

"How'd you know?" Lorraine asked warily.

The girl bent down again and went back to loading fresh

crumb donuts into the case. "Sea Port's small. We've been waiting for you. Word's already out that you're here."

"Damn," Lorraine breathed.

She laughed as she put the last donut in place and closed the latch. "Get used to it."

Lorraine heard her, but she was too busy inspecting every sweet little treat in the display case to care about small town surveillance.

"Anything you want to try?"

"Um... I shouldn't," Lorraine said, eyeing those crumb donuts closely.

"Everyone says that before they cave," the girl said with a knowing smirk on her mouth.

Lorraine didn't know how much Mary was paying this girl, but she was earning every cent.

"I had some of Mary's muffins this morning. I'll be big as a house if I don't watch myself." She said the words, but she heard them in her mother's voice, and that unsettled something in her gut.

The girl was unfazed. "You're in the South now. Men like women with a little meat on their bones down here. But who cares what men think, anyway?"

"I like you," Lorraine smiled.

"I'm likable," she said, shrugging adorably.

"Is Mary here? We're supposed to go on a tour."

The girl's smile shifted and her light brown cheeks flushed prettily. "She's in the back in a...meeting. She'll be out in a second."

Lorraine thought that was an odd response, but something in the display cases caught her attention. "Okay, what's a teacake?" she asked, moving to stand in front of the middle case.

"Oh, those are my favorites," the girl beamed. "They're like a light, fluffy cookie. Not too sweet, not too soft or hard. It's hard to explain. You have to try one!" She slid open the back of the case while she spoke, not giving Lorraine a chance to change her mind. Lorraine had worked in food service when she was a teenager, but this girl was a professional. She grabbed a cookie with tongs and placed it on a small yellow napkin that matched the décor, then put it on the top of the case and slid it toward Lorraine.

Lorraine reached inside her purse. "How much do I owe you?"

"Not a cent," Mary called loudly, walking through the swinging door. Lorraine caught a glimpse of the bakery's kitchen before her view was eclipsed by a man too beautiful to look at up close, but she couldn't look away. Medium brown skin, dark eyes, gorgeous jet-black hair, and serious eyebrows. If DeJuan was here, he'd be beside himself.

Lorraine cleared her throat. "You already brought me muffins. You have to let me pay for the cookie."

Mary shook her head, a pretty smile on her face as the man reached around her to open the swinging counter and let her through. And a gentleman? Yeah, DeJuan would need to know about this.

"Nope. This is part of my marketing strategy. I give away all the free things at first and as soon as you're hooked, I start charging."

"Works every time," the girl behind the counter added, sliding the cookie across the counter.

"Thanks, Charlie," Mary said, carefully picking the cookie up and offering it to her.

Lorraine shook her head, but her traitorous stomach growled again and Mary seemed too pleased at the sound.  There were only four people in the shop and the other three watched her closely. Lorraine was going to eat this entire teacake, but before she took it from Mary's hand, she pulled a five-dollar bill from her purse and dropped it in the tip jar.  And *then* she grabbed the cookie from Mary's hands.

"I like you so much," Mary mumbled as Lorraine took her first bite.

"The feeling's mutual," Lorraine replied around her bite  of cookie.

"See, I told you she was great," Mary aimed at the beautiful man behind her. 

"You did," he said in a dry, serious tone. He sounded bored — or annoyed — until his eyes landed on Mary and lit  up with adoration. A tiny smile fought for a place on his lips. Mary looked back at him with the same warmth.

Lorraine wasn't personally interested in dating, but if this man was a sample of what Sea Port had to offer, she  would keep her eyes open for a man DeJuan might like, just in case he was open to moving down South.

"Lorraine, this is Miguel Santos, the new police chief."  Charlie clapped for him and Miguel shook his head, offering his hand to Lorraine.

"It's nice to meet you. You can call me Santos. Mary's  been gushing about you all morning."

"I have!" Mary said, practically bouncing on the balls of her feet.

They were a study in contrasts. He was tall, lean, and

severe where she was short, round, and warm, but they were definitely in love.

"I've gotta go," Santos said. "See you at home."

Mary lifted onto the balls of her feet and offered her mouth to him for a kiss. Lorraine and Charlie looked away to give them some privacy. Lorraine ordered a Danish to go.

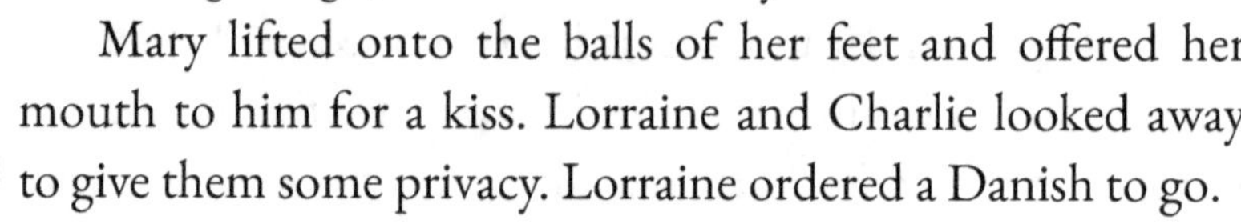

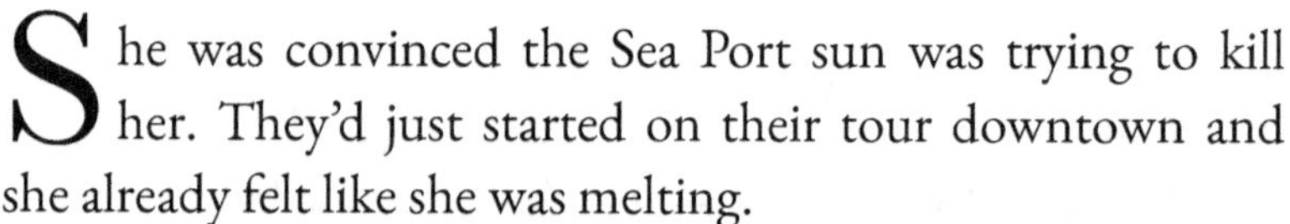

She was convinced the Sea Port sun was trying to kill her. They'd just started on their tour downtown and she already felt like she was melting.

"So there's Mr. Wright's diner," Mary said, pointing down the street. "There aren't too many restaurants in town. We'll see them all, but all you need to know about the Sunnyside is they have great burgers and terrible fries."

Lorraine nodded. "Good to know."

"I also make their pies now, so you know those are good," Mary bragged with an adorable grin. "And here's Main Street."

Lorraine hadn't driven this far into downtown, but she recognized it from the town website. "It seemed bigger and longer online," Lorraine whispered.

"That's what she said," Mary whispered back, and the two giggled together.

"You can walk most of the town in an hour, maybe two if you stop and sit for a spell," Mary said.

"Wow," Lorraine breathed as a spurt of panic entered her bloodstream.

"Yeah, I know. Freaked me out too, but you get used to the size eventually. Promise."

Lorraine squinted in disbelief, but she just shrugged.

"Promise," she said again. "And here's Sully's!" Mary  pointed through a large picture window into a surprisingly popping coffee shop. "It's the best coffee in town, which isn't saying much, but it's good. They grind their own beans, and if you drop in on Thursdays in the late after-  noon, the head barista, Keith, plays nothing but rare disco cuts."

"Why?"

Mary shrugged. "No idea, but the playlist is impeccable.  Almost no repeats."

"Almost?"

"Keith is a Donna Summer stan," Mary said seriously.

Lorraine laughed. "Okay, I'll allow that."

Mary turned away from the coffee shop and pointed across the street. "The main administrative building has all the stuff you'd expect. Mayor's office, police department, fire department, courthouse — you know, all the things. Come 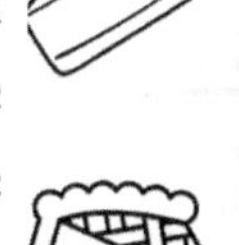 on, let's cross here. We can cut through the building to get to the library faster."

"Faster than what?" Lorraine asked before she could stop herself.

Mary laughed, stepping into the street. Lorraine rushed after her and quickly overtook the other woman because Mary wasn't in a rush. Her laughter intensified as Lorraine realized they hadn't passed a single car on the road yet.

"There's not much traffic here." A small pack of kids on bikes turned onto Main and Mary pointed them out.

"Beware the local biker gang. They're adorable but some-times forget how to use their brakes."

Laughter bubbled from Lorraine's mouth. "This place can't be real."

"I thought the same thing at first. I still do sometimes, but it is, and I've *never* been happier."

"How long have you been here?"

"Just over a year, and I'm still getting used to it, small as it is. It's not perfect. I'm not trying to sell you on this place. Every other day I wish some things were easier or that Sea Port was big enough for things to be easier." Lorraine nodded, hanging on every word. "But then something'll happen that could *only* happen in Sea Port and it's amazing. And then I can't imagine living anywhere else."

Mary's happiness was infectious and it soothed Lorraine's exhausted nerves. She pulled the front door of the main administrative building open and the air conditioning welcomed them like a long-lost lover.

"And does Santos have something to do with that?" Lorraine asked playfully.

Mary's face lit up. "He *definitely* does," she said with a wink.

"Well then, you're lucky. I can't imagine what the dating scene is like here." Lorraine laughed, and Mary joined her.

"You don't have to tell me how lucky I am. Believe me. But now that you mention it, I don't know what the single population is like. Small, I'd guess."

"And old," Lorraine said.

They laughed together as they continued their walk. There wasn't much to see on the way to the library, but

Lorraine thought getting to know Mary while on an easy walk was a great first impression of life in Sea Port.

WELCOME TO SEA PORT

SIX

Jonah

What Jonah hoped would be a quick meeting turned into a couple hours of intense conversation, not about the new wiring but Jonah's plans for the renovation and what Knox thought was possible. 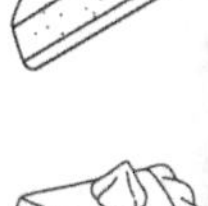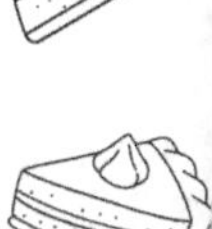 He used to have these conversations over the phone with his dad and he missed his father something fierce, but he trudged through those two hours like he'd been trudging  through the last few weeks.

"I mean, how much can that really cost?" Jonah's drywaller, Ezequiel, asked, walking up behind them.

Now that the building had been pulled back almost to  the studs, they'd found one surprise after another. Today, they were staring at the plans for the library's new electrical,  their next and biggest project.

The first library in Sea Port had been in a shack right in  the center of downtown, back when it was barely a town and all the roads were made of packed dirt. It burned down in 1915 right along with the AME church. It was officially labeled as an accident, but all Porties knew it was arson, which is why they only talked about it in hushed tones.

How this new library had avoided catching on fire was a miracle as far as Jonah was concerned. In the entire building, his father's crew hadn't been able to salvage a single inch of wiring. His crew now, he had to keep reminding himself.

Thankfully, his dad had budgeted for that possibility, but Jonah had been hoping to save a little money if he could.

"I can't imagine you getting a quote under twenty-five grand," Knox sighed.

"Damn," Zeke said.

"And that's just for the wiring. We're not talking about getting supplies or any of the labor," Jonah added in a matching sigh.

Zeke shook his head and walked away without another word.

"Who does electrical on your team?"

"No one I'd trust with a project this big. We're gonna have to call in an electrician from the city," he said. This, too, was in his dad's budget. There really wasn't anything for Jonah to fret about yet, but he found himself with his hands on his hips frowning up at the ceiling.

Knox, however, had moved on. He turned to Jonah with a curious smile on his face. "So...when you people—"

"You people?" Jonah asked.

Knox rolled his eyes. "Porties," he clarified. "When y'all talk about the city, where exactly do you mean? 'Cause Freetown is barely any bigger than this place."

Jonah could see why people liked Knox so much. It was a tricky question that only a Transplant would ask because they weren't from here and they'd never be a *real* Portie, or at least that's what some Porties believed. A few Transplants Jonah had met tried their best to avoid topics that made them stick out like a sore thumb, but not Knox. Never Knox.

"How long you been wanting to ask that?" Jonah asked, chuckling around the question as his shoulders relaxed. 

Knox laughed right along with him. "At least a year and a half. I've been trying to figure it out on my own, but I just can't make sense of it. Some of these places are just as small as us." 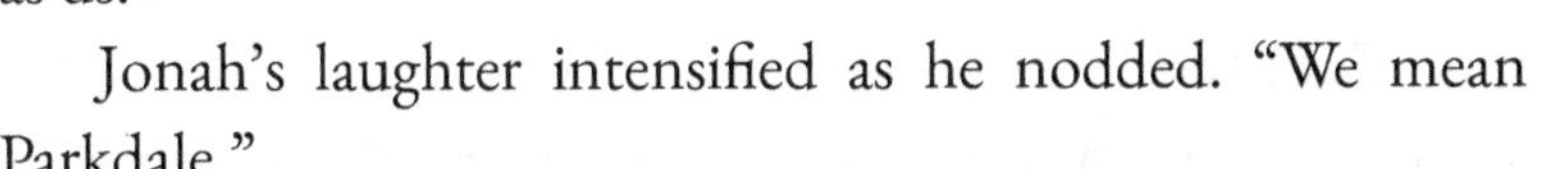

Jonah's laughter intensified as he nodded. "We mean Parkdale."

Knox stared at him for a second, a blank look on his face. "Really?" he gasped. 

Jonah's shoulders were bouncing with laughter but also a more determined shrug. "They got fast food restaurants, a bowling alley, *and* a strip club." 

Knox's eyebrows lifted. "There's a strip club in Parkdale?"

Jonah grimaced. "It's terrible, but it's there. Been there since 1987. Unfortunately, it looks like it." 

Knox's face crumpled. "Ugh."

"I know. Anyway, my dad knows every electrician in three counties. I'll start making some calls." 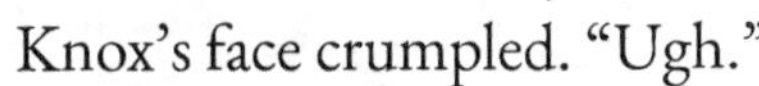

"This gonna hold you up?" he asked. 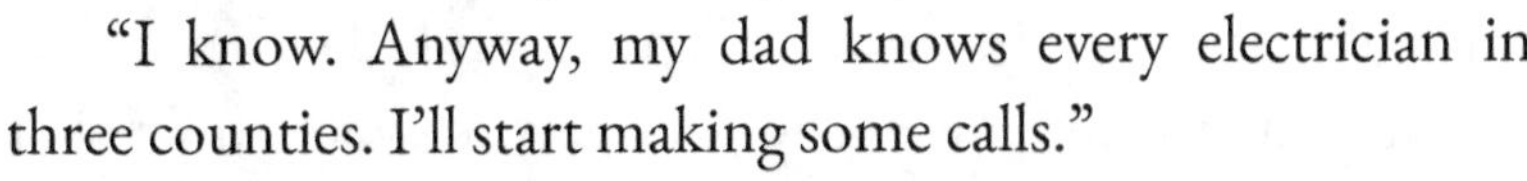

"Probably, but that's fine. There's so much damn work to do, it won't matter. We got more than enough to keep us busy in the meantime. Don't worry." 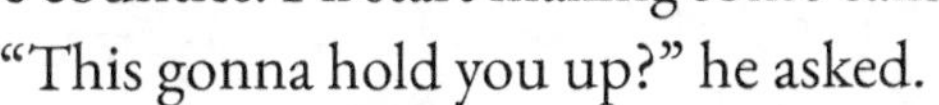 

"I don't care about you looking busy," Knox chuckled. "I ain't paying y'all. Just give me a heads up when you need 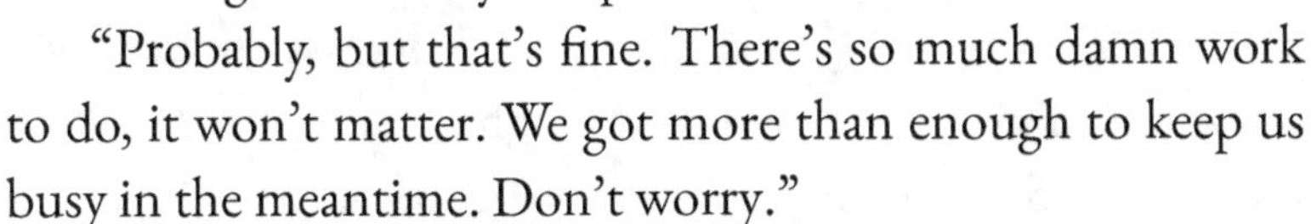

me back out here. And hey, if you can schedule it during a Council meeting, even better."

"I'll do my best," Jonah laughed. "Lemme lead you outta here. The floor's tricky."

"Please. I wanna get out of my new job but I don't wanna break my neck to do it."

Wesley used to tell Jonah to pray for problems in the morning so the afternoon was easy. It was just one of those things he said and years later, those words still rang true. If they'd had to wait until Friday for the meeting as scheduled, Jonah would've had to wait until after the weekend to call up to Parkdale, but now he had a couple days' head start. Of all the surprise inspections he'd weathered, this was one of the best. And if this was the worst part of the day, he'd be eternally grateful. Most days were hard as hell and he just wanted a few hours of relief.

He led Knox back down to the ground floor. They stopped in the open doorway; the twelve-foot-tall door Jonah's crew was hoping to salvage in the renovation was covered in pads and left open to minimize any accidental damage. Jonah turned to Knox and offered his hand to shake again.

"I'ma head on back to my office," Knox said. "I'll try to get my portion of the report filled out and filed by tomorrow, but if it's not 'til Friday, I hope you won't hold that against me."

"That's alright," Jonah said, but Knox's attention was elsewhere. The man leaned to the right to look around him, a soft smile forming on his face. When Jonah turned around to see what had caught Knox's attention, he wasn't at all shocked to find Mary walking straight toward them.

Jonah liked Mary. She was cute, funny, and sometimes he dreamed about her sweet potato pie. He'd dated women with less to offer, so Jonah could understand why Knox and Santos had agreed to share her, but it was the woman next to her that caught his eye.

Sea Port was small enough that most people knew one another at least by sight, if not through generations of tangled family history, but Jonah didn't recognize the woman in the slinky black dress at all — not her face or those curves.

"Who the hell is she?" Jonah whispered.

"I'm guessing that's the new librarian," Knox offered.

"Goddamn," Jonah responded before he could stop himself. He was so caught up in ogling her, he dropped the notebook in his hands. He bent down and picked it up but kept it at waist level because his dick was hard — for the first time in a long time. Grief had sapped his libido for a good long while, but apparently that might be on the mend. It was an inconvenient time for his hormones to reassert themselves, but Jonah couldn't even remember the last time he'd felt anything besides sadness and exhaustion, so he just rolled with it.

"Smooth," Knox laughed, walking around him to greet Mary.

"What are you doing here?" he called to his girlfriend.

Her face lit up as she gasped happily. "What are *you* doing here?"

"Working," Knox yelled back.

Jonah followed behind the man at a distance.

"I'm working too. Well, volunteering," she laughed. "This is Lorraine the Librarian—"

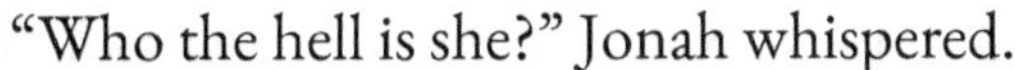

"Oh, that's gonna stick," Knox laughed.

"Right? Anyway, I'm showing her around town."

"You're just now getting here? I thought you did that this morning?"

They stopped in front of one another, the toes of their shoes touching. "She was tired. I helped her move in and gave her the muffins."

"And then what?" he asked, putting his hand under her chin. Jonah moved to Knox's right side, inching close to Lorraine the Librarian.

"And then I went to work," Mary said. "Someone's gotta make the cookies that keep this town running."

Knox leaned forward. "You coulda brought your cookies home," he whispered.

The moment turned unexpectedly intimate and Jonah spun quickly away because this was none of his business. He turned toward Lorraine and made accidental eye contact with her shocked face. He'd been in this position with Knox and Mary and Santos before, but to get thrown into their sexual tension on her first day seemed to be breaking their new Transplant.

Jonah cleared his throat, but it still took Knox and Mary a few seconds to pull their mouths away from one another. When they finally separated, Mary threw an arm around Knox's waist and turned to him. "Hey, Jonah, how are you?"

"I'm fine," he mumbled. "But since you're here, when are you gonna send another rhubarb pie over to the diner?"

"You liked that?" Mary didn't need to be as humble as she was, but sometimes her ego got a nice, slow stroke. Metaphorically speaking. Anyway, she deserved it.

"Obviously. I liked that salted caramel brownie too, if you're looking for feedback."

"Always," Mary beamed. "I've been thinking of setting up a focus group, actually."

"Since when?" Knox cut in. "You ain't told us that."

Mary rolled her eyes prettily, leaning into Knox's body. "I don't tell y'all everything about the bakery. Just like you don't tell me everything about the firehouse."

"That's 'cause there ain't nothing to tell. But how you gon' start a focus group without me?"

"You just want more cookies," Mary teased.

Jonah could see Knox's reply forming in his brain and he cut in. "So you're the new librarian?" he asked.

"Oh, I forgot," Mary said.

"I bet you did," Knox mumbled, and Mary laughed before pushing away from him.

"Lorraine, this is the fire chief, Billy Knox. Everyone calls him Knox. And Jonah's handling the library renovations. I bet you two are gonna get sick of each other before this place is done," Mary laughed.

"I don't know about that," Jonah mumbled under his breath.

"Lorraine, you alright?" Mary asked.

Lorraine rolled her eyes in Knox's direction. "Huh?" she gasped.

Mary's big smile started to slip, but Knox just chuckled and threw his arm around her shoulder.

"You met Santos already?" he asked.

Lorraine's eyes went wide. "You know about Santos?"

Understanding dawned on Mary and she giggled loudly.

Jonah covered his mouth with his hand, trying to muffle his own laughter.

"I mighta heard of him," Knox said with a grin so wide, Jonah's skin tingled.

"We're all together," Mary laughed. "Me, Knox, and Santos. There's no funny business. Well…some funny business."

"*A lot* of funny business," Knox corrected.

"What kinda small town living is this?" Lorraine asked in a voice teetering between an accusation and playfully scandalized.

"Sea Port's changing. That's the point of all this, right?" Knox said, gesturing toward the gutted library and between him, Mary, and Lorraine.

Jonah might've lived in Atlanta, but he was a Portie forever. Wesley had kept Jonah up to date on the Relocation Program and all Willie said it would offer their town. Right from the beginning, Portie opinion had been evenly split between those who supported the program and those who hated it. Jonah had expected his father to fall into the latter camp, but Wesley thought the Relocation Program would be good for Brown & Son, and he'd been right. With new people applying each week, there were houses, farms, and city buildings that needed more work than Brown & Son could do, but Wesley was committed to trying. And now Jonah was trying for him.

Jonah had been on the fence about the program, but he'd been living in Atlanta with no plans to return, so he'd decided his opinion didn't matter. But now that he was home and so much was changing around him, some days he still struggled to welcome the new, especially now that his father was gone.

"Girl, two men? Two *fine ass* men?" Lorraine hissed, staring at Mary, mouth agape. "For real?"

"Aw," Knox said.

"I told you I've never been happier!" Mary beamed. Knox pressed a kiss to Mary's temple.

"Somebody's gotta tell the Mayor to put this on the brochures," Lorraine said. "I, for one, could have used this information with the job offer, at least."

Mary and Knox laughed.

"Does that mean you're single?" Jonah blurted out, finally pulling Lorraine's attention to him.

"Oh," Mary whispered excitedly.

Lorraine's eyebrows lifted and she smirked. "And if I am?"

She had beautiful, big, dark eyes and having her gaze on him made the hair on Jonah's arms stand on end. "Sea Port's a small town. We know each other here," Jonah managed to say even though his tongue felt heavy in his mouth.

"And?" she asked, lifting an eyebrow up at him, her grin widening. "You trying to get to know me?"

Jonah felt like butterflies were having a rave in his stomach. "Yes, ma'am."

"Smooth," Knox whispered.

Lorraine's tongue moved over her lips and Jonah watched it hungrily. It was Mary's turn to clear her throat. Lorraine's eyes moved away, but Jonah's gaze didn't budge an inch from her profile.

"How about Jonah show you the library?" Mary offered.

"I can do that."

"What about the tour of downtown?" Lorraine asked Mary, who giggled in response.

"We did that already. Besides, I can show you anything we missed another time. Jonah... Jonah?"

He didn't realize she was calling his name until Lorraine turned toward him again. "Huh?"

"I said after her tour, can you get her either back to her place or the bakery?"

"Yeah. Wait, where's she staying?"

"The cottage on Maple," Knox answered.

"Oh, yeah. Of course. I've got her. *It*," he corrected quickly.

"Not so smooth," Knox whispered with a sad shake of his head.

"Can you take me back to the bakery?" Mary asked.

"Depends. What's in it for me?"

Before Mary could answer, Jonah cut in. "Come on, Lorraine. Lemme show you around."

If Mary and Knox were at all offended by Jonah, they covered it with a laugh as they walked toward Knox's car. Jonah shook his head and gestured for Lorraine to follow him.

"Something tells me you're not a newbie," she said.

Now that they were standing close, her voice sounded deeper, velvety soft. His dick had relaxed for a few moments, but it started to perk up again.

"We call y'all Transplants and no, I'm not one of you. I'm a Portie," he said. "My family's been here since before the town charter, but I just moved back from Atlanta."

"That's a big move,' she said. "I'd love to hear what brought you back."

Jonah had only wanted to flirt a little, but as he walked Lorraine into the library site, he felt a warm shiver of antici-pation run up his spine.

WELCOME TO SEA PORT

SEVEN

Lorraine

Mayor Waltham did tell Lorraine the library was undergoing a total renovation, but Lorraine thought she was exaggerating. She was not.

Hell, now that she was literally staring up at the sky from the ground floor, she thought Mayor Waltham had under-sold just how much work was being done. This wasn't a renovation, it was a gut job, and it wasn't anywhere close to being done. If DeJuan had been here, he would've been laughing his way through a laundry list of 'I told you so's' and she wouldn't have been able to argue.

"What the hell am I supposed to do with this?" she hissed under her breath as a bird flew by.

"Be patient, I guess," Jonah muttered.

Lorraine startled at his voice. Honestly, she'd forgotten about him, which was surprising because he was fine as hell. She'd been momentarily distracted from his beauty by the lack of a roof, but when she tilted her head to look at him, his dark cocoa skin glistening in the midday sun took her by

surprise again. She didn't know what was in the Sea Port water that had all these fine ass men in one place, but there had to be something. Three sexy men just roaming the streets before lunch! How?

Jonah was frowning down at her feet.

"What?" she asked, pulling his attention to her face again.

He had the nerve to have beautiful eyes to boot. "Your shoes."

"Are expensive."

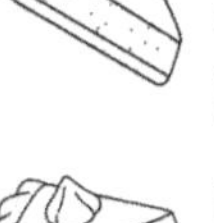

He laughed softly, just once. His eyes moved up and down her body. "I bet they are," he mumbled under his breath. That sentence and the way he said it had serious potential to get her pussy wet. "This is a construction site. Your expensive—"

"And cute," Lorraine added, making Jonah laugh for real this time.

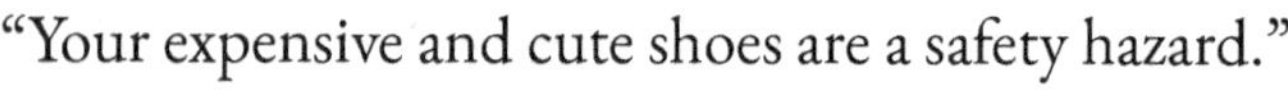

"Your expensive and cute shoes are a safety hazard."

"I'll be careful."

He shook his head. "That's a liability. Our insurance won't cover that."

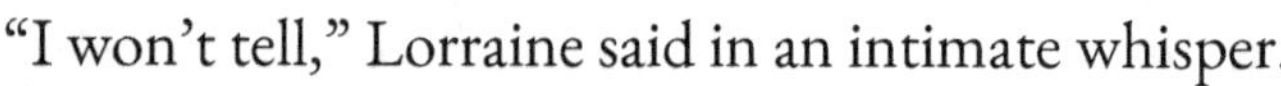

"I won't tell," Lorraine said in an intimate whisper.

Jonah swallowed loudly. He looked left and right, but Lorraine kept her attention squarely on his face. He grimaced and Lorraine saw a peek of a dimple. She loved men with dimples.

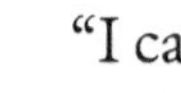

"I can show you a little of the first floor."

"A little?" she asked in that same soft voice.

He put his hands on his hips and looked seriously at her. "That ain't gonna work twice."

"Had to try."

"Step where I step and stay close," he said, shaking his head and smiling like he didn't know how fine he was.

"I can do that," she said.

Jonah stared at her for a few silent seconds. Lorraine kept a smile on her face; she always blossomed under scrutiny, especially when the person scrutinizing her was sexy.

Finally, Jonah turned into the room. "Come on."

"Yes, sir," she laughed.

A muscle jumped in his neck, but he didn't respond.

She was lucky DeJuan wasn't here. He'd be calling her all kinda hussies and he'd be right.

JONAH

The list of things Jonah needed to do today was a mile long and these impromptu meetings were fucking up his schedule. At the top of his list was a check-in with the foreman at the Mayor's basement remodel and those calls to Parkdale for an electrician, but Lorraine smelled like warm flowers blooming in the morning and every time he turned even slightly in her direction, he got a new whiff of her perfume. It was starting to make his balls ache.

Jonah gave Lorraine a brief tour of the library, mapping out plans for the new circulation area, reading rooms, a couple of multipurpose meeting rooms, and whatever he could remember about the plans off the top of his head. He tried to paint a picture, but that was harder said than done since there were fewer walls than she was probably expecting. If he'd known the new librarian would be stopping by, he would've brought the aesthetically pleasing render he'd created and Willie had quickly approved, but he did the best he could.

Unfortunately, he couldn't tell if Lorraine hated it or not.

"When'd the renovation start?" she asked.

"About ten months ago, technically. This place took forever to clear and gut."

"Ten months is a long time," she breathed, barely hiding the shock on her face.

Jonah's chest tightened. "We had to stop for a couple months because of...something else. Not related to this project." He stumbled over his words. This was the first time Jonah had spoken about his father's death to someone who hadn't known him in a long time and it left his mouth tasting like ash. He didn't have the right words to describe what he'd lost yet. He might never.

Thankfully, Lorraine's next question moved the conversation back on track.

"Do you know where the books are?" she asked, looking around again.

"I heard they're in storage, but I don't know exactly where. You'd have to ask Willie about that."

"I'll bring that up with Mayor Waltham," she said, stressing the title.

Jonah laughed softly at the sharp tone in her voice.

"What's the plan here?" she asked, gesturing across the room to the tall floor-to-ceiling windows covered in plywood. They were old and leaky and some of the frames had rotted out, but the glass was good, so they were doing their best to keep them safe until they could rebuild the frames.

"You can't see it now, but there's a garden back there. It's beautiful in the spring and summer. We're gonna build a little pergola, outdoor seating, stuff like that."

She looked over her shoulder. "It's spring," she reminded him with a smirk.

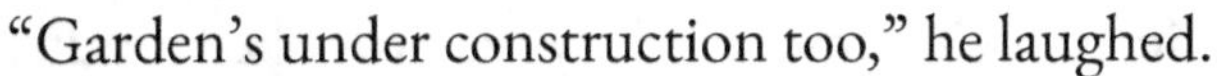

"Garden's under construction too," he laughed.

She huffed out a hard breath and tipped her chin up to the sky. "And the roof?"

"There will be one."

Her laughter got better each time. "Good to know. I was worried for a second."

"Happy to ease your fears." Jonah didn't crowd her space, but he watched her like a hawk, drinking in the contours of her profile and the beautiful curve of her neck,  before turning away and leading her back to the circulation area. He stepped onto the 'x' he'd marked out in tape in the center of the floor and looked up. "There'll be a skylight right above here."

She followed him, her heels tapping carefully on the  hardwood. "Oh, yeah?"

Jonah nodded and turned to face her, standing in the middle of their soon-to-be circulation area.

"Was that your idea?"

"It was. You like it?" he asked, stepping forward, dropping his voice to a whisper.

"I do," she whispered.

"Good."

She sucked her bottom lip into her mouth and his gaze dipped for a quick second. "Is this all you can show me?" Lorraine asked, not even trying to pretend that question was above board.

Jonah's heart started racing. The back of his neck was hot like the sun was beating down on him. He opened his mouth to respond professionally — or recklessly — but a loud crash ruined the mood.

Lorraine jumped and Jonah wrapped his arm around her waist, pulling her close to his side while he looked around for the cause of the disturbance.

"Why the hell did you let go?" Angelo yelled up the scaffolding at Sean.

"You said to!" Sean yelled back.

"I said *don't* let go!"

"Oh," Sean breathed.

Jonah sighed, shaking his head. Lorraine turned in his hold, her soft body sliding against his. A bead of sweat fell down his spine.

"I should go," she whispered, close enough for her breath to rustle his beard. "Don't wanna ruin my cute and expensive shoes."

His fingers tightened on her hip as he smiled. "Yeah. Yeah, okay. Let me just check on—"

She pressed her palms against Jonah's chest. "No, you're okay. I'll walk back."

Jonah shook his head. "I told Mary I'd get you back."

She laughed and Jonah had to ease his groin away from her body. "Sea Port is tiny," she said. "I would say the only thing I need to worry about is getting hit by a car, but I don't even think that's true."

Jonah tried to laugh, but Lorraine was too close. It was all he could do to keep his hand where it was, which was inappropriate as is. "Do you know how to get back?"

Her eyes were on his mouth. "Huh?"

Jonah pulled a half-smile onto his face. "Do you know how to get back downtown?" he asked again. 

"Oh, yeah. Probably. This town isn't big enough to get lost."

"You'd be surprised," he mumbled under his breath. "I'll get someone to walk you back if you don't want—" 

"No, thanks," Lorraine said. "I need to think. I'm taking in a lot. A few minutes alone will help clear my head." 

"Okay," Jonah said eventually, squeezing her waist before loosening his hold. "But I'm gonna call on Mary in half an hour to make sure you made it back okay." 

Lorraine pressed herself against his side. "You gonna check up on me? I'm a grown woman." 

Jonah couldn't help but smile. "Believe me, I noticed. But you're living in Sea Port now, and I was raised right."

Her smile made the next breath hitch in his chest, which seemed to please Lorraine as she finally stepped out of his  hold. "Good to know," she said before turning toward the door and walking away.

Jonah's eyes were trained on Lorraine's ass in that dress.  "Goddamn," he breathed to himself.

"I'm glad you said it," Zeke said, scaring the shit out of Jonah. 

He turned to find his drywaller standing a little too close for comfort. "Can you back up?"

Zeke looked offended. "What? You didn't mind when she was close."

Jonah rolled his eyes. "*She* is sexy."

"Wow. So you're saying I'm not sexy?"

Jonah laughed, and the tension caused by Lorraine's presence started to dissipate. "Get back to work," he said, heading for the stairs, glancing at the entryway one more time even though Lorraine was long gone.

WELCOME TO SEA PORT

EIGHT

Lorraine

Lorraine coped with emotional turmoil in one of three ways — sleeping, eating, or drinking. If DeJuan were here, he'd already be opening a bottle of champagne so they could gossip, but she was alone in a town she wasn't sure had a liquor store, let alone sold champagne, and DeJuan was far, far away, so she called him instead.

"Regretting your decision, huh?" he asked as soon as he picked up.

"No," she lied. "I'm calling to let you know I made it here in one piece."

"Mmhmm, sure. How was the drive?"

"Long." She was about to tell him how boring most of it was. The closer she got to Sea Port, the less inspired the scenery. She'd struggled to stay awake because on either side of the two-lane road, all she saw was fallow farmland as far as the eye could see. But she couldn't tell DeJuan any of this;

he'd just try to convince her to pack her stuff and come on home.

But she didn't want that, so she changed the subject. "So, what are you up to?"

"Same thing as usual. Working and hating it. Spending recklessly to cope. Turn your camera on. I want to see where you ran away to."

"I didn't run away," Lorraine lied again.

"And I love my job," he responded sarcastically. "Now show me Shreveport."

"*Sea Port*," Lorraine corrected.

"Whatever."

She stopped and looked around, cringing at the view. There wasn't much of Sea Port that Lorraine would say was aesthetically pleasing. The little downtown area wasn't overly developed, but it looked the best of what she'd seen so far. Unfortunately, she was strolling down a concrete path that connected the neighborhood around the library to the center of town and her view consisted of the shell of a library on one side and the city administrative building on the other, with more of that fallow land filling in the gaps. DeJuan would *not* approve.

"Oh, shit," Lorraine said, "I've gotta go."

"Why? What's wrong?"

"Library emergency," she said. "Love you. Talk later."

"Wait, you're working on your first—"

Lorraine hung up before DeJuan could finish asking a question she wouldn't be answering. She had a mild existential crisis to handle and apparently, she'd have to do so on her own. Maybe it was the sunshine or the quiet, but by the time she made it back to Main Street, she did feel less stressed. She considered calling DeJuan back now that she could give him a better view, but then she spied the Mayor walking from the café with a paper cup in one hand.

Lorraine shoved her phone back into her purse and started power walking in her direction. "Mayor Waltham," she called. 

The woman stopped at her name and turned in Lorraine's direction, a smile already on her face. "Ms. Freeman, you made it. Welcome to Sea Port." 

"Thanks. Can we talk?" Lorraine said, wiping the sweat at her hairline into her hair.

"Of course. Your contract is legally binding, though,"  she replied with a professional warning in her voice. Her smile stayed firmly in place as she spoke and Lorraine admired that about her.

"Yes, I know, and don't worry, I'm not trying to quit.  Besides, I don't want to have to pay back my relocation fees."

Mayor Waltham nodded slowly. "It wasn't cheap."

"And my stuff's not even here yet. Anyway, that's not what I want to talk about."

"I'm all ears." 

"I've just been by the library."

"It's beautiful, isn't it?"

"It's a frame," Lorraine shot back. "A few walls, no roof,  no floors."

"The stairs are still intact, though," the Mayor cut in.

"Okay. I thought I was going to get here and get immedi-  ately to work. There's no building. When were you going to tell me that?"

"I was hoping for never," the other woman admitted with a grin and an elegant shrug of her shoulders. Lorraine's mouth fell open at her honesty. "We started the search for your position before we started the renovations. The original plan was that the renovation would get underway when the job ad closed and the bulk of the work would happen while we were interviewing, and then you'd get here to find a brand-new, state-of-the-art building."

"Not a bad plan," Lorraine conceded.

"Thanks, but we all know things rarely go to plan. We had an unfortunate setback unrelated to the library. It caused a significant delay right after we cleared the building."

"Yeah, Jonah told me."

"Oh, good, you met Jonah," Mayor Waltham laughed. "He's great at his job. His family's been in Sea Port since the beginning. It's pretty fitting he's here to guide the renovations."

"But how long will they take?" Lorraine asked. "My contract is a year. As much as I like doing nothing, I didn't come here to sit on my butt waiting for contractors to do their jobs."

"Of course, you didn't. And you shouldn't. We've set up a small library site in the admin building. I was going to show you next week when your contract *officially* starts."

"Oh. Okay."

"Also, our delay provides you with a fantastic opportunity," Mayor Waltham continued. "Since the library renovation is ongoing, you can make it your own." Lorraine's eyes closed to slits, but Mayor Waltham was unfazed. "Instead of walking into a building that's been designed in a way you don't like or dealing with a collection that doesn't represent the wealth of knowledge and experience you bring, now you can rebuild our library from the ground up. How does that sound?"

"It sounds like you're blowing smoke up my ass," Lorraine deadpanned.

"I prefer finding a silver lining. How does that silver lining sound?"

Unfortunately, it sounded fantastic. Lorraine had worked in a lot of libraries over her career and most of them were great, but she'd left them all for one reason or another. The opportunity to build a library from the ground up, literally, had been her dream, and Mayor Waltham was dangling it right in front of her.

"Sounds good," Lorraine muttered.

The Mayor's face lit up. "Perfect, I'll see you Monday morning. Enjoy the rest of your first day in beautiful Sea Port," she said, already rushing across the street.

It was a quick conversation where the Mayor had unfortunately neutralized Lorraine by stroking her ego. It was diabolical, and Lorraine respected it.

Now that was over, Lorraine followed the scent of sugar back to Mary's bakery.

MARY

"You made it!" Mary cried as soon as Lorraine stepped into her shop.

She'd just returned to the bakery herself after a quick little detour to Knox's office. She left him slumped in his chair with his pants around his knees. She popped into Santos's office to share the news of Knox's disheveled state before finally making it back to work.

Mary and Charlie were just filling the breadbasket for Porties who liked to stop by the bakery to pick up a fresh loaf for dinner. Bread wasn't originally part of Mary's plans, but now she had a sourdough starter in her kitchen and a dozen or so loaves of bread to sell before they closed.

But first, Mary was ready for some gossip.

"So, what'd you think of the library?"

"You mean the construction site?" Lorraine shot back.

"It can be both," Mary replied.

"Can I buy a water?" Lorraine asked.

"No bottled water," Mary said, pointing toward the corner, "but there's a fountain."

"Thanks." Lorraine walked to the water cooler in the corner and filled up a little paper cup three times in a row before she managed to take the edge off her thirst.

"Feel better?" Mary asked, coming into the storefront.

Lorraine filled the paper cup again. "A little."

"Want a croissant?" She moved to one of the small tables next to the cooler and set two croissants on the tabletop. Lorraine raised an eyebrow. "Almond and regular," Mary said.

"Absolutely," Lorraine replied, taking a seat. She pulled the almond croissant toward her and broke off the flakiest end of the pastry. She popped it in her mouth and danced happily in her seat. "Very good."

"Thanks. Now, spill."

Lorraine sighed and thought about all she'd seen in the last couple of hours. "The construction site was alarming, but I can see the vision. What little of it I saw. Sea Port is beautiful, but so small." 

"So damn small," Charlie said from behind the counter.

Lorraine hadn't even registered the other woman was there, but she smiled at her. "Are you from here?" she asked.

Charlie leaned her hip against the counter. She nodded. "Yeah, but my family's only been here since the Great Depression. Not a First Family, but still old." 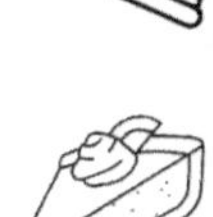

"First Family?"

"Founding families," Mary clarified. "It matters a lot here." 

"A whole lot, and until you Transplants started showing up, people never shut up about it." Charlie rolled her eyes with a smile. "But now that y'all are here, almost no one cares about that. So thanks!" 

Lorraine laughed around another bite of her croissant.

"You're welcome," Mary said. "If you want to get off early, you can." 

"Oooh, tempting, but if you let me off early, my dad's just gonna put me to work. I'd rather be covered in flour over printer ink. So, if it's all good, I'm going to start on some dishes." 

"Excellent," Mary said as Charlie turned toward the kitchen. "I love her." 

"I'm definitely telling Bria you said that!" Charlie called over her shoulder.

Mary rolled her eyes and turned back to Lorraine.

"Who's Bria? Do you have a girlfriend too?"

Mary laughed. "No, Bria's my baker's apprentice. This is her day off, but you'll meet her soon, I think." She nodded toward the table.

"Damn," Lorraine said, popping the last of her croissant into her mouth. Mary pushed the other toward her. "Oh, you're diabolical."

Mary shrugged. "I've got a business plan and I'll do whatever it takes to succeed." She shook her head. "Okay, not *whatever*, but you know what I mean. Anyway, what'd you think about Jonah?"

Mary mentally patted herself on the back that she'd managed to hold out asking about him for this long.

Lorraine shrugged. "I didn't think anything about him."

"Bullshit," Mary gasped. "He's fine. Good with his hands. Likes my pies."

"This sounds like you should date him."

"Santos would have a fucking fit."

"Not Knox?"

Mary sighed happily. "He's too calm for that. But if I talked about wanting someone else, they'd do their best to convince me otherwise." She licked her lips and looked out the window. "Actually, I might try that out."

"Again, when are they going to put you three on flyers? Sea Port would be twice the size in a year," Lorraine cried.

Mary laughed. "Some people would not be happy about that. But anyway, what about Jonah?"

"You're relentless."

"I'm nosy. Are you single?"

"Very."

"So is he. I think. Actually, I'm not sure. But I can ask around if you want."

"I don't," Lorraine said.

Mary frowned and slumped down in her chair.

"I'm here to do a job, and as long as Jonah keeps on pace with that renovation, that's all that matters."

"That's the saddest news of the day and I heard one of the farmers might have to slaughter his favorite pig soon," Mary sighed.

Lorraine pulled the croissant apart and took a big bite. "You should have one of your croissants," she said, covering her full mouth. "They're improving my mood significantly."

And just like that, Mary's mood was on the upswing.

WELCOME TO SEA PORT

NINE

Jonah

J onah could cook; his dad made sure of that. Now neither man could open a restaurant, but they hadn't starved.

When she was alive, his mother did all the cooking, his dad did all the yard work, and they worked together on cleaning the house. Jonah was too young to remember this arrangement on his own, but even mundane lessons about the importance of dusting and cleaning the baseboards was an invitation for his father to reminisce about Jonah's mother in his lifelong effort to keep her alive in Jonah's memory. But now, whenever he tried to do more than make coffee or heat up leftovers in his father's kitchen, he was overwhelmed with memories of his father most of all, so he ate out whenever he could, and more often than not, he ended up at the Sunnyside.

"Oh good, you're here," Moses Wright said as soon as Jonah stepped into the diner.

Jonah froze and squinted his eyes at his father's best friend. "Why?"

He loved Moses and Terra like family, but he was also tired as hell. After Lorraine left, he and his crew got down to business. Some people had worked on the scaffolding for the roof repair while Jonah and a few workers started ripping up concrete. His back was aching, and all he wanted to do was eat and go immediately to sleep. He didn't have the energy to troubleshoot their alarm system or fix a wobbly chair. Not tonight.

"Mary dropped off a rhubarb pie for you," Moses said.

Jonah pointed at his own chest. "For me?"

Moses rolled his eyes. "I just said 'for you.'"

Jonah's feet started moving again and they led him right to the pie case. He'd grown up on Terra's pies and cakes and had never had a complaint about her chocolate cream pie or banana pudding. They were good, but he'd been dreaming about Mary's rhubarb pie ever since the first bite.

"You can gon' head and just box the whole thing up for me," he told Moses.

Terra laughed. "I told him you'd say that. What do you have a taste for, Jonah?"

They didn't need to bother with menus; Jonah had memorized it long ago. And if Jonah had a taste for something that wasn't on the menu, they'd make it special — just for him.

"What's the special this week?"

"Meatloaf," Moses said.

"That sounds good. What's..." Jonah's voice trailed off as the door opened and Lorraine's small figure caught his attention.

Instead of that thin black dress she was wearing earlier, she had on a pair of blue leggings and a black tank top, just as formfitting and just as arousing. Jonah noticed her hard nipples immediately.

"Welcome to the Sunnyside Diner," Moses called. "Where'd you come from?"

Jonah startled. "Moses," he warned.

"What? I don't know who she is, so I asked where she's from. What's wrong with that?"

"You didn't have to say it like that," Terra sighed.

Moses turned around to face his wife, throwing his hands out to the side. "Well, how the hell am I supposed to say it?"

"Milwaukee," Lorraine called. They turned their attention back to her. "I moved around a lot as a kid, though, but I liked Milwaukee so I claim it as my hometown." She smiled at Moses, then leaned to the side to see Terra behind the lunch counter and waved.

"I've never been to Milwaukee," Terra said.

"Me neither," Moses echoed before turning to Jonah. "You?"

"For what?" Jonah asked.

"Well, I don't know. You the one that moved to Atlanta," Moses said.

"Which ain't Milwaukee," Jonah shot back.

"You wanna sit at the lunch counter or in a booth, sweetheart?" Terra called over the men's heads.

Jonah turned his attention back to Lorraine to find her looking at him. Her smile was fragile. "It's my first night here and I... I don't want to have dinner alone. I don't know why. You can say no, but—"

"That booth in the back corner is my favorite," Jonah said. Lorraine's shoulders relaxed. "You want some water?"

She nodded and leaned to the side to see Terra again. "I'm Lorraine, by the way."

"The new librarian," Jonah offered.

"Oh, we've heard good things about you."

"Have you?" she asked.

"Willie eats here a couple times a week," Moses said proudly.

"*Mayor* Waltham," Jonah said. Lorraine's eyes moved to his and she smiled brightly at their inside joke.

"Now that could be her or her daddy. Just 'cause he's dead don't mean he don't come up in conversation," Moses said, swatting his hand dismissively in the air. "Come on, lemme show you to your seat."

She smiled at Jonah before turning to follow Moses in the other direction. He turned to the counter and found Terra smiling at him.

"I just met her today," he blurted out guiltily.

She smirked and pushed two red plastic cups full of water across the counter.

Jonah balanced the cups in one hand. His first job was helping his dad on job sites and his second was being a waiter at the Sunnyside whenever the Wrights needed an extra hand. He turned toward the table when Terra cleared her throat. He turned back as she plucked a menu from the wire basket attached to the dessert case.

"I don't need—"

"She does," Terra reminded him.

"Oh," he said, taking the laminated menu from her frail, bent fingers.

"You want me to send Moses to get a bottle of wine?" she whispered.

Jonah pursed his lips as she tried to get her smile under control. He passed Moses in front of the display case. 

"Don't fuck it up," the old man whispered.

Jonah sighed and shook his head as he came up behind her. He put the menu on the table in front of Lorraine and placed the cups of water down before sliding into the booth  across from her.

"Thank you," she said.

"You're welcome?"

"For agreeing to eat with me. You didn't have to." 

"I was gonna eat dinner by myself anyway," Jonah said, which wasn't quite true. If Lorraine hadn't walked in, he'd have been sitting on his favorite stool at the lunch counter,  eating his dinner while Moses and Terra told him about their day. In Sea Port, he'd only ever be truly alone in the mausoleum of his parents' home.

Jonah took a long sip of water. "So, how was your first day in little old Sea Port?"

Lorraine laughed dryly and scratched at her chin. "It was  interesting, that's for sure." She seemed to be thinking, nodding her head slowly as her eyes drifted toward the window.

There wasn't much to see, not even with the town's new  development, but he watched her stare off into the night, not in a rush to look away.

"I saw the Mayor earlier," she said, turning her gaze back  to him.

"Did you find out where the books are being stored?"

"I did. And then I ended up back at Confections. Ate

two croissants and bought a cinnamon roll the size of my face for later."

"Which flavor?" Jonah asked, lifting his eyebrows.

"There's flavors?" she gasped.

"If you see the caramel, just get it. Get two," Jonah corrected.

"Oh my god. It's a good thing this city is walkable. I'm gonna need to get every step in so I can try it all."

Jonah laughed softly. "And then what'd you do?"

"I was gonna go home and have a sugar nap, but then I remembered I didn't have any food or anything, so I went to the..." She shrugged. "It feels wrong to call it a grocery store, but yeah."

Jonah squinted at her. "If you just went to the grocery store, why are you here?"

She looked at him like he was a child. "No one wants to cook after they go grocery shopping; too much work. Besides, I need a vegetable or two after an entire day sponsored by Confections by Mary and a three-day road trip before that. I feel like one long stick of beef jerky, dry and salty."

Jonah laughed. "Long?" he said, squinting at her.

Lorraine sucked her teeth. "I'm tall in spirit."

He laughed louder and she smiled along with him, batting her eyelashes as she took a sip of water.

"Now I love Moses and I love Sea Port, but this ain't the kind of place to eat out if you want a vegetable that ain't been stewed to all hell or fried."

She shrugged. "Can't say I didn't try. I'll make a salad tomorrow."

"Smart."

She picked up the menu. "Is there anything you'd recommend?"

"Oh, lots of things. I've been coming here all my life. I've eaten everything on the menu and some stuff they took off."

She glanced up at him and they got stuck looking into one another's eyes. He'd been thinking about her pressed against him earlier, replaying it in the back of his mind all day, but now it jumped to the forefront of his brain.

She licked her bottom lip, and Jonah dropped his head to hide his smile. Reaching across the table, he flipped the menu over and walked her through his favorite items, dusting off his skills as a waiter.

LORRAINE

"So, did you enjoy what you saw of Sea Port at least?" Jonah asked just as Lorraine took a bite of her burger.

She looked at him over the bun, mid-bite, with wide eyes.

Jonah tried his hardest not to laugh, but he couldn't stop himself. "My bad," he said, choking on his own mirth.

Lorraine chewed with a smile, watching him as he downed another cup of water.

Lorraine didn't mind eating alone. She'd moved around enough in her life that she was skilled at doing everything by her lonesome — lunches, dinners, movie dates, whatever —

but Jonah had just looked so goddamn cute leaning on the counter that she couldn't pass up the chance to spend a little time with him.

And she hadn't regretted it for a second.

She wiped her mouth and hands and took a sip from her own cup before she answered. "After seeing the library looking like a matchstick diorama..." she started.

"Alright," Jonah cut in, shaking his head. "It wasn't that bad."

She pursed her lips and smirked at him. "If you say so. Anyway, after that, nothing could shock me. Well, almost nothing."

"Oh, yeah?"

She nodded quickly. "I know I must sound foolish, but I was not prepared for this heat," she cried softly.

Jonah nodded and scooped some mashed potatoes onto his fork. "Welcome to the South."

Lorraine grabbed a small bunch of fries and popped them into her mouth. She chewed for a few moments, thinking. "Mary gave me so many free pastries, though. That was definitely nice."

"Free?" Jonah said, his fork freezing between his plate and his mouth.

Lorraine sighed, reaching for her burger again. "Don't worry. She told me her plan is to get me hooked for free and *then* charge me. I'm gonna have to give her so much money tomorrow." She shook her head sadly, but then Jonah smiled and she couldn't help but smile back.

"That explains so much," Jonah laughed.

"So, you lived in Atlanta?" Lorraine asked.

Jonah nodded, ducking his head to scoop some more of his dinner onto his fork.

"But you grew up here, right?"

"I moved away for college."

"That makes sense," she said, plucking a piece of bacon from the middle of her burger. "I bet Atlanta felt like another world compared to this place." 

"Definitely," Jonah said, nodding as he moved the food around his plate. 

They ate for the next few minutes in silence and Lorraine didn't let that silence go to waste. She took the biggest bite of her burger she could manage, closed her eyes, and chewed. The Sunnyside was like a time capsule from the Sixties. It had definitely seen better days, but the food was to die for. In a few bites, the Sunnyside became Lorraine's favorite place in all of Sea Port. Well, second favorite after Confections. 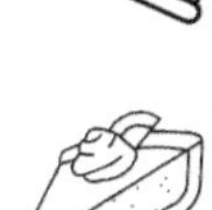 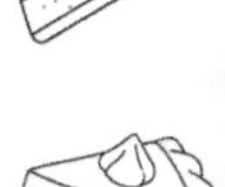

"Does that mean it's good?" Jonah asked.

Lorraine stopped dancing in her seat, an embarrassed smile on her face. "You don't dance when you taste something good?"  

He shook his head before wiping his mouth with a napkin. Lorraine looked at his empty plate. "Damn, does that mean the meatloaf was good?" she asked. 

"Always is," Jonah said, leaning back in his seat. 

"I'll remember that." She grabbed another fry and popped it into her mouth. "So you eat here a lot?" 

"You asked that like an accusation."

"It's just a question."

"And if I say I do come here a bit, you'll say what?"

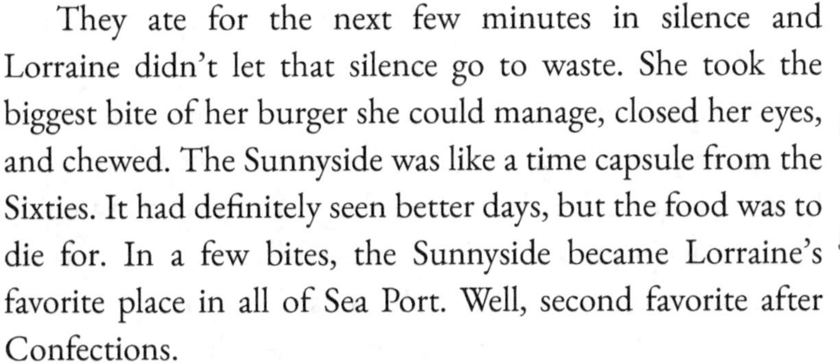
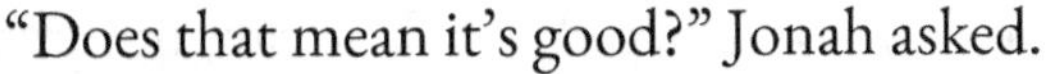
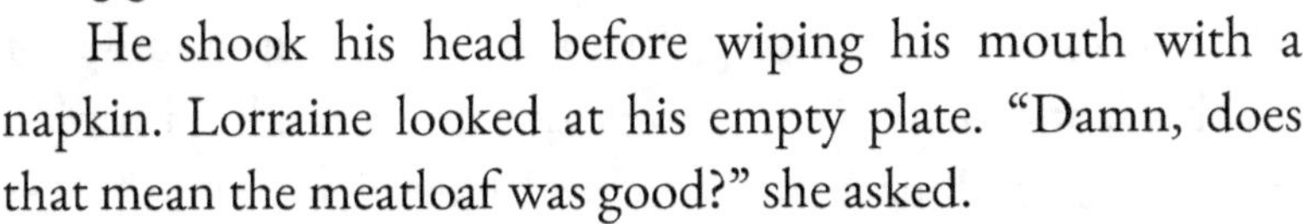

Lorraine shrugged and ate another fry. "So, you can't cook?"

"Ah, there it is," Jonah said, rolling his eyes, but his smile didn't budge. "*It's just a question*," he mimicked.

"I'm just sayin'," Lorraine teased. "When men eat out a lot, it's usually 'cause they can't cook."

"You're eating with me," he said.

She made eye contact and held it. Jonah's smile wobbled, and then she smiled wider. "Yeah," she breathed seriously, "'cause that salad I'ma make tomorrow is about all I can cook."

He tipped his head back and burst out laughing.

Lorraine smiled at him, but she didn't let herself laugh as hard or loud as Jonah because she was too busy watching him, the length of his neck, his dark, lush beard, his Adam's apple bouncing in his throat. He was already beautiful, but seeing Jonah from this angle hit her in her gut. She clenched her thighs together and breathed through a wave of lust that would've knocked her on her ass if she'd been standing.

Lorraine hadn't had sex in four months, which for her was a drought of the worst kind. But breaking up with a situationship, interviewing for a job in the middle of nowhere, and then dismantling her old life had her running around like a chicken with its head cut off; no time to get laid. But the wave of lust that rushed through her veins as Jonah laughed a little too hard at her mid joke had her thinking she should've fucked her ex one more time before she blocked him.

She took the last bite of her burger just to keep her mouth busy.

Jonah drained the last of his water after his laughter died

down, chuckling every now and again while Lorraine finished her food.

"Y'all want some more water?" Mr. Wright called down from the kitchen.

"I'm good," Lorraine said. 

"You want some dessert, sweetie? We've got some pie."

"Not rhubarb," Jonah said.

Mr. Wright sucked his teeth and glared at Jonah. 

"No, thank you. All I've been eating all day is dessert. It was good to get some real food in me."

"She inhaled her burger," Jonah said. 

"That's the best burger I've ever eaten," Lorraine agreed.

"That's what I like to hear," Mr. Wright said. "Won't be  no other diners in Sea Port if I got anything to say about it."

Lorraine started to laugh but a loud yawn came out  instead. She rushed to cover her mouth. "I'm sorry," she said, yawning again.

"No need to apologize. It's been a long day," Jonah chuckled. "Come on, I'll walk you home."

"Why? I basically live around the corner. What can  happen to me between here and there?"

"Famous last words," Jonah joked, and then he shook his head. "You're in the South now. This is just how we do things. I'll pay the bill and we can go." 

"You don't have to do that," she said.

"I know." He slid from the booth and offered his hand. She eyed him carefully before taking it. His skin was a  little rough, but his grip was firm as he helped her stand. Her stomach was doing flips.

"Thanks for dinner," she whispered. "But I don't like strangers knowing where I live."

"Seriously?"

"Seriously."

Jonah sighed. "I already know where you live. I've known that house all my life."

"So you know where I'm going and that I'll be just fine getting there."

"Are you always this stubborn?" he asked, putting his hands on his hips and frowning down at her.

Her thighs clenched, but she powered through it. "I am."

They stared at one another for a few seconds before he shook his head. "Then I think you're gonna fit in here better than you think," he replied. "Goodnight, Lorraine."

"Bye, Jonah," she said, winking and walking toward the door. "Nice to meet you," she said to the Wrights as she passed.

"I got her dinner," Jonah called.

"As you should," Mrs. Wright said. "Have a good night, sweetheart."

"Goodnight," Lorraine called.

She would've felt like a goddess if she strutted from the restaurant without a second glance, but she looked over her shoulder just before stepping outside and found him watching her with a soft, knowing smile on his face.

She thought about his smile on the walk back to her cottage. She fished her vibrators from one of her suitcases, masturbating to that image of Jonah in her head, and *then* she had a great night's sleep.

WELCOME TO SEA PORT

TEN

Jonah

A few days later, Jonah woke up in his old twin bed, curled up in the fetal position, his feet still hanging off the end. Another day in Sea Port. It took him a few minutes to remember where he was and the heartbreaking why. The sting of his grief had dulled some, but never faded completely.

He turned onto his back and stretched the best he could, even though his hands and feet touched the walls in his small bedroom. He missed the king-sized bed in his condo in Atlanta, but the longer he stayed in Sea Port, the less he thought of that place as home. Home would always be Sea Port. Home was this house and this small ass bed.

It was still dark outside and Jonah closed his eyes, just for a few more seconds of rest, but his brain and his dick had other plans. He thought about her in those leggings at the diner, smiling around a French fry, Lorraine sitting across from him in his favorite booth at the Sunnyside, hard nipples pointing in his direction.

The room was cool, but it was still warm under his covers and he pulled the sheets up to his chin. He shoved his left hand into his sweatpants and grabbed his stiff shaft.

If he'd met Lorraine at any other time in his life and any place besides home, he would've asked her out already, but things were different in Sea Port. The last girl he'd dated here was his high school girlfriend, Dayna Marshall. She left town the day after their high school graduation because she always felt suffocated in a town this small. He left a couple months later. Last he heard, she was engaged to a high school basketball coach in Michigan, but there were people in town who still thought they'd get back together one day. Some Porties didn't think events that happened beyond the town's boundaries were real life. Jonah had joked with his dad once that the next woman he brought home would have to be his wife, because the town gossip wasn't worth it otherwise. That was the excuse he used for never bringing Angie home.

But Angie was back in Atlanta and Lorraine was just across town.

He groaned when his fist closed around the length of his shaft, but when he started to stroke, he opened his eyes and frowned. Chafing ruined the fantasy. He rolled over and snatched the drawer in his bedside table open. The bottle of lotion had been there for years and for this exact reason. Some things never changed. He pumped some lotion into his palm and ducked back under the covers, smearing it into his shaft with a sigh. It was messy but it always got the job done.

When Jonah closed his eyes again Lorraine was smirking at him, popping a French fry in her mouth, and it made his gut clench. He rubbed his slick palm over the head of his dick and a shiver moved across his back.

He gave up on reality now and imagined Lorraine in a bedroom. Not this bedroom. He couldn't imagine his father would approve of that — not even from the afterlife — so he pictured her somewhere luxurious and as far from Sea Port  as they could get. The Lorraine in his head was wearing a cute little business suit only because Jonah wanted to watch  her take it off.

For the first time in months, instead of waking up and crying for half an hour, Jonah imagined Lorraine standing in  front of him, getting more naked by the minute, until he  came all over his hand.

LORRAINE

"This is more than I was expecting, to be honest," Lorraine said as she strolled through the top floor of the city's administrative building.

"I'll take that as a compliment," Mayor Waltham said.

It was her official first day as Sea Port's head — and only  — librarian. She'd gotten dressed this morning hoping for the best but prepared to be pissed just in case. Thankfully, it wasn't bad at all.

It wasn't the largest collection she'd ever worked with,

but she hadn't expected it would be. It was also dated, but Lorraine was prepared for that as well. What she hadn't thought to consider was how much she'd learn about the town based on the books lovingly cared for on its shelves — or in storage, as it happened.

"A lot of Black history," Lorraine murmured, running her thumb over a leather copy of *The Negro in Our History*.

"And true crime," Willie said. "Nothing Porties love more than our people and big city serial killers."

Lorraine glanced in Willie's direction to find a small, playful smile on her face. She looked the part of a small-town mayor, if a bit young, but her smile made Lorraine consider that Mayor Waltham had once been a girl running around the old library and it softened her heart to her and all that she was seeing.

Willie was an interesting woman. Lorraine had thought she was a little quirky while interviewing for the position. There hadn't been any red flags, just question marks. She was maybe in her mid-thirties but carried herself like she'd been in this position for half her life. She was professional but not stiff, and every now and then, she'd say something that would subtly change the way Lorraine saw her.

"Has anyone ever told you you'd make a decent cult leader?" Lorraine blurted out. Her cheeks warmed immediately. "I can't believe I said that."

Willie's face did something odd, but for her maybe it was normal. Instead of bunching up in anger or disbelief, it softened as if she was giving what Lorraine said some serious consideration. "No," she finally said. "And now I'm wondering why not, 'cause I can see it. Anyway, before she left the position, our last librarian combed through the books, culling the ones in disrepair or that no one had checked out since my grandmother was Mayor."

"Oh! You're from a political family," Lorraine nodded. "That makes sense."

Willie sighed. "It's in my DNA."

"So this is what's left?" Lorraine asked, turning around the room.

"Technically there are some more upstairs, mostly reference books. They're accessible, but I'm going to require you to only go up there in the company of Knox or Santos. Safety precautions."

"Okay. Your last librarian, was she a...was she from here?" Lorraine asked, stumbling over her words.

"Yes and no. She's from an old Portie family, but her parents left sometime during the Great Depression. She came here in the Sixties to visit her grandmother before she died. She was expecting to be here for a few weeks, a couple months at the most, before she got back to her life in a big city somewhere."

Lorraine smiled. "Let me guess, she came here and realized there was more to little old Sea Port than she thought and decided to stay?"

"She met a man," Willie said with a grin.

"Of course. Was he a hardworking farmer or..."

"Serviceman," Mayor Waltham said, her voice turning serious. "He came home with an amputated leg and his brother's ashes."

"Oh my god," Lorraine breathed.

"Don't worry. They took one look at each other and it was love at first sight. She got a job at the library and he

started working at his father's garage like he did before the war."

"Did they have kids?"

"Three. Oh, but I'm not one of them," she laughed.

"Granddaughter?"

Willie shook her head. A braid fell from the bun atop her head and she wound it back into place. "Nope. That would have been cute if this was a movie or a romance novel, but it's just a story. Not all Porties are related. The important part is that when Mrs. Jones became the library director, she didn't play about her books. She applied for every grant to upgrade our systems to the best of her ability. She worked with my campaign to make sure the library was part of our early renovation plans. And when we got the money to completely renovate the building, she was the one to figure out the temp control for our book storage."

"Does that mean she's still around?" Lorraine asked.

"Of course, she is. And the only reason you haven't met her yet is because she can be...a lot."

"I don't mind," Lorraine said with a shrug.

"We'll see. Do you have any questions so far?"

"So many," Lorraine breathed.

There was a rectangular table in the exact center of the room, and Mayor Waltham gestured toward one of the chairs while she took the other.

"Temperature control is great, but what about fire? Flood?"

Mayor Waltham sat easily. "Flooding is why we didn't store these books in the basement. Fire's a perpetual hazard. We're gonna need to gut this place soon, but right now, it's all we have. All we can hope is that Knox is on top of his game," she said with a smile.

Lorraine nodded in agreement. "This is a small collection."

Mayor Waltham nodded. "We have a small budget for you to start updating and moving to digital, but I won't lie, it's not much. Which brings me to the most important part of your position." 

Lorraine smiled. "Grants."

"So many grants." 

"I figured."

"Wonderful. This experiment is just that, an experiment. We hope all the things we're doing will help us stabilize in the future." 

"But libraries always need money."

"They do. We have a very small tax that goes to the library, but any more will involve *a lot* of political goodwill."  Lorraine stared at the Mayor, waiting for her to continue. "Mrs. Jones had the connections, but you don't." 

Lorraine sighed loudly. "So, I'm a show pony."

Mayor Waltham laughed. "Oh, honey, we're all show ponies. But if it gets the job done, that's all that matters." 

"Spoken like a true politician."

"There have been Walthams in the Mayor's office for over a hundred years," she said. "This is the job I was raised  to do."

"Is it the job you wanted?" Lorraine asked.

Mayor Waltham's face pinched, as if she was in pain, but her smile stayed in place. "When I was younger, I didn't  think so. I left for college like lots of Porties do. I stayed away through law school. I traveled a little bit in Europe, but everywhere I went, I never forgot about home. So, I guess yeah, this is the job I wanted."

They sat in silence for a few moments, each woman lost in their own thoughts. Even though she claimed Milwaukee as her hometown, the city hadn't stuck with her in the way Sea Port clearly had with Mayor Waltham. Memories of her hometown followed Willie around the world, but Milwaukee had never done the same for Lorraine. She didn't dream of it when she traveled or go back on the holidays. There was no one there she loved anymore; everyone she used to know had long forgotten about her or moved away themselves. If she had a home, it was wherever DeJuan was, but that wasn't quite the same.

"Well," Mayor Waltham said, pulling Lorraine from her thoughts. She pushed her chair back from the table. "Now that you've approved of our storage methods, I'll show you the lending library."

"Was that Mrs. Jones's idea as well?"

"Of course, it was," she laughed. "And it was a good one. Her ideas usually are."

"I'll remember that," Lorraine said.

Mayor Waltham led Lorraine from the room. Lorraine waited behind her while she locked the door. She was just about to put the key back into her pants pocket when she stopped, turned to Lorraine, and offered her the keychain. "I guess these are yours now."

Lorraine stared at the keys for a few seconds before taking them from Willie's hand.

"Don't lose those," she said. "I don't even know if there are duplicates." And with that, she brushed past Lorraine, heading for the stairs.

Willie was at least half a foot taller than her and Lorraine had to work up to a gentle jog to keep up with her stride. She didn't even think the woman was in a rush, but Lorraine was happy she chose flats today instead of heels.

The lending library was set up in a large room on the main floor of the city's administrative building. There was an old metal music stand next to the door with a printed sign indicating the library's temporary home. The Mayor stepped aside and gestured toward the door. Lorraine raised her eyes in confusion.

"You can unlock it," Mayor Waltham said in a mild rebuke.

"Oh. Right," Lorraine laughed. There were three keys on the ring, and she stared at them.

The Mayor pointed at each in turn. "Storage upstairs. Lending library. Unlocks the old front door. I guess you can get rid of that one," she said.

Lorraine unlocked the door, turned the handle, and pushed. Nothing happened.

"Weather," Willie said. "Put your shoulder into it." Lorraine leaned against the door. "Harder."

Lorraine sighed and shoved her body into the door and stumbled inside.

"There you go," Willie said, walking in behind her with an elegant stride.

The room was larger than Lorraine was expecting and it was set up rather nicely. There were two small square tables in the middle of the room with a few book stacks lined along some of the walls, keeping books as far from the light as possible.

"This used to be our second courtroom," the Mayor

said. "But we don't have enough people committing enough crime to justify keeping it, so we repurposed it."

"That's a good thing," Lorraine replied.

Willie shrugged. "I guess. A little boring, but that's alright. Hopefully in a year or two, we'll have enough people to put Santos to work."

"Is that really the goal?" Lorraine asked, whirling around to look at her.

Mayor Waltham only winked.

"Knock, knock." They turned to find Mary leaning into the doorway. "You open?"

"Just giving our new librarian a tour of her workspace."

"Sounds boring. Want a donut?"

"Is it free?" Lorraine asked, already stepping forward.

Mary frowned and stepped back. "Sorry, not this time."

"Damn," Lorraine sighed, slowing her steps. Not stopping, though.

"We're doing a fundraiser for the Community Center to refurbish the wheelchair ramp. Apparently, it's been feeling a little wobbly," Mary said.

"How much?" the Mayor asked.

"Five dollars a donut."

"That's steep," Lorraine laughed.

"It's for charity."

"How many you have left?" Mayor Waltham asked.

"Six, but I'll give you a deal if you want to buy a few," Mary offered, tipping the basket in her hand forward so Lorraine and Willie could get a good glimpse of her treats, individually wrapped in clear plastic cellophane. There was an adorable little cupcake sticker on each package indicating the ingredients and allergens.

Lorraine eyed the chocolate donuts seriously and was just reaching for her wallet when Mayor Waltham pushed past her with two crisp twenty-dollar bills in her hand.

"No change necessary."

Mary's face brightened. "Thank you! I recommend the—"

Mayor Waltham shook her head. "I'm actually not a huge fan of sweets."

"What?" Lorraine and Mary gasped.

Willie rolled her eyes. Clearly, she'd had this exchange before. "Give the donuts to whoever wants them."

"Like me," Lorraine offered.

"Willie, that's so nice!"

"Can I call you Willie?" Lorraine asked.

The woman eyed her. "*If* you make it to four months,  we'll talk about it."

"Well, you have to let me thank you if you're not going to eat my donuts," Mary said with a frown.

"No, I don't," Willie said.

"You do," Mary said, a firm smile on her face.

Willie sighed again. "I tried to get them to fix that damn  ramp eight months ago. There's money to do it, but the place needs a full gut reno as well and the director is worried about using money we have for small things when there's so much work to be done."

"Is the ramp a small thing?" Mary asked warily.

"No. Mr. Brownley was my high school math teacher,  but he still talks to me like I'm fifteen and skipping his class every Friday."

"*Every* Friday?" Lorraine asked.

"Allegedly. He won't listen to any of my advice, but if he

wants to fundraise, fine. Let's just hope no one gets hurt on that ramp before you meet your goal."

"Oh, we're really close," Mary said brightly. "Louis convinced Jonah to donate his time, so we're just fundraising for the cost of parts."

Willie's serious face broke into a smile and she nodded, reaching into her wallet. She shoved another couple bills into Mary's hand. "Don't tell him I gave you this. He'll be annoying about it."

Mary pressed her lips shut and pretended to lock it with a key. "Let me make you dinner," she said. "To say thank you. Do you have plans tonight?"

Willie nodded. "I'm always busy," she said. "And like I said, there's no reason to thank me." She turned to Lorraine. "Lending library is closed on Mondays, so take all the time you need to orient yourself. I have a call I need to prepare for." She sounded very unhappy about that last part. "My office is one floor up and my door's always open."

"Okay," Lorraine said. "Thanks."

She shook her head again. "No reason to thank me. This is the job. And we're very happy to have you here," Willie said before she nodded at Mary and walked from the room at that same fast clip.

Mary turned back to Lorraine. "Well, do you want to have dinner with us?" she asked.

"Luckily for you, I don't care about feeling like second best when there's food involved." She punctuated those words by plucking both chocolate donuts from the basket.

Mary beamed at her. "We're only about a hundred dollars to our goal."

Lorraine was already pulling at the sticker holding the

wrapping closed. She stopped and made eye contact with Mary, who was still smiling.

"Fine," Lorraine said, reaching into her purse, offering Mary a twenty-dollar bill.

"Thank you!" Mary trilled.

"You're welcome," Lorraine replied, snatching a red velvet donut as well.

WELCOME TO SEA PORT

ELEVEN

Lorraine

Lorraine started second-guessing Mary's dinner invitation only when she was standing at the end of their paved stone walkway staring up at their house and trying to stifle a yawn. Mary, Knox, and Santos's house was set right in the middle of an adorable little cul-de-sac. There were three other houses around this curved street, but since their windows were all dark, Lorraine guessed they were empty. She had a bottle of her favorite Italian wine — packed to give away in moments exactly like this — but she was tired; she'd been talking to people all day.

At the Sunnyside when she popped in for lunch and had the last of their meatloaf. Jonah was right, it was amazing, so she talked to Mrs. Wright about the recipe while she ate. At Sully's when she stopped by for her afternoon pick-me-up. And of course, all afternoon at the lending library. She hadn't known what to expect of her new patrons, especially in a town so small, but after her first day on the job, Lorraine

could say for sure that Porties loved to read and yap, not necessarily in that exact order. Between the mystery book club talking her ears off about new series they needed her to buy ASAP and a teenager who decided to read her book in the corner rather than check it out, Lorraine hadn't had a moment of peace all day.

She wanted to sleep.

She was considering texting Mary her apologies and asking for a rain check when Knox moved past the picture window lit with a warm light and stood in what looked like their living room.

"Lord, that man is beautiful," she whispered to herself as Santos moved into view. The men laughed with one another and moved closer and closer together. Lorraine couldn't look away, not even when Santos grabbed Knox's face, still laughing as they kissed.

She sighed and started up the path, nosy as ever. Lorraine understood polyamory...for the most part. What she didn't understand was how in the hell they were doing all this in this small ass town and everyone just seemed fine with it. It was fascinating, and Lorraine wanted to get to the bottom of it more than she wanted a quiet night in.

Also, she thought she smelled caramel as she stepped onto the porch and knocked on the front door.

Santos opened the door with a smile on his face. It wasn't as warm as Mary's or Knox's, but it immediately struck Lorraine that he looked far more relaxed than the first time they met.

"Hi," Lorraine called.

"Hello."

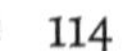

"Come on in," Knox called from behind him.

Santos stepped back and pulled the door open wide for her to enter. He accepted the bottle of wine and her purse, hanging the latter on the coat rack bolted to the wall while Lorraine kicked off her sandals.

"You want something to drink?" Knox called from the bar cart they'd set up in the dining room.

"Do you have wine?" she asked. "Or I brought some."

"You didn't need to bring anything," said Mary, stepping into the dining room as Santos led her toward the table.

"I can't show up empty-handed. That would be rude."

"We got red and some white in the fridge," Knox said. "Unless you want to open yours."

"Oooh, I'll take a glass of white, please."

"Gotcha," Knox said, walking toward the kitchen. He deviated from the straight pathway there to wrap an arm around Mary's waist and press his face into her soft curls.

There was something about the intimacy of that moment that tugged at Lorraine's heart. She wasn't particularly sentimental. In fact, each and every one of her exes probably would've described her as cold by the time she broke up with them. There was a kernel of truth she couldn't deny in the accusation. And in her mind, the fault was theirs since they hadn't inspired her to thaw in their hands like Mary melted in Knox's.

"Were the directions okay?" Mary asked, laughing as Knox let her go.

"Yeah. Definitely. I mean...it's kinda hard to get lost in Sea Port."

"Not as hard as you think," Santos said. He'd taken

Knox's place at the bar cart, refreshing two cups with a light-yellow premade cocktail. "This salesman came here last year and started pounding the pavement. He took the wrong turn and ended up in the pasture *behind* the Johnson farm. He said his GPS kept glitching."

"His GPS loaded?" Lorraine gasped.

"Not for long," Knox said, walking back into the room, sliding past Mary to offer Lorraine a beautiful long-stemmed glass with a generous pour of wine.

"Ooh, these are pretty," Lorraine said.

"Housewarming gift," Mary said.

"I'll give you a map of the city," Knox offered, meeting Santos at the bar cart. "Sea Port's too small for GPS. The system keeps thinking you're on a different street because everything is so close together."

"Hell, sometimes I'm not sure I'm on the street I think I'm on," Lorraine said.

"Does it even matter?" Santos asked, his mouth tipping into a smile.

"No," they echoed in a comforting chorus, laughing with one another.

Lorraine could nap later; this dinner was exactly what she needed.

JONAH

J onah thought he knew his dad's job inside and out. He'd spent his entire childhood riding in the passenger seat to one worksite after another, but after only seven months in his dad's shoes, he was still discovering parts of the job he hadn't noticed before. Like right now, instead of  going home and crashing out or stopping by the Sunnyside for a quick dinner, Jonah was jogging across town to drop some paperwork off with Knox.

Business in a small town was a double-edged sword. On  the one hand, he knew everyone in town, so filing paperwork and getting approvals he needed was easier than it had ever  been in Atlanta. Hell, some people who still worked in the city knew Jonah's father, mother, *and* grandparents and were happy to just fill out the paperwork for him and call  him into the city offices to sign his name.

On the other hand, the work schedule seemed never-ending. He would never do a half-assed job, but even if he  wanted to, he couldn't — every job was personal, every client got a friends and family discount, every job was just as important as the other. Sea Port was too small for anyone to  be a nameless face in a crowd and Jonah took every mistake or delay personally.

So, when he discovered one of his crew members had  fucked up the paperwork for the new ramp at the Community Center, Jonah took them home to fix, but now, it was late. He could accept the delay in his timeline or he could  stop by Knox's house and ask the man to submit the forms on his behalf, specifically so Knox could charm Ms. Bordon, the county clerk, to stamp it with the right date — another perk of small-town living.

He knocked on the front door and waited. He wasn't sure if it was his brain playing tricks on him but Jonah thought he smelled warm chocolate and it made his stomach growl.

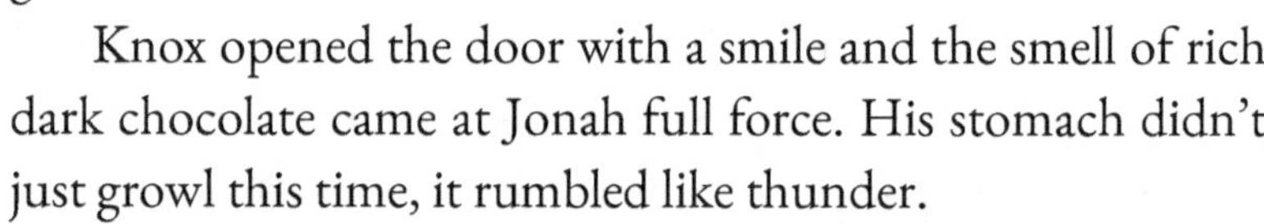

Knox opened the door with a smile and the smell of rich dark chocolate came at Jonah full force. His stomach didn't just growl this time, it rumbled like thunder.

"Well, hello to you too," Knox laughed.

Jonah smiled and offered the manila envelope with the paperwork inside. "Thanks for doing this."

Knox grabbed the envelope and used it to bat the air. "No worries. I've been trying to sweet-talk Ms. Johnetta into cutting me a deal on a side of beef for the longest time anyway. Might as well just add this to the list."

Jonah laughed, shaking his head. "Alright, I'll let you get back."

"You don't gotta run so soon. I'd ask if you had dinner, but your stomach already told me no. Come on in. We're having lasagna. Mary made too much."

"I didn't make too much," Mary yelled from farther in their house. "I made enough to eat for lunch. It's called meal prepping."

Knox rolled his eyes but his face was full of gentle fondness. "We've got enough for a few lunches," he said. "You're more than welcome to a plate."

Jonah shook his head. "No, I don't wanna interrupt. You three probably want to be alone."

Knox lifted his eyebrows and took a step back. "We're not alone."

Jonah recognized the back of Lorraine's head immediately. She turned slowly around, a fork still in her mouth. She smiled around it and winked in Jonah's direction.

"I made a German chocolate cake for dessert," Mary cried happily.

"You had me at cake," Jonah said, stepping into their entryway, even though his eyes were focused on Lorraine.

WELCOME TO SEA PORT

TWELVE

Jonah

"So, is it good?" Mary asked Jonah in a soft, sultry voice.

Jonah froze at her question. Every eye in the room was on him and the spoon between his lips. They waited in silence for him to answer.

He pulled the spoon from his mouth. It was clean. He wasn't letting a drop of icing go to waste.

Knox laughed, taking the edge off the moment as Jonah scooped up another bit of cake. "That's his second slice. I think we know the answer."

Mary was sitting at the head of the table with Santos and Knox crowding in on either side of her chair. She was happy and a little tipsy when she leaned forward, forearms resting on the table, her eyes happily boring into his.

"Yeah, but I want to hear him say it," she said in a seductive whisper, batting her eyes at him. "Go on. Stroke my ego, Jonah."

Santos covered his mouth, not that it did much to

muffle his laughter, but it was Lorraine's soft giggle that really broke the tension, and then everyone laughed at Jonah.

"You're an easy mark," Lorraine whispered, scooping up more of her second slice as well.

"No," Mary laughed. "You've just got such an expressive face and we're assholes."

"Speak for yourself," Knox laughed, throwing his arm over the back of Mary's chair. "And Santos."

Mary rolled her eyes fondly. "We know people still gossip about us."

Jonah dropped his eyes to his plate. "Oh, really?" he asked unconvincingly.

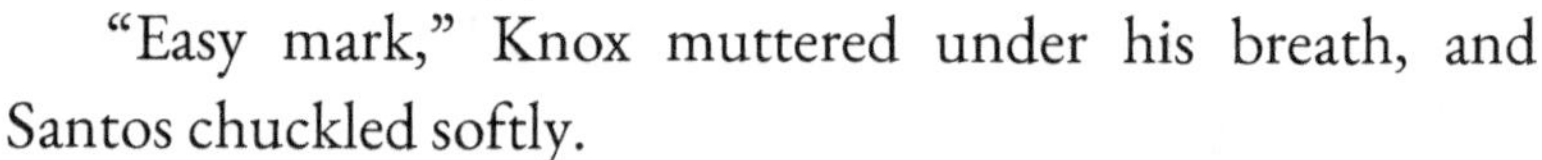

"Easy mark," Knox muttered under his breath, and Santos chuckled softly.

"I haven't heard anything," Lorraine said.

Knox, Mary, and Santos turned their attention to Lorraine. Jonah scooped another spoonful of cake into his mouth now that their attention was mercifully elsewhere.

Knox's chuckle was deep and rolling. "No offense, sweetheart, you've been here five minutes. You ain't heard about us 'cause they're gossiping about you too."

Her mouth fell open. "About what? I haven't done anything interesting yet."

"And they're probably getting mad about that," Jonah added helpfully. He leaned back in his chair with a happy, full belly and chocolate flooding his veins. He hadn't even had a drop of alcohol; the cake was all he needed.

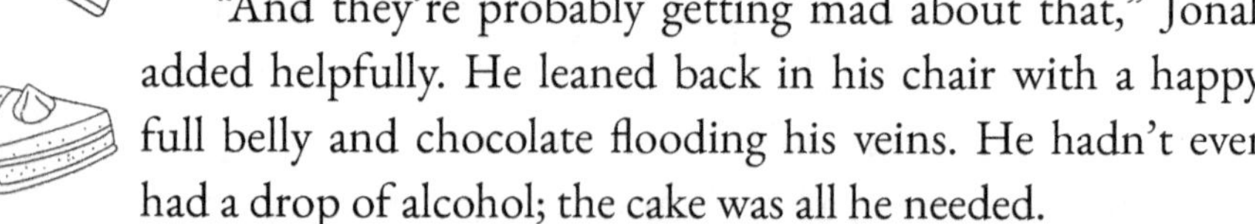

"Hold on," Lorraine said, reaching for her wine glass. "Do I want to hit the town gossip mill or not?"

Jonah laughed and shook his head. "You don't have a choice. None of us do."

"Us?" Lorraine asked. "So it's not just us transfers?"

"Transplants," Santos corrected. "And it's not just us, but apparently the three of us have been the hot topic for the past year."

"You've been together a year?" Lorraine gasped happily.

"A little over a year," Knox corrected quickly. "And while the attention has been nice, we can't wait for someone else to take over the top spot on the gossip train." 

"Good luck with that," Jonah said. "Good gossip lasts forever. When I was a kid, my dad used to tell this story about Willie's grandfather. Maybe her great-grandfather? I don't know. Anyway, when he was young, he was a rolling stone, and he didn't care if the women he was sneaking around with were married or not."

"Oh no," Lorraine gasped.

"Oh yeah," Jonah laughed. "One day, he snuck in the wrong back door. Nobody knows exactly what happened, but apparently her husband came home early, pulled out a pistol, and next thing you know, half the town saw him running home butt naked." 

"Oh my god," Mary laughed as the table burst into laughter.

"I don't even know when that story happened exactly, but my daddy told me and now I'm telling you, and that's the power of good gossip in a place like Sea Port." 

"And now we're part of the problem," Lorraine laughed.

Jonah made the mistake of glancing in her direction. All through dinner, he'd been trying not to look directly at her if he could help it, but sometimes he couldn't stop himself.

Every time he looked her way, his brain wished he hadn't, but his dick was happy he did. The conversation moved along, but all Jonah could see was Lorraine's tongue gliding along the back of the fork. He swallowed a groan and shifted in his chair. He reached for his glass of water and downed the rest, trying to get his brain back on the right track and off Lorraine's mouth. He set his glass down and looked up, making eye contact with Santos for a second before the other man looked away and laughed with everyone else.

Sprinkled in amid the condolences for his father's passing were promises that eventually, his life would get back to normal — that one day, he'd be able to think of his father without the sharp pain of grief stabbing him in the gut. Jonah hadn't believed them and still wasn't sure he did now, but he couldn't deny that the possibility felt more real tonight than in the last few months.

Jonah's father was his blueprint. He couldn't imagine getting over losing him, the same way his father had never gotten over losing Jonah's mother. And the fact that Jonah had lost them both and was all alone in the world heightened the intensity of his grief. But it was different tonight. Knox, Mary, and Santos had known his father in passing, but to them he was just another Portie, not someone they remember carrying Jonah around town on his shoulders. And Lorraine hadn't known Wesley at all. Hell, he wasn't even sure if she knew his father had recently passed. Jonah certainly hadn't told her. For the first time in months, Jonah had a few hours where he didn't feel like his father's ghost was sitting on his shoulders, reminding him of all he'd lost. With these four people, Jonah could mention his father and the conversation would still move along for all of them,

Jonah included. He didn't know how he felt about that just yet.

Mary stood from her chair and reached across the table for their dishes, smiling down at him. "Done? Or you want me to wait for you to lick the plate?" she asked in that same sultry voice. 

Jonah's face was hot and he shifted his eyes away. "I'm done," he said as his gaze landed on Santos, who was staring at Mary's ass. 

"Mmhmm," Mary hummed.

She grabbed the plates and turned toward the kitchen while Santos took their empty glasses and followed her. 

"So, Lorraine, how long's your contract?" Knox asked.

"A year," she replied, taking another sip of wine.

"You planning to stay longer than that?" 

"It's basically my first day on the job," she laughed.

"Yeah," Knox conceded, "but a lot can happen in a year."

They were in the kitchen, but as if to accentuate his point, a soft peal of Mary's laughter drifted in, followed by a soft groan. Or at least that's what it sounded like to Jonah's ears. 

If Knox heard the same, he didn't let it interrupt the flow of conversation. "So..." he asked, nudging Lorraine again. 

She set her wine glass down. "Did Mayor Waltham put you up to this?" she asked.

Knox laughed loudly, holding onto his stomach as he sat up straight. "That sounds like some shit she'd do, but no. Not yet. I'm just nosy." 

"He is," Mary said, walking back into the room. Instead of sitting back in her chair, however, she trailed her hand over Knox's shoulders. He pushed his chair back just enough for her to slide onto his lap.

"Be nice," Mary whispered to Knox.

"I'm always nice, baby," he whispered in return as Mary ducked her head. Their mouths brushed together. Jonah's eyes went wide when he caught a glimpse of her tongue moving between their lips.

Santos sauntered back into the room with a small smile on his face. He stopped behind Mary and Knox and smiled down at Jonah and Lorraine. "So, Lorraine, how long's your contract?"

Knox laughed into Mary's mouth and pulled away. "I already asked that," he said as Mary kissed her way across his face down to his neck.

"I missed it. What'd she say?" Santos asked, watching Lorraine. She took another sip of her wine.

"She told me she'll be here for a year, but she also accused me of prying for the Mayor," Knox said, his eyelashes fluttering.

Jonah turned to Lorraine, who was smiling against the rim of her glass. Her eyes shifted to Jonah and their gazes locked for the first time all night. His muscles tightened under her gaze, including his groin. Her tongue moved over the rim of her glass and Jonah took in a shuddering breath that was drowned out by one of Mary's soft laughs. This one definitely sounded like a moan.

Jonah tore his eyes away from Lorraine to find something that would've had the gossip mill turning for the next decade. On its surface, it was a cute, slightly tipsy tableau of three people in love, but without even scratching the surface, Jonah realized that whatever was actually going on over there was something far more serious.

Mary had lifted her head from Knox's neck, her face blowing their cover more than anything else. He knew Mary was tipsy, but her eyelids were almost fully closed now and that wasn't because of the alcohol. Santos's eyes were aimed in her lap and whatever was happening there had all three of them breathing heavily. 

Lorraine's knee bumped into his and he jumped, pulling them all out of their sugar and wine stupor. 

"You alright?" Knox asked Jonah, licking his thumb with a smile. His hand dropped back to his or Mary's lap and she squeaked as she shifted on top of him, but he held her close. 

"Yeah, I'm fine. Sorry, it's just been a long day."

"Tell me about it," Lorraine hiccupped, breaking the tension again. 

"We accidentally got Lorraine drunk," Mary said, another laughing moan falling from her lips again. 

"It might have been an accident for you, but not me," Lorraine giggled. She ran her fingers through her hair and licked her lips.

Jonah wanted to look away but knew if he did, all he'd see was whatever the hell was happening with Mary, Knox, and Santos; this small dining room was a minefield. 

"I haven't been able to let my hair down for real in weeks. This feels great," Lorraine said, tugging gently at her braids. 

"Jesus," Jonah mumbled under his breath and reached for his glass of water, but it was gone because he'd finished it. 

He looked up and made eye contact with Santos again. The man had a soft smirk on his face. Jonah looked quickly away, only to latch onto Santos's hand on Knox's shoulder, his fingers slipping into the neck of the man's t-shirt.

"Let's get you home," Santos said.

Jonah looked up to find him looking at Lorraine. She set her glass on the table and licked her lips again. "I'll take her," Jonah blurted out.

"You sure?" Mary asked. "There's still more cake."

Jonah swallowed. "Uh...yeah. I got an early morning tomorrow, and uh...her house is on the way."

"You don't know where I live," Lorraine teased.

Jonah rolled his eyes, but then her knee bumped his again, except this time, she didn't shift away. In fact, she turned into his side and smiled at him, her tongue peeking out of the corner of her lips. Her lipstick had faded over dinner to a soft, bruising red that made his dick swell in his jeans.

He was for sure going to dream about this later.

"I told you, I've known that house all my life."

"Prove it," she whispered.

"I guess that settles that," Mary sighed sensually while Knox and Santos chuckled softly.

LORRAINE

Lorraine had been to worse dinner parties in her life, but dinner at Mary's — and Santos and Knox's — was lovely. The food was good, the cake rich and delicious, but ultimately, it was the company she enjoyed the most, especially the man walking beside her. 

She tried to watch Jonah from the corner of her eye, but Sea Port didn't have a single streetlight outside downtown.  They didn't have sidewalks either, so they walked in the middle of the street and she caught glimpses of him in the moonlight. His skin was a deep, dark brown, the firm cut of his jaw and soft rounding of his nose only accentuated by  the shadows.

There was nothing but room and yet Jonah's arm brushed hers every few steps, making the hair on her arms stand on end while her nipples hardened outside of her  control.

Finally, he spoke. "You think they wanted to get rid of us  so they could fuck?" he asked.

Lorraine's laughter echoed in the silent street, and after a few seconds, Jonah's deep rumble joined hers. "Of course,  they did. You see how Santos's right arm was under the table the whole time we were eating?"

She felt Jonah turn to her. "What? No."

Lorraine nodded, laughing harder. "Now, I'm not saying  nothing for sure, but I'm saying."

"That's how town gossip starts," Jonah laughed.

Lorraine gasped and turned to him, stumbling over her  next step. "Oh no, I don't want to—"

"Calm down," Jonah said, grabbing her around the waist and holding on as she steadied herself. "I won't tell anybody. I like them, I'm just saying."

"I like them too," Lorraine sighed.

"I also don't want Mary to ban me from the bakery."

"You think she'd do that for real?"

"If she wouldn't, Santos would, and I don't need those kinda problems." His hand slid along her waist to the middle of her back. Her dress was so thin she swore she could feel his fingers on her bare skin, and it made her wet.

Lorraine had to press her lips shut to stop from saying or doing something she might regret — definitely enjoy but possibly regret. She'd kept her libido in check for hours, but with Jonah's hand on her, she was quickly losing the war.

"This is your house, ain't it?" Jonah asked with a smile in his voice.

"Shut up," Lorraine whispered as she turned toward him and his hand dragged along her lower back to settle on her hip. She'd left the porch light on just in case she forgot which cottage was hers. In the afterglow of warm light, she saw his tongue move over her lips and she followed his lead. "Thanks for walking me home."

He shook his head. "I'll walk you to the door."

"Why?"

He sighed loudly. "Can't you just let me be a gentleman?"

"Why?" she shot back, mostly playing but also curious because he was so goddamn beautiful and she liked getting under his skin just a little bit.

"Why not?" he shot back, squeezing her hip. "I'm not trying to take advantage of you or hurt you, this is just how I was raised."

"To follow women home?" she teased.

"I led you home, actually," he said, squeezing her hip. "I just wanna make sure you make it in okay."

"Is there something out here I should be afraid of?" she whispered.

"You mean besides the raccoons?"

"Raccoons?" Lorraine cried out, stepping away from the warmth of his body.

"See, you didn't even know about them. Come on,"  Jonah laughed, gently nudging her forward.

Halfway up the path, she remembered she needed keys and fumbled in her purse as she took the stairs slowly, but  she stopped when Jonah's hand fell away from her hip. She turned to find him still on the middle step, waiting with a soft smile on his face. She didn't think anything could top  the warmth of his hand on her body, but his small, lopsided grin broke through the last threads of Lorraine's self-control.

"You gon' stay there?" she asked, fully turning around.

His head tipped forward and she felt his gaze move down  her chest. She wasn't wearing a bra or panties and that hadn't mattered until right now when she wished there was  nothing between Jonah's gaze and her body.

"Don't want you thinking I'm trying to rush inside," he said. "Your house, I mean."

"I don't think you'd rush," she said. "You look like the  kinda man who'd like to take it slow."

Jonah laughed softly, shaking his head, but he didn't refute her claim.

"Is that all you wanna do?" she rasped. "Make sure I get  in safe, I mean?" She swore she heard Jonah swallow.

"That's all I'm willing to say out loud," he said in a heated whisper.

That was all the opening Lorraine needed. "So, don't say it. Do it."

She was planning to hold her breath and wait, but Jonah didn't give her the chance. As soon as she finished speaking, he took that last step onto her porch and stalked toward her. By the time he was right in front of her, she was panting in excitement as his chest brushed her already hard nipples. He pushed her back against her front door.

"You sure about that?"

Lorraine lifted onto the balls of her feet, pressing herself against him like a needy cat. "Please quit teasing me," she moaned.

She didn't know much about Jonah yet, but so far, he'd proved himself to be the kind of man who'd give her some of what she wanted but not everything, and the denial was just as delicious. He bent forward until they were breathing the same air. His bottom lip grazed hers, but he didn't kiss her the way she wanted. It was torture. Lorraine couldn't get enough.

Jonah wrapped his arms around her waist and pulled her into his body. "You sure you want me to stop teasing?" he asked, his smile touching hers.

"For now," she breathed and then captured his top lip between hers. Their kiss was hot from the moment their lips touched. She moaned against his mouth. His tongue tasted like chocolate, and his dick grinding into her stomach was hard as steel. Lorraine wanted to stay in that moment forever, but they were interrupted by some animal Lorraine didn't want to know anything about howling in the distance, and they pulled apart.

"That wasn't a raccoon," Jonah laughed, rubbing her back in soft, soothing circles.

"Well, I don't want to know what it was," she said.

"I should let you get inside."

"Why? Is that coyote coming for us?"

He moved his hands to her hips and squeezed. "It wasn't a coyote."

"I said, I don't want to know."

She moved her hands behind his neck and pulled him back down to her mouth. He came willingly, a gorgeous smile on his face.

"Your neighbors," he whispered against her lips.

She froze, looking into his eyes. Honestly, she'd forgotten there were other people in the neighborhood. Hell, at some point while Jonah was sucking on her tongue, she'd forgotten where she was, but now that he mentioned it, she glanced left and right. She could see the houses in her peripheral vision, but they were all dark. It was only her porch light that was on, perfectly illuminating their embrace. If anyone was looking, they'd already seen a lot, and that should've straightened her right up.

But for some reason, it had the opposite effect on her.

Instead of pulling away, Lorraine trailed one hand down Jonah's chest. She felt his chest rise and fall under her palm and his abdominal muscles hitch as her hand moved to the front of his pants. She smiled against Jonah's mouth while dragging her palm down the length of his long, thick dick.

He hissed and pulled away for a second before stepping back into her hold again.

"Someone could see us," he whispered, echoing her own thoughts.

Her blood started pounding in her ears. "I know," she said as her fingers brushed the zipper of his jeans. She toyed with the tab but didn't pull it down.

Not yet.

They took a few shared breaths, letting the silent night engulf them.

Lorraine could take rejection, but that's not what she felt from Jonah. There was excitement running through him, heating his skin and the air between them. But she could feel the nervous energy as well, maybe even a little fear at their exposure. He hesitated for a few seconds and she waited patiently for him to make the next move.

And he did.

Jonah's hands slid over her hips. He stared deep into her eyes as he pulled her short jersey dress up with one hand while the other moved over the curve of her ass.

When his hot palm hit her warm, bare ass cheek, they groaned in unison.

"A thong?" he groaned.

She licked her own lips and then licked his. "Keep touching me," she whispered into his mouth.

Jonah held his breath while his hand moved between her ass cheeks and then down until the tips of his blunt fingers brushed her wet slit.

"Jesus, Lorraine," he groaned softly.

She loved the way he moaned her name. She spread her legs for his seeking fingers and popped the button of his jeans open before pulling the zipper down.

They stared deep into one another's eyes while he stroked her lips and she spit into her palm. Lorraine shoved her hand into his boxers and pulled his dick out into the cooler night air. They stroked one another in tandem, the only sound between them hungry, panting breaths.

If Jonah still cared about them getting caught, he didn't show it. Lorraine cared. She hadn't met any of her neighbors yet, but the thought that one of them might see her and  Jonah touching one another had her hot and wetter by the second.

They masturbated one other until Lorraine couldn't keep the volume of her voice in check. Thankfully, Jonah was on top of it, covering her lips as soon as she started to moan, licking her loud cry from the cavern of her mouth. This kiss was messy and desperate. Lorraine was so wet, his fingers started making sounds as they sawed in and out of her hot hole.

She was close, but Jonah was closer.

His mouth fell open as he groaned against her lips and came, wet and sloppy in her hand. She felt his come wet her  dress and shuddered, clenching hard around three of his fingers pushed deep inside her.

They held onto each other and waited until their bodies stopped shaking and their breaths returned to normal. 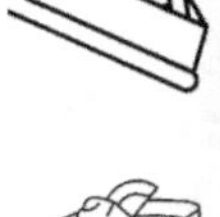 When it was time to disentangle their limbs, Jonah squeezed her ass with his wet fingers and pulled her dress back into place with a soft caress and one more squeeze. Lorraine tucked his soft dick back into his pants with gentle fingers.

Almost as if nothing happened. Almost.

"I'm still gonna wait 'til you're inside," Jonah said in a  soft but rough voice that tickled her lips.

Lorraine smirked and wiped her wet hand on her already soiled dress. She pulled her keys from her purse and this time unlocked the door. She stepped inside, but Jonah pulled her back into his chest and kissed her on the cheek. The sweetest goodbye.

She closed and locked the door but watched Jonah walk away through her living room window. She caught the smile on his face before the night's shadows engulfed his retreating form.

She got ready for bed with her own smile, dumping her dress into the washing machine to soak overnight and crawling into bed with her favorite vibrator.

She still wasn't sure what to make of Sea Port, but if tonight was any indication of what was to come, Lorraine thought she'd made a very good decision to move here. And she wore out her vibrator's battery feeling surer and surer of her decision with every climax.

WELCOME TO SEA PORT

THIRTEEN

Lorraine

The first month of Lorraine's life in Sea Port flew by, and it was a mixed bag.

As was common whenever she completely upended her life, there were many days of regret. Days when her new library's limited resources made her seriously  consider packing up and leaving because she was a librarian, not a miracle worker. Thankfully, she'd kept those moments of panic to herself instead of calling DeJuan — who  would've come to collect her immediately — and just stopped by Confections on her breaks for a cookie or two. Those sweet treats made most things better, and the things  they couldn't fix, Lorraine just moved to the next day's to-do list.

She considered putting herself on a Confections budget  but tabled that, too, for another day.

Actually, once she thought about it, her transition to Sea Port had been the smoothest of her life. The only thing that hadn't quite gone to plan was the morning after Mary's dinner party and the hot embarrassment that moved through her when she remembered all but begging Jonah to fingerfuck her on the front porch for the entire neighborhood to see. Her quick commute to work felt like a walk of shame. Even with her neighbors' houses as still as the night before, Lorraine couldn't shake the feeling that they were all watching her from behind their drawn curtains and judging her.

Nerves took her by Confections for a donut, which instantly lifted her mood, but she resolved to keep her distance from Jonah Brown. Clearly, she couldn't trust herself around that man.

A couple days after that dinner party, Lorraine was just leaving the lending library for her lunch break. Her plan had been to stop by the Sunnyside for a burger and a little bowl of banana pudding before she got back to grant writing, but as soon as she stepped into the hallway, she heard the echo of Jonah's voice and froze. She heard Knox's laugh mix with his, her heart beating up into her throat.

She wouldn't even acknowledge what the sound of Jonah's laugh did to her pussy.

Lorraine held onto the doorknob like her life depended on it, knees knocking together in lust, but then she heard their shoes on the old laminate flooring and ducked back into the library. She eased the door open and flipped the sign promising her prompt return before closing the door again. She listened as Jonah and Knox's voices got louder and then drifted away. She pressed her forehead against the door and decided to skip lunch. Lust had eaten away her hunger anyway.

Lorraine had been worried it would be impossible to

avoid someone in a town as small as Sea Port, but she'd managed just fine over the last couple of weeks. All she had to do was stay the hell away from the library renovation site, which was easier than breathing. She stuck to her desk in the lending library and pretended like her little encounter with  Jonah on her front porch never happened. It was easy as long as Lorraine didn't get cocky.

She didn't know how much longer she could avoid  Jonah, but she wouldn't let herself think that far ahead. She was, however, reaping the rewards of her hiding to eavesdrop on that gossip mill she'd heard about. One day, she  happened to see the back of Jonah's head in the administrative building, so she ducked inside an empty office and accidentally overheard Charlie's father lecturing her about  wasting her time at Confections rather than helping out at the family business, also known as the *Sea Port Sentinel*. Lorraine hadn't read a single issue, but she had run across  boxes of old issues on microfiche. It was too early to think about reviving the local archive, but she made a mental note to stop by the offices and inquire about their newer issues  when she had the chance. Whenever she found out where their offices were, that is.

Another time, she'd had to dip out of a conversation  with Santos on Main when she spotted Jonah a block away. But since he'd been telling her Mary wanted to have another dinner party, she'd been happy to exit that conversation  considering how the last one ended. Not the cake, but the public touching.

Some days, the stress got to her and she considered  burning the whole town down to hide her shame. But usually, she ate a cookie and calmed down. It was a rough start, but Lorraine thought she was acclimating pretty well to her new job and town and avoiding Jonah seemed easier every day.

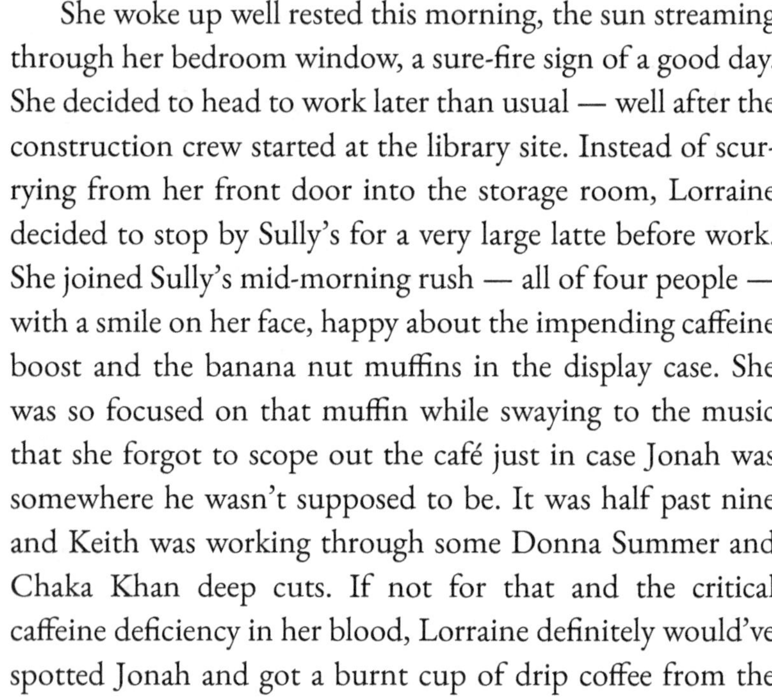

She woke up well rested this morning, the sun streaming through her bedroom window, a sure-fire sign of a good day. She decided to head to work later than usual — well after the construction crew started at the library site. Instead of scurrying from her front door into the storage room, Lorraine decided to stop by Sully's for a very large latte before work. She joined Sully's mid-morning rush — all of four people — with a smile on her face, happy about the impending caffeine boost and the banana nut muffins in the display case. She was so focused on that muffin while swaying to the music that she forgot to scope out the café just in case Jonah was somewhere he wasn't supposed to be. It was half past nine and Keith was working through some Donna Summer and Chaka Khan deep cuts. If not for that and the critical caffeine deficiency in her blood, Lorraine definitely would've spotted Jonah and got a burnt cup of drip coffee from the diner instead.

But she was singing along to "Pandora's Box" when she turned her head and locked eyes with Jonah, and her stomach dropped into her pussy.

"Fuck," she mumbled under her breath, turning quickly away.

JONAH

Brown & Son was created for Jonah, obviously, but it had always been an uneasy legacy to inherit. He ran away to Atlanta for college with a dream of being an architect, a dream his father had hoped he would bring home to grow the family business, to make something Jonah's children would inherit and so on and so on. In theory, Jonah had wanted that as well, but he'd always thought Sea Port was too small to hold all his dreams.

It held all his history, though.

Jonah was grieving Wesley's death in slow waves of anger, but the work made him feel close to his father in ways nothing else could. The work also kept his mind off Lorraine throughout the day.

Ever since the dinner party, Jonah had been waking up hot, sweaty, and hard. He hadn't masturbated this much since he was a teenager, but he hadn't been so indiscriminately horny since then either. He expected his hormones to level out after a while or at least after he saw her again, but he *never* saw Lorraine again. It had been two long weeks since that night on her porch and every day, he woke up, masturbated, showered, and looked for her everywhere he went.

For the first few days, he rationalized they were just missing each other. Sure, Sea Port was too small to miss someone, but Lorraine was new and busy, so it almost made sense. But then he started smelling her perfume in hallways or he would hear stories about Lorraine just leaving Confections or picking up a coffee at Sully's, and he started to wonder. He knew something was up when he couldn't even catch her at the lending library. The sign taped to the door

said they were open, he walked inside, but she was nowhere to be found.

She was avoiding him.

He thought about showing up at her house, but that sounded a little too close to stalking for his liking. So, he woke up, jacked off to memories of her, showered, and kept an eye out for her.

He knocked on Knox's open door.

"Come in," Knox called from his desk.

"How'd it go?" Jonah asked.

"Well, good morning to you too," Knox laughed.

Jonah sighed and sat in the chair across from his. "Sorry. Good morning. How'd it go?"

Knox leaned back in his chair with a smile. "Everything went fine. The Mayor agreed to hold some special City Council meetings on how to make the town more accessible."

"Just like that?" Jonah asked. He'd taken a class on accessible urban planning in college and what he remembered the most about all that he'd learned was that it wasn't just an uphill battle, it was a fight damn near every step of the way. Even with the ADA's guidelines, most cities and all towns were as inaccessible as possible. Making buildings easier to navigate for people with physical disabilities cost money, and most cities wanted to spend the absolute bare minimum on all their citizens, even less on their disabled ones. And if accessibility got in the way of the city making money or possibly made it easier for unhoused people to live comfortably, most cities would spend all that money just to get in the way of social progress.

"What's the catch?" he asked, squinting across the desk.

Knox chuckled gently. "No catch, just another round of fucking grant applications and more fucking meetings." He sighed and let his head fall into his hands. Jonah waited for Knox to pull himself together, but the angst on his face was obvious. "But beyond that, it was a green light. Damn near every city-owned building in this town is barely accessible to people in wheelchairs and the elevators are hanging on by a thread. We were gonna have to do the work, anyway, why not just do it all at once?"

Jonah's excitement was battling with his horror at the state of the elevators. He decided to take the stairs from here on out.

"Anyway, it's gonna be a lot of work, but if it means we get more grants, Willie's all about it. Oh, shit." Knox looked at his watch. "I've got a meeting, come on. I'll fill you in on the way."

Knox led Jonah to the stairwell, thank god, and ran through the rest of his meeting with the Mayor and City Council.

Jonah didn't really want to know the details, but in a town as small as Sea Port, he needed to know everything. Who was on his side? Who was in opposition? And crucially, who would be filling out the grants because Jonah surely wouldn't be volunteering for that job.

Outside, they jogged down the front steps and crossed the street. "Where are you going?"

"Confections," Knox said. "I've got a little date."

Jonah stopped walking in front of Sully's picture window and cut the man's steps short. "I'm heading in the other direction."

Knox sighed in frustration, clearly mad Jonah was

getting in his way. "Alright," he said dismissively, trying to step around him.

Jonah cut him off again. "Boy," Knox muttered in an amused threat.

"I just wanna know if there's anything else I need to know."

Knox rolled his eyes. "Nah, not really. Whenever we schedule the first meeting, you'll obviously hear about it. You can make your case there with me and the Mayor's support. I'm not writing those fucking grants, though."

Jonah sighed and was about to tell Knox that he wasn't writing them either, but then he looked right, and for the first time in weeks, he came eye-to-eye with Lorraine and lost track of what he'd been about to say.

Knox took the break in the conversation to skirt around Jonah, throwing a quick "Have a great day," over his shoulder before rushing down the street.

He thought she was avoiding him, but when he saw her eyes widen in shock and guilt, he knew it for sure. Jonah had never needed to chase after a woman in his life, not even in tiny ass Sea Port. He should've turned and walked away, but he pulled Sully's front door open instead.

The plan he'd been pulling together in his head was thin. He was more than happy to just let her off the hook if she wasn't interested in him, but only *after* he told her he still remembered the taste of her pussy and he wanted to taste it again.

It was only right that he gave her all the options.

WELCOME TO SEA PORT

FOURTEEN

Jonah

"Jonah? Jonah, come here."

Lorraine's head flinched in the direction of the voice but then she quickly looked forward.

"Boy, I know you hear me," Celia Johnson called to him.

Jonah glared at Lorraine's back for another second before turning to one of his mother's oldest friends — and one of the town's two garbage women. "Yes, Auntie Celia." He wove his way through the tables to get to hers. "Yes, ma'am. What can I do for you?"

She immediately placed her hand over his and patted his skin with a smile. "How you been holding up?" she asked.

It took a lot of energy not to break down at that question, although breaking down would've conveyed the message that he wasn't holding up very well. Still, he had a script. "One day at a time," he whispered, emotion invading each word.

"One foot in front of the other."

"Yes, ma'am."

"Good. Now who you got haulin' materials outta Willie's basement?" she asked with a wink.

"How did you even know about that job?" he said, dropping into a chair.

Celia rolled her eyes. "I know everything. Answer the question."

"I was gonna call you. I've just been busy running 'round for all these jobs."

She looked at him with pursed lips and disbelief written all over her face. Jonah sighed and reached into his pocket to pull out his cell phone. He put it on the table. Celia reached inside her shirt pocket for her reading glasses, slipping them onto her face.

"What am I looking at here?"

"My to-do list," Jonah said, opening his notes app. His dad used to scribble notes on a small spiral notebook he kept in his back pocket whether he was working or not. Jonah never knew what happened to all those notebooks until after his father died and he found a box full in his closet. There was maybe a decade of project planning notes for jobs he couldn't even remember, but the sight of his father's handwriting — thin, slanting chicken scratch —brought him to tears.

That was the first time he'd cried about something unexpected, but not the last.

"And there you are," Jonah said, pointing to the entry to call the Johnsons and arrange a material pick-up. "I just ain't get around to it yet."

She tapped his phone screen and marked that task as

completed. "We can come by next Tuesday," she said. "Same rate as normal."

Jonah sighed, sitting back in his chair. He was preparing himself to fight with Ms. Celia, to explain that he couldn't schedule the pick-up without talking to his foreman at least, but then he heard Lorraine's laughter. He turned to find her, coffee cup in hand, chatting with Sully over the cold display case. She waved at Sully and turned to leave. Her lipstick was a deep red like the night of the dinner party, dredging up memories of the taste of wine and chocolate on her tongue.

"Alright, Auntie Celia. See you Tuesday," he said, grabbing his phone and standing from the table.

"Alright now," she said as Jonah's attention laser-focused on Lorraine.

She'd clearly forgotten all about him because as soon as she spotted him in her peripheral vision, her eyes went wide and she froze in place. Jonah felt a pang at that, but he kept moving in her direction. If the last couple weeks was any indication, he needed to talk to Lorraine now before she disappeared again.

She had an iron grip on her coffee cup with both hands and she refused to look him in the eye. He wondered if she even realized she was licking her lips.

He got close enough to speak in low tones without crowding her, but that was close enough to smell her perfume and get his pulse racing. "Lorraine," he whispered.

"Jonah." She whispered his name and it brought him right back to that night on her porch. It was too damn early to be getting hard so publicly, but Lorraine had his blood running hot in an instant.

Jonah put his hands on his hips and crowded closer. "So you've been avoiding me." It wasn't a question.

Her gaze darted left and right before she lifted her chin to finally look him in the eye. Her mouth fell open and Jonah had to swallow a groan. "I have. I thought it was the best course of action."

"Why?" he asked, eyebrows hurting they were furrowed so deep, dick already hanging heavy in his pants. He didn't know how she did this to him, and when she ran her pink tongue over her red lips again, he didn't care.

"You gotta stop doing that," he groaned softly.

"Doing what?"

He licked his own lips and she mimicked him without thinking. "That," he growled gently. He hadn't realized how close he was — that he'd moved even closer — until she lifted her hand to run her fingers through her braids and her arm brushed his stomach.

Her gaze moved left and right again. He didn't know her well enough to read this emotion on her face, so he cut to the chase. "You afraid of me?" he asked, his own icy cold fear making him take a step back.

"No," she said quickly and a little too loud.

"Do you think I took advantage of you? 'Cause I swear I didn't mean that."

"No," she said again. "It's not— I can't—"

Jonah jumped when Ms. Celia cleared her throat and appeared at his right side. He leaned away from Lorraine and forced his mouth into a hollow smile.

"I try not to get into other people's business," she said. Jonah's smile turned to a knowing smirk, but she continued undeterred. "But if you two don't want to be the center of town gossip, maybe you should have this conversation somewhere a little more private." Celia didn't wait to see if they took her advice, she just waved and turned toward the door.

Jonah watched Ms. Celia leave only so he had time to figure out how to approach this. When he turned back to Lorraine, however, she was watching him, the tip of her tongue peeking out of the corner of her mouth. He swallowed another groan and then wrapped his arm around her back. 

"What are you doing?" she gasped.

"Moving this somewhere more private so we can talk?" he said, leading her across the room to a booth far enough away from everyone else that they wouldn't be overheard. 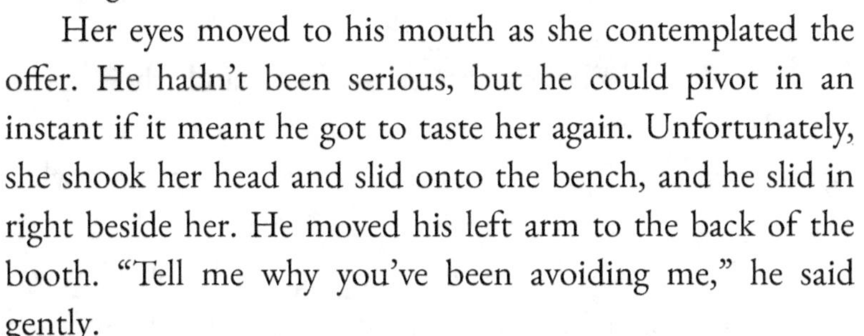

"Is this private enough?" she asked when he motioned for her to sit.

He lifted an eyebrow and looked down at her. "You wanna go somewhere else?" he asked.

Her eyes moved to his mouth as she contemplated the offer. He hadn't been serious, but he could pivot in an instant if it meant he got to taste her again. Unfortunately,  she shook her head and slid onto the bench, and he slid in right beside her. He moved his left arm to the back of the booth. "Tell me why you've been avoiding me," he said gently.

"This town is small," she whispered, her eyes shifting behind him.

He smoothed his fingers down the braids at the side of her head. "Look at me," he said just as gently, but with a little more bass. 

Her gaze snapped to his. The vinyl booth squeaked as

she shifted in his direction. Their knees touched. Lorraine let out an obvious and slow breath.

"Tell me," he said, all bass.

"We shouldn't have done all that," she said. Jonah's eyebrows lifted into his hairline. "On my porch, I mean. We shouldn't have done all that on my porch, and I was worried if we saw each other, we'd do it again."

Jonah laughed softly. For weeks, he'd been thinking about exactly that — waiting impatiently for it, actually. "And that would be a bad thing?" he asked slowly, leaning close. His fingers moved through her braids and brushed her scalp.

Lorraine sighed softly. "Yes," she said in a whisper just on the verge of a moan. "Anyone could've seen us out there."

He was just about to tell her it was late enough that most of her neighbors had likely been fast asleep, but his fingers were massaging her scalp and she closed her eyes, exhaling softly again. Her tongue poked from between her lips and it was Jonah's turn to shift in his seat.

Lorraine's eyelashes fluttered open, and their gazes locked for a second before hers shifted to the café and back again. It was the look in her eyes that finally explained what Lorraine seemed to be struggling to articulate.

He didn't know Lorraine well enough to know what was feeding the shame he saw briefly in her eyes, but he focused on her gaze boring into his as lust made her nostrils flare instead. The worry she had about someone seeing them that night was real, but it wasn't the whole picture at all.

He moved his hand down, brushing the back of his hand against her jaw. Her eyes fluttered closed again, but only for a second. Lorraine was used to being in control. He'd figured that out already, but watching lust and apprehension and need war on her face made him think she might like to loosen her grip on the reins for a little while. Sometimes, she might like a little bit of danger.

He moved his hand from the tabletop to her right leg. He felt her shudder and used his fingers to pull the hem of her skirt over her knee. Her skin was hot to the touch and he wasn't even between her thighs yet.

"Jonah," she whispered.

He lifted her leg and set it over his left thigh. "Lorraine," he whispered back.

She shook her head slightly. "You're playing with fire."

He rubbed small circles up her inner thigh with his index and middle finger. "Yeah, I can feel that." She barely swallowed her next moan. "You want me to stop?"

"No," she said quickly. He smoothed his hand up her thigh and she spread her legs to give him more space to touch her, which he did happily.

Her hands were folded neatly in her lap, but when his fingers brushed the seam of her leg, Lorraine lifted her hands to her breasts. He watched with a slow smile spreading across his lips while she toyed with the indents of her nipples through her shirt.

"Then what do you want?" he asked.

He wanted to sink his fingers deep inside her pussy again, but first he wanted to get them on the same page.

"You know," she whispered.

He moved his arm over the back of the booth and inched closer again. "I do, and I want it too." She licked her lips again, but this time he was so close he couldn't help himself. He pressed his mouth against hers and she hungrily licked

the seam of his lips just as his fingers brushed the gusset of her underwear.

"All you gotta do is tell me, Lorraine," Jonah moaned into her mouth. The pads of his fingers found her clit through her damp panties.

"I want your fingers inside me again," she admitted in a hoarse whisper. Jonah immediately started pushing her panties to the side. "B-but I shouldn't want that. We shouldn't be doing this."

Jonah leaned away so he could see her clearly. They locked eyes and stared at one another while his fingers massaged her clit. "'Shouldn't' is doing a lot of work. We probably shouldn't be doing this here," he admitted, "but you can want something without shame. And we can both feel how much you want this." He punctuated this statement by moving his fingers down her very wet lips, enjoying the smooth velvet folds of her skin.

"Anybody could see us," she said.

Jonah thought she meant that as a warning, but she pinched her nipples and shivered through an orgasm while she said it.

He wasn't the smartest tool in the shed, but he wasn't the dullest either. "You're right. Anybody could see us," he said, pushing two fingers into her opening while he spoke.

Late at night on Lorraine's porch was one thing, but this was so many degrees more dangerous, and he guessed that explained why Lorraine's pussy was wetter. A beautifully lewd wet squelch filled the silence around them.

"Do you want me to stop?"

"No," she moaned, a little louder than he would have, but he also didn't give a shit.

"I want to make you come," he whispered.

"Fuck," she muttered.

"Shhh. You need to be quiet so I can make this pussy happy."

She pressed her lips shut and moved her thigh into his lap. "You're hard."

"Don't worry about that right now," he told her just as the pads of his fingers found her g-spot.

She opened her mouth and his eyes widened, preparing himself for her to blow their cover. He didn't stop pushing his fingers in and out or massaging her clit, though. She managed to hold herself together and snapped her lips shut, letting go of her right breast to grab at his shirt.  

"Fuck, you feel good. I want to kiss you," he admitted.

Her hips started moving against his hand. "I want to kiss you too." She smiled nervously, as if kissing was too far when his fingers were pumping inside her pussy.  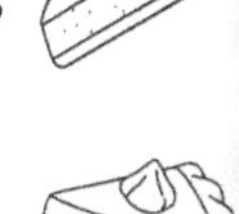

"Anyone looking?" he panted, the effort to keep his movements as discreet as possible starting to take its toll. 

Her eyes darted from his face to the café again. The reminder of just how many people were close by had her clenching his fingers so tight it was almost hard to push another inside her, but he made it work. 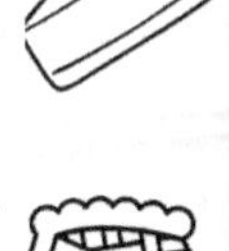 

She shook her head quickly. "Doesn't look like it."

"Good," he said and moved his thumb to her clit. 

"My god," she sighed, shutting her eyes tight. Her back bowed and Jonah felt the tremors of a small orgasm move through her core. "If you keep touching me like this, I'm going to leave a puddle on this seat." 

"I'll clean it up for you," he whispered in her ear.

She whimpered softly before gasping and lifting her

head to look him in the eye while she soaked his fingers in her release.

"All anyone would have to do is look at your face right now and they'd know what we were doing."

She smiled. "And then you'd have to stop."

"We don't want that," he said, slowing his strokes. "So, this is what gets you off? Fooling around in public?"

"It never has before," she said, as shyly as any woman could say anything when a man she barely knew was currently fingerfucking her pussy in a moderately busy coffee shop in a small town where everyone was on the lookout for everyone else's business. "What about you?" she asked, lifting her fingers to his beard, caressing it with delicate care.

"This is new to me too, but I'm as stiff as you are wet."

"Is it weird?" she asked adorably, worry written across her brow.

He made sure his next stroke was harder. The light slap of his hand against her pussy sounded louder to their ears and she smiled immediately.

"Don't do that. Don't make yourself feel bad. You like what you like. And if I thought we could get away with it, I'd let you put your hand in my pants so you can get me off too."

She groaned in frustration and he finally leaned down to kiss her quickly.

"You can't be impatient *and* into public sex," he laughed against her lips. "That feels like a bad combination."

"Sounds like a great way to get arrested," she panted as her pussy tightened around his fingers again.

"You like that?" he asked, even though the answer was dripping off the back of his hand.

"I'm gonna come," she whined against his lips.

"Can you do it quietly?"

She thought about it for a few seconds before nodding.  "But it'll be so obvious on my face."

"Good point," he said, scooting closer to kiss her again. He was still worried about too much attention, but as long  as he got to make Lorraine come, he was willing to accept any and all consequences.

It didn't take too many more strokes of his fingers or  hard circles on her clit to get Lorraine off. Her body seized as she came, muscles tightening deliciously around his digits. She managed to contain her moan to a soft cry that he  happily licked from her tongue. He pressed the heel of his hand into her swollen clit and her entire body jerked as she came again. If they were in a more private location, he would  have kept going and going, draining her until she was a sweaty, shaky mess. If they were anywhere else, his dick would be in her hands at least.

But someone dropped a mug behind him, pulling them  out of their embrace.

He finally stopped his hand, but he kept his fingers buried deep inside her as they pressed their damp foreheads  together.

"That was better than last time," she panted.

He laughed hoarsely and nodded.

"Did you come in your pants?" she asked, that hint of  fire in her eyes again.

"What do you think?" He brushed his mouth against hers.

"I wish I could feel it," she admitted.

His dick lurched in his pants and he groaned against her lips. She put her hand at the back of his head to keep his mouth on hers. They breathed the same air for a few more seconds before he pulled his hand from between her legs.

"Anyone looking?" he whispered.

Her eyes moved to scan the room and he started counting her eyelashes, wanting to know everything about her in that moment.

"No."

"Good," he said, and then shoved his wet fingers into his mouth.

Lorraine snapped her thighs shut and shivered against him.

A damn good morning indeed.

WELCOME TO SEA PORT

FIFTEEN

Lorraine

It was simple, but the smile Jonah's text message put on her face should've been criminal. It made her now ice-cold latte taste like it was freshly brewed and she sipped it happily as she walked to work.

On the drive down, she'd kept an eye out for other towns and cities she could travel to for things Sea Port didn't have — like movie theaters, malls, and a grocery store that sold almond milk — but it struck her as she enjoyed her ice-cold coffee and deliciously loose muscles after all those orgasms that she hadn't left Sea Port since she arrived. Apparently, this little town had everything she needed. If anything, Lorraine was even less inclined to leave than she might have been just a couple hours ago.

Her heels clacked against the old tile floor as she reached into her purse for her keyring. She'd just unlocked the door when her cell phone started ringing, but she ignored it to get

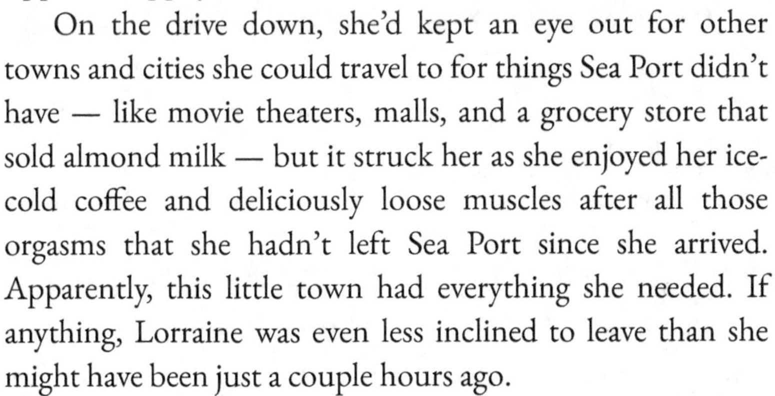

the library open. She was already late. She opened the door and kicked the doorstop into place, then walked to the small desk she'd pushed in the corner to make her base of operations. She'd spent an entire hour one day searching for an old microwave Ms. Bordon said was stored somewhere in the basement. While spelunking, Lorraine had also tracked down a welcome mat and a banker's chair, all of which Santos and Knox had promptly brought up to her desk. They grumbled about not being movers or something, but Lorraine was too excited by her discoveries to worry too much about their complaints.

She slipped her coffee into the microwave and rushed back to the door to flip over the sign to let anyone wandering the halls know that the lending library was open, then sat at her desk and waited for her coffee to warm.

Her phone had stopped ringing, but it started again just as she pulled it from her purse.

"Have a little patience," she said, putting the phone on speaker.

"Have you met me?" DeJuan asked.

Lorraine laughed, dropping her purse into the bottom drawer of her desk. "I have, that's how I know this is a lesson you need to learn."

"I don't like what this place is doing to you. Come home."

"Home where?" Lorraine laughed. She and DeJuan met in college as two of the only kids who stayed on campus through summer break because they didn't really have anywhere else to go. Their families were complicated in different ways and together, they learned that there were perks to not having a home to return to, so they traveled together in their twenties and moved around as their hearts and job prospects allowed.

"Wherever I am," he shot back, reminding her of the glue that held them together. DeJuan was her family and he was her home, but Sea Port was giving him a run for his money.

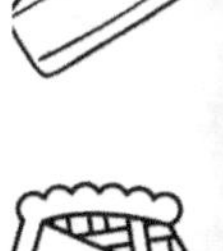

She rolled her eyes and opened the library's ancient laptop. Her first grant application was with the Mayor to replace this thing immediately. She got back to her conversation and reheated coffee while she waited for it to boot up, assuming it would boot up this time.

"Which is where?" she asked because DeJuan spent more time traveling for work than anything else, even getting on her nerves.

"Right now, I'm in Indianapolis, but I'm calling because I'm thinking of taking a trip to Scottsdale."

"Okay," Lorraine said.

DeJuan sucked his teeth. "And I'm calling you because I found a spa I want to visit. I *wanted* your ornery ass to join me, but now I'm rethinking that."

"Is this the invitation?" Lorraine laughed. "'Cause it's a shitty one."

"Well, I'd had something better planned but didn't expect all this attitude. Who pissed you off today?"

Lorraine's face was hot thinking about how shameless she and Jonah had been in the coffee shop. "Actually, I'm in a great mood."

"If this is great, then that place must be tearing you down."

"You know you can just tell me you miss me?"

"Well, obviously I miss you."

"Good, 'cause I miss you too. That's why *you* should come visit *me*."

"Mmmm, no, thank you. You know I only do two transfers if there's a beach at the end of my travels."

"Well, you got me there, but this place is so cute. We could have so much fun on your visit?"

"Doing what?"

Lorraine squirmed happily in her seat. "So much. First, you *have* to visit Confections. Mary's so nice and I'm trying to eat my body weight in teacakes."

"Girl, what the hell is a teacake?"

"You'll find out when you get here. Okay, so after that, we can walk around town. It's so picturesque."

There was silence on the other end of the line for a few seconds. "So you want to get me hooked on pastries and then exercise?" DeJuan said, voice dripping with disbelief.

"I mean, when you put it like that..." Lorraine mumbled.

"When *you* put it like that, the answer's still no."

"Anyway," Lorraine said, trying to change topics before DeJuan ruined her post-orgasmic high. "What's up with you?"

"So you're really saying no?" DeJuan asked.

She sighed. "Yes, Juan, I'm saying no. I just got here."

"You don't got PTO?"

"Not yet." This was a lie, but since DeJuan already thought Sea Port was on another planet, she leaned into it.

"Seriously?"

"Seriously," she said. "It's a small town with super limited staff. They need me." 'Need' was a strong word to describe her daily tasks, but since she was already lying, why stop now?

"I can't wait 'til your sentence is over," he sighed.

"I'm not in prison, Juan," Lorraine laughed.

"You're right, I am. Free my friend! I have vacations to schedule." 

Lorraine laughed and their conversation drifted toward less contentious matters, like the man pursuing DeJuan like  his life depended on it. Lorraine loved other people's relationship tea, so she put an earbud in one ear and gasped her way through the update on DeJuan's dating life. 

She didn't tell him about Jonah, though. It was too soon, and she wanted to protect the warm, gooey feeling he  gave her this morning.

DeJuan wouldn't understand yet.

"Knock, knock," Mary said, breezing into the library.  Empty-handed. "What?" she asked, stopping halfway toward Lorraine's desk.

"No cookies? A spare donut? Nothing?" Lorraine asked. 

Mary smiled at her. "No, but I appreciate the enthusiasm."

Lorraine rolled her eyes. "What's up?" 

"Nothing much. Just here to pick up a cookbook."

Lorraine stood from her desk and followed Mary to the small but very active cookbook section of the library. Lorraine was doing a full and official review of popular titles with Sea Port readers through the library's records, but she was also keeping track of the walk-ins, especially the patrons who came in, plucked a book from the shelves, and read for hours.

So far, she'd figured out that while the lending library was never packed at any one time, it was busy throughout the day. Her first patrons of the day were usually seniors looking for a quiet place to sit in the middle of their morning walks. By the time the elderly people were ready to migrate over to the Community Center for their senior dance class, Knox dropped in to hide from the Mayor and the City Council. He liked to hang out at a small desk on the far side of the stacks, just out of view from the door, and work, but he was also reading through the library's surprisingly exten-sive collection of Walter Mosley novels. He told Lorraine he never checked them out because he enjoyed his little hour of peace in the middle of the workday.

Knox left right around when Lorraine closed for a quick lunch break. When she opened back up, it was to Sea Port's board game club, Checkers & Chess, who showed up for an afternoon of gaming and stayed until they closed. Lorraine was still trying to figure out the contours of her job, but her time in the lending library were the best part of her day.

And that didn't even include the gossip!

"So, you and Jonah," Mary whispered excitedly.

Lorraine immediately stopped walking and felt her eyes widen quickly. "What?"

Mary rolled her eyes. "Don't bullshit me, I heard about this morning."

Lorraine could feel her soul trying to exit her body through her butthole. "Nothing happened," she wheezed.

Mary cocked her hip and crossed her arms. "You look like I caught you literally red-handed, so I know that's a lie."

Lorraine tried to speak, but nothing but squeaks came out of her mouth. She'd never been a goody two-shoes, but she'd always stayed mostly on the right side of the line. She had a clean record and goodish credit, and public sex was definitely not part of that plan.

Mary sighed and threw her hands down in exaggerated exasperation. "Come on, girl, I'm nosy. Knox told me Jonah's entire body froze when he saw you. He damn near forgot Knox existed. Just tell me if y'all are dating. I promise I won't tell anyone," she pleaded. "I mean, no one besides Knox and Santos, obviously."

Lorraine's brain was whirring as she tried to keep up with Mary's words and what they meant. She exhaled loudly in relief that Mary didn't know what Lorraine thought she did. She felt like a thousand-pound weight was lifted from her shoulders and the flash of panic passed. "We're not dating," Lorraine breathed.

Mary's face and shoulders fell at the same time. "Really?" She looked legitimately sad and Lorraine was sad for her.

"We've kissed," she said, offering her a little crumb to lift her mood. "A couple of times."

"I'm listening," Mary said.

Lorraine shooed her toward the cookbooks. "There's not much else to tell. We've kissed, but I don't know if I'm ready to date." She whispered the last word, surprised at her own discretion. Her last relationship had ended a few months later than it should have, but right on time to suit Lorraine's needs. She wasn't hung up on him, so dating Jonah wasn't out of the realm of possibility. It was just that

dating felt like too weak a word for whatever the hell she and Jonah had just done in Sully's.

Mary rolled her eyes. "Okay, don't date, but what about sex?" She didn't whisper any of those words.

"Seriously?" Lorraine hissed.

Mary stopped in front of the cookbooks but didn't even glance at the shelves. "No one cares," she said, nodding. "The latest gossip is about a pick-up flag football game last weekend."

"What happened?" Lorraine asked. She'd wanted to go to that game, actually, but the Mayor had forced her to take a virtual seminar on grant writing.

"Nothing," Mary cried. "Literally nothing. But Santos and Knox were on different teams and apparently, they like competing against one another. It wasn't long before they were shirtless and sweaty." Mary's gaze drifted to the right and took her story with it. "They were kinda in their own world, I guess, tackling each other and throwing the ball. At some point they definitely hugged, and maybe Santos gave Knox a quick peck on the lips, but seriously, that was it."

By the time Mary was done with her story, Lorraine was fanning herself. "That don't sound like nothing to me."

"It was a whole lotta something *after* the game." Mary smirked.

"You are truly the world's luckiest woman," Lorraine breathed.

"Don't I know it. Jonah was *also* at that game, shirtless and sweaty."

"Damn," Lorraine said sharply.

"Exactly. So keep kissing."

Lorraine cut her eyes at Mary. "What the hell has gotten into you? Wait, not like that," she added quickly at the end.

Mary chuckled happily. "That's a good one. Knox is gonna like it."

"You know what I mean."

Mary pressed her palms against her cheeks. "Look, I'm sure you've noticed that the average age of Sea Port residents is close to sixty. Maybe even seventy. They're great people, but if I wanted to invite someone over for dinner, it would have to be before sunset or at least before their evening medication. I need friends who don't remember the war." 

"What war?"

"Any of them," Mary laughed. 

"There's Willie and Bria and Sully," Lorraine pointed out.

"Yeah, we hang out with them too. And I want to add you and Jonah to our little under-fifty club. We almost have enough people to be a sports team." 

"Will we be shirtless?" Lorraine asked, then shook her head. "Never mind. Don't answer that. Look, I've only known Jonah a month. He's a good kisser," she said and then forced herself not to go any further down that path. "We're just getting to know each other." 

Mary sighed. "Fine. I guess that's okay for now, but remember that this isn't about you and Jonah, it's about all of us." 

"Just?"

"Huh?"

Lorraine sighed. "This isn't *just* about me and Jonah. You said it wasn't about us." 

Mary smirked. "Yeah, I know what I said." 

Lorraine couldn't hold her own shocked laughter inside. "You're a mess."

Mary was also laughing. "And I'm fun. If you stay in Sea Port, we can all have fun."

"I'm here for the rest of my contract," Lorraine reminded her.

"See, that's what I'm talking about. We've gotta work through that indecision."

They laughed together just as her cell phone chirped with a new text message. It was Jonah, and Mary saw it on her face.

Have dinner w/me tnite?

WELCOME TO SEA PORT

SIXTEEN

Jonah

Jonah rushed home after work to get ready for his date with Lorraine. It was the only thing he could think about all day besides what they did in that booth in Sully's.

He ate dinner at the Sunnyside more nights than not, but Lorraine had already eaten there and he didn't need his godparents any more in his business than they already were. Besides, La Bella Rosa was good and he wanted Lorraine to see the best Sea Port had to offer while she was here.

The walk to the Italian restaurant was just long enough to ease his nerves. He kept a lookout for Lorraine on his way, but when he finally made it to the restaurant, he pulled the door open with a nervous smile on his face...only to come face-to-face with Bria's bored, blank stare from behind the hostess stand.

"Welcome to La Bella Rosa," she said in the blandest voice ever.

"Is Lorraine here?" She rolled her eyes and turned to

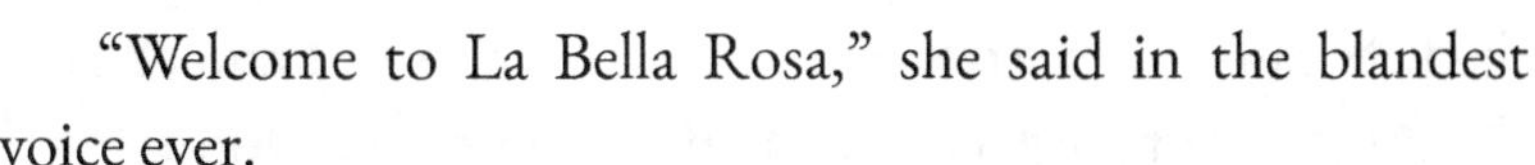

look at the almost-empty dining room. Jonah followed her gaze. "Oh. Okay. I'll wait."

When he turned back to Bria, there was a little more life on her face. He'd piqued her interest and that was a bad sign. "You gotta date?" she asked with a smirk.

"Don't you work at Confections? What are you doing here?"

She rolled her eyes. "Some of us gotta work a couple jobs to make rent."

He rolled his eyes right back. "What rent? You live with your mom."

Jonah had known Bria her entire life. Their families were close in the way most Sea Port families were — at least three generations of Browns and Stones had grown up together, but they weren't related, not even by marriage — and Jonah still saw a younger, slightly annoying distant cousin when he looked at her. Apparently, Bria felt the same.

She sucked her teeth but refused to respond.

"Thought so. I'll wait outside."

"We'll see if she shows up," Bria called as Jonah pulled the door open.

He cut his eyes at the door before it closed, but he should have expected this because it was the exact kind of thing Jonah loved and hated about Sea Port; here, he was never truly alone. When he came back to see his father, he didn't have to tell anyone he was in town. Someone saw him at the small hospital, and within a few hours, everyone in town knew. He didn't have to tell anyone when his father died because the town's whisper network handled the announcement and coordinated dropping off food for a freshly grieving Jonah as well. There were no secrets in Sea

Port, and now that Bria knew he was going on a date with Lorraine, it was only a matter of time before Keith — who *was* related to Jonah on their mothers' sides — would know, and from there, the news would go everywhere. At least if they'd gone to the Sunnyside, Terra and Moses would've  gossiped amongst themselves. He was just second-guessing his decision to even eat here when he spotted Lorraine halfway down the block. She took his breath away. 

The sun was setting behind Jonah's head, so he had an unobstructed and perfectly lit view of Lorraine walking toward him like a runway model. He still didn't know much  about her, but the first time he saw Lorraine, he'd thought she stuck out like a sore thumb in a small place like Sea Port and she hadn't even been dressed up. But she was very  dressed up tonight in a short, clingy black dress that seemed to find a different curve to hug with every step. The thin shoulder straps exposed her bare shoulders and chest. Her  small, perky breasts swayed softly as she sauntered toward him. He had to tear his eyes away just to keep his gaze moving down her body. Thankfully, her legs were just as exciting — a little thick around the thighs and delicate  ankles. But it was her heels that had his heart galloping in his chest. She was at least four inches shorter than Jonah, but in those heels, he thought there was a good chance he might  have to look up at her a little bit, and he wasn't mad at that at all.

"Stop looking at me like that," she called.

"Like what?" he asked, dragging his gaze back up her body without an ounce of urgency. There was just so much to admire.

He lifted his gaze to her face just as a soft laugh fell from her lips. She wasn't wearing much makeup and she didn't need it, but her eyelashes were definitely longer, thicker, blacker, and her lips had a perfectly sexy smudge of that red lipstick again.

"Like you want to eat me up," she whispered.

Now it was his turn to smile. "I already know you taste good. Who's to say that's not exactly what I was thinking?"

He'd planned to keep his hands to himself as long as physically possible, but she was wearing a different perfume and he wanted to sniff it directly from her skin. Jonah grabbed Lorraine around the waist and pulled her into his body, happily shoving his face into her neck, sniffing loudly. She laughed softly into his ear and wrapped her arms around his shoulders.

"You smell like you're trying to get ate," he whispered.

She pressed her smile against his ear and then sighed softly against Jonah's skin before she pushed out of his hold and backed away. They stared at one another for a few seconds before he remembered how to speak.

"I was worried you wouldn't show up," Jonah admitted.

"If I didn't want to be here, I would've said no. I don't like to lie if I can help it."

"Me either," Jonah said.

"Good. I'm surprised you didn't ask to pick me up."

Jonah shoved his hands into his pockets. "I thought about it, but if I'm real, I was worried we wouldn't make it to dinner if I did that."

Lorraine's smile widened. "Good call."

Jonah walked to the restaurant's front door and Lorraine followed him. She inched close, and he left his hand on the long brass handle. "But I'm definitely gonna walk you back."

Her tongue wet the width of her smile. "Good," she whispered. "I've been looking forward to that all day."

LORRAINE

"Well, well, well," Bria trilled as soon as Lorraine and Jonah walked into the restaurant.

"Girl, you work here too?" Lorraine asked.

"Sometimes," Bria said with a frustrated sigh.

"She's gotta make rent, apparently," Jonah said. Lorraine could hear the teasing note in his voice and Bria rolled her eyes, but their inside joke went over her head.

Bria focused on Lorraine. "If he's holding you hostage, blink once."

Lorraine let out a small burst of laughter and slapped her palm over her mouth.

"Can we get a table?" Jonah asked in annoyance.

"Sure thing. I'm guessing you want a little privacy?"

Lorraine turned to look in the mostly empty restaurant. "Um..."

"Our dinner rush hasn't started yet," Bria said quickly.

"Define rush," Jonah muttered.

Bria cut her eyes at him and caught Lorraine's eyes when she looked back. "Choir practice lets out in fifteen minutes."

Lorraine didn't know how big the choir was or which church they were coming from, but she nodded in understanding. "Then yes, we would like a table with a little privacy."

"Great, follow me." Bria grabbed two menus, smiled at Lorraine, glared at Jonah, and then flounced away from the hostess stand.

"Be nice," Lorraine whispered.

Jonah screwed up his face. "Absolutely not. I've known her since she was in diapers. She's been annoying all her life." He put his hand on her left hip and nudged her forward.

La Bella Rosa was as different from the Sunnyside as it was possible to get. Where the diner was bright, lively, and loud with a kind of mid-century yellowy tinge, Sea Port's Italian restaurant was dark and cozy — the perfect setting for a sexy date.

"Good call," she whispered as she took in the ambience. He squeezed her hip in reply.

Bria led them to a small, dark corner of the dining room. She flipped a switch on the wall and illuminated the space.

"Ooh, can we dim those? Or turn them off?" Jonah asked.

Bria and Lorraine turned to look at him. His eyes went wide, but there was a sheepish grin on his face.

"It's a date," Lorraine said, trying to cover for him. Bria was rolling her eyes when Lorraine turned back toward her. "It's nice ambience."

Bria smirked and shook her head, then placed the menus on the closest table and shrugged. "Whatever that is. I'll see if we have some candles, I guess."

"Thanks, Bria," Lorraine said.

"Yeah, thanks," Jonah echoed.

"Shut up," Bria muttered before disappearing.

Jonah shook his head for a second before turning his full attention back to Lorraine. He stepped closer at her back, squeezed her soft waist, and kissed her shoulder. 

"God, you make me wet," she whispered, turning in his arms.

"I remember," he replied, leaning forward to brush his mouth against hers. 

"Seriously?" she said before licking his bottom lip.

"A closed mouth don't get fed."

"Anyone could see us." 

He lifted his eyebrows. "Bria's probably told half the people under the age of thirty already."

She sucked her teeth. "And what if I don't want  everyone in town to know about my personal life?" It was a ridiculous question to ask considering what they'd discovered about each other just this morning, but she said it anyway. She was willing to say anything to stay in Jonah's arms right now.

"Then you shouldn't have moved to a town like Sea  Port. And you *definitely* shouldn't have let me put my hand in your panties in the middle of Sully's." He moved his mouth to her ear. She thought he was going to say something dirty, but he kissed a path from her earlobe along the  shell of her ear instead. She shivered in his arms and her eyes drifted closed.

"Excuse me," Bria said in a sharp tone. 

Lorraine jumped in Jonah's arms, but he held her close for a second before turning and glaring at Bria. She had two small tea lights in her left palm. 

"We're a respectable establishment." Bria aimed her disappointment at Jonah. "Take all that lollygagging back to Confections."

Jonah sighed heavily and shook his head.

"I'm gonna tell Mary you said that," Lorraine teased.

"The queen of lollygagging," Bria laughed softly. "She'll be so proud of me for the organic advertising."

Even Jonah had to laugh at that one as they stepped out of Bria's way. She set the candles on their table, adjusting the placements subtly, before stepping back to check the aesthetics and make a few tweaks.

"It looks good," Jonah said impatiently.

"I didn't ask you," Bria replied.

She turned to Lorraine. "You want some wine?" she asked. "He can afford it."

"Come on, man," Jonah sighed.

"A red would be lovely," Lorraine said.

"Perfect," Bria laughed, flouncing away, switching the overhead lights in their section off as she passed the switch.

As soon as she was out of sight, Lorraine wrapped her arms around his neck and pressed her smile to his.

"She's gon' charge me an arm and a leg for that wine," he laughed into her mouth.

She licked his bottom lip. "I'm worth it."

His hands moved down her back and cupped her ass cheeks in a firm hold.

She sucked his top lip into her mouth, tasting him without the pressure of her impending workday. Lorraine thought you could tell a lot about a man from the way he kissed, but every time she'd kissed Jonah, he felt just a little bit different. Drunk and happy on her front porch, adrenaline racing through her veins in Sully's, and now tender in a secluded dining area, each with its own taste and tease. If nothing else, Lorraine had learned that Jonah — and his tongue — were very flexible and she couldn't wait to learn if there was more where that came from.

"So, the only two restaurants in Sea Port are a diner and an Italian restaurant?" she asked. "That's random as hell."

Lorraine dipped a piece of bread into the best pesto sauce she'd ever had and popped it into her mouth. She'd stopped dancing in her seat at every bite a while ago, but that was only because she wanted to focus on eating. Even talking was becoming a chore.

"Sea Port is random as hell," Jonah said with a shrug.

"Is that why you moved to Atlanta?"

"You remember that?"

"I have a good memory. Don't read too much into it."

"I will," he laughed. "But yeah. I wanted to live in a place where no one knew me and at least three generations of family history."

"I bet that was a culture shock." She laughed.

"Yeah, definitely. I almost failed out my first semester, but I got it together."

"I bet you did. How long were you there?"

"All college, and then I got a good internship and a better job."

She speared some pasta onto her fork. "Oh, you had a whole life there."

Jonah nodded, ducking his head into his plate. "I did."

If he hadn't spoken, she might not have noticed the change in his mood so quickly. If she were a decade younger, she might've changed the topic and tried to cheer him up, but she was too grown to let a potential red flag go unnoticed. "When'd you come back?"

Jonah twirled spaghetti onto his fork, but he didn't bring it to his mouth. He kept twirling it until he set his fork down and sat back in his chair. He picked the cloth napkin from his lap and wiped his mouth.

The feeling of dread rose in Lorraine's gut, but that was a different part of her stomach, so she popped another piece of pesto-soaked bread into her mouth.

"A little under a year," Jonah sighed, but he wouldn't meet her eyes.

"Why?" He glanced up but only for a second. "What made you come back?"

Jonah wiped his mouth again and reached for his wine glass. He started to take a sip but then dropped his arm, resting the bottom of the stem on his thigh. "My... I came back 'cause my father had a heart attack."

Lorraine froze and her mouth fell open. She covered her mouth. "Oh my god. I'm so sorry."

Jonah shook his head and then drained the last of the wine in his glass. Lorraine reached for the bottle, but Jonah shook his head. "I'm good. I mean, I'm... I don't need any more."

Lorraine nodded. "When— I mean, if you don't mind me asking. When did he pass?"

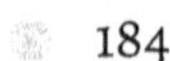

"Seven months." Those two words were rough with emotion. A few seconds later, he lifted his gaze to hers. "My dad died seven months ago. My construction company was his. The truck I'm driving to the library and our other sites, all his. All the jobs I'm working on were his. The life I'm living was his and the one he wanted for me."

"Because your life is in Atlanta?" she asked gently.

Jonah rubbed a hand over his beard. "I guess. I don't know, if I'm honest. I've got a condo there that's more like living in a frat house 'cause I rent out all the rooms. And I left my job once I ran out of PTO and FMLA. I thought I had a life there, but it was so easy to leave."

"But you've got friends there," she said. "People?" The word she'd wanted to use was *girlfriend*, but that seemed like such a petty thing to bring up in the face of his grief.

"Sure," Jonah sighed. "Of course, I do, but..." He smiled sadly, and the dim, romantic lighting only accentuated the moment his eyes started filling with water. "Losing my dad made everything and everyone feel less important because they are."

Lorraine nodded. "That makes sense."

"Does it?"

"Yes," she replied quickly.

Jonah laughed softly, wiping at his eyes. "What about you?" he asked, sounding relieved at the chance to change the subject. "Why'd you move here?"

"A job," she laughed, snatching another piece of bread.

He pursed his lips and squinted his eyes. "Willie's been running around town telling everybody who'll listen about your qualifications. I feel like you coulda gotten a job anywhere else if you wanted."

"In this economy?"

"Yeah," he said simply.

She shrugged and sat back in her chair, patting her tummy to his laughter. "I left a job to take this one. Simple."

"Did you hate it?"

She shook her head quickly. "Not even a little bit. It wasn't a perfect fit, but I liked most of my coworkers and I was living in the same city as my best friend for the first time in a long time. Life was good."

"And you left all that to come...*here*?"

Lorraine laughed. "We moved around a lot when I was a kid," she said, launching into a comfortable version of her life story. "Moving around makes sense to me. Why spend forever and a day in one place if you can see a new place, make some new friends, and just..." She shrugged. "I don't know, see a little more of the country? Or the world? I've never been tied to a place before. Why start now?"

Jonah wiped his eyes and nodded. "When I was a kid, I used to want to be literally anywhere but here. I used to go to the old library where they had a wall with a big ole map of the world. And every day I went there, I chose a new country, province, city, town, island. Whatever. It just had to be somewhere that was far away from here 'cause I just knew this place was too small for me."

"Do you still feel that way?"

Jonah massaged his beard again. "I don't know," he said sadly.

Lorraine wanted to burst into tears, but she could see the discomfort on his face, so she did something else — something much less melancholy. She slipped her right foot from her heel and stretched her leg until her toes brushed

Jonah's shin. He jumped in his seat and lifted his gaze to Lorraine's face. They locked eyes for the first time in minutes as she brushed her toes up his shin to his knee.

They watched one another as she teased his legs open, as the sounds of the busier restaurant filtered into their quiet little alcove, hidden just behind a little screen with their tea lights making shadows dance on the crimson wallpaper. 

No one could see Lorraine pressing her foot against his inner thigh, massaging the outline of his hardening dick. No one could hear him grunt when she curved her foot along his length. 

"Fuck," Jonah breathed softly, bringing a smile to Lorraine's face. 

That smile made her almost as happy as the pesto.

WELCOME TO SEA PORT

SEVENTEEN

Jonah

Jonah could see the closest table through a small tear in the screen next to them. It was empty, thankfully, but he could hear the sounds of other people having dinner nearby — forks scraping plates and laughter — all while Lorraine was using her bare foot to jack him off.

"Fuck. Fuck," Jonah whispered under his breath.

"Does that feel good?"

He tried to roll his eyes but then her heel nudged the head of his dick, making him jump in his seat, rattling the table. She laughed softly, steadying her wine glass, never letting up on the pressure on his shaft.

"Yes," he finally managed to say.

"Good," she breathed, taking a sip of her wine, watching him with a small smirk on her face.

A few seconds ago, Jonah had been fighting back uncomfortable tears from the endless well of his grief, and now he was holding his breath, trying not to come before they even finished their dinner. Lorraine was multitasking, however, stroking Jonah while spearing more pasta on her fork.

"I'm not bringing you any more bread until you order," Bria said, her voice carrying from elsewhere in the dining room.

Her voice felt like a bucket of ice-cold water over Jonah's head. He scooted his chair closer to the table, using his napkin to hide Lorraine's foot in his lap before he realized that Bria wasn't talking to them. His heart was racing, but when he finally locked eyes with Lorraine, she seemed amused by his fear.

"Still feel good?" she asked, sliding her foot up and down his length.

Jonah swallowed the fear in his throat. "Yeah," he said, shuddering as her foot shifted and her toes nudged his balls.

"Y'all alright over here?" Bria asked, breezing into their little alcove.

"We're great. Who are you yelling at?" Lorraine asked.

Bria rolled her eyes. "My Aunt Christine, and I'm not yelling. Well, I am, but she's hard of hearing and refuses to wear her hearing aid."

"Ah," Lorraine said, sliding her foot down Jonah's shaft.

He pretended to cough to cover his moan, mortified that the fear of being discovered had his dick hard as a rock.

Bria looked at him and begrudgingly refilled his water glass. "So, how was everything?" she asked Lorraine.

"Amazing. Honestly, I didn't know what to expect from Italian food in this small town," she said carefully.

"In the middle of nowhere," Bria corrected with a nod.

"Yeah," Lorraine laughed. "But everything was so good."

Jonah agreed with her. He hadn't been to La Bella Rosa in years, but everything was as good as he remembered. Unfortunately, he couldn't tell Bria that because Lorraine was still jacking him off while holding a full-on conversation with her. He downed half the water in his glass in one gulp. 

"I'll tell Sal. It'll make his night. Now, did we leave room for dessert?" Bria asked with the same enthusiasm she offered a teacake for the road at Confections. 

"Oooh, I don't know," Lorraine said.

"No," Jonah choked out, trying to catch Lorraine's eye. He could've reached under the table, put his hand on her foot, and pushed it away, but he didn't want that. 

"Confections took over the desserts and we're still working on the menu. So in the meantime, we're making granitas in-house." 

Lorraine frowned. "That's it? No cookies? Nothing?"

Bria frowned. "No, sorry. But hey!" She reached into her apron and extended a card toward Lorraine. "We're putting together a tasting event in a couple weeks." 

Lorraine snatched the little flyer from Bria's hand.

"For ten bucks, you get access to all the dessert samples you can eat. And in exchange for your honest feedback, we'll give you a coupon to Confections." 

"Yep, that's all I needed to hear. I'll be there."

"Perfect," Bria said, then turned to Jonah. She frowned at him and pulled another flyer from her apron. "You can come too, I guess." 

Jonah rolled his eyes and snatched the flyer from her hand. "Can we get the bill, please?" he ground out. 

"Sure thing," Bria said cheerily, as if she suddenly remembered that Jonah was in charge of her tip.

As soon as Bria was out of earshot, Lorraine pressed her foot against his shaft, pulling a louder groan from his lips.

"Fuck. Someone's gonna catch us," he said, closing his eyes and trying to breathe through his feelings.

"They will with that attitude," Lorraine laughed, stroking her foot against his dick.

He opened his eyes, ready to plead with her to slow down before he came, but as soon as they locked eyes, he knew trying to convince her would be futile even if he could speak.

Lorraine's face was a picture of hungry concentration. "It's your turn," she whispered, licking her lips while the table shook softly from her movements.

"Fuck," he bit out as his back tingled and his orgasm washed over him.

It was a good thing he wore black pants.

LORRAINE

L orraine was tipsy and horny, signs of a great date as far as she was concerned.

Jonah reached around her to push the restaurant's front door open. His arm brushed the side of her breast as Lorraine stepped out into the cool evening air. It wasn't uncomfortably cold but chilly enough to make her nipples hard, and when she turned toward Jonah, his gaze went immediately to her chest.

When they'd gone inside for dinner, the sun had been setting and the streets were empty. They hadn't lingered too long, but it was dark outside now. The tall streetlamps gave downtown Sea Port just enough glow to make Lorraine feel like she was stepping inside a painting. It was beautiful.

Sea Port didn't have anything like a nightlife, but the cute little downtown area was by no means empty. There were small handfuls of people out for an evening walk, enjoying the spring air.

"You gonna fight me about walking you home again?" he asked.

"Looks like you're gonna have to ask me to find out."

Jonah shoved his hands into his pockets and let his gaze wander down her body. Lorraine took a step back and cocked her right hip, posing for him. It wasn't the same as having his hands in her panties or her foot on his dick, but it made her pussy slick nonetheless.

"Lorraine," Jonah said as his gaze started to move back up her body.

"Jonah?"

"Can I walk you home?" She smiled, the word *yes* already on her lips, but Jonah wasn't done yet. "And can I come inside and eat your pussy for dessert?"

Her mouth fell open on an excited sigh. "Well, when you put it like that, how can I say no?"

Jonah moved forward, pressing right up against her with the sexiest smile on his face. "Do you want to say no?"

"No," she sighed. "I want to sit on your face."

"I'm glad we're on the same page. Now turn around. I wanna watch that ass while you lead the way."

She leaned forward and brushed a soft kiss on the side of Jonah's mouth. "Wait 'til you see it naked."

"Hey, Jonah," someone yelled from across the street.

They both turned toward the sound. "Hey, Mr. Freeman," Jonah called with a wave of his hand.

"Who's your friend?"

"The new librarian," Jonah called.

"I'm a Freeman too," Lorraine said with a bright smile.

"She's not from around here," Jonah said quickly, hoping to cut the genealogy conversation off at the root. He knew how the Freemans could be. "You have a good night," he said, steering her down the street.

"That's one of Charlie's uncles," Jonah said. "Both sides of her family will talk your ear off about their family tree if you give 'em half a chance. So *never* give 'em half a chance. Let's go."

Lorraine was professionally interested in Sea Port history, but tonight was anything but professional. She was well-fed, tipsy, and horny as hell, so she turned in the direction of her house. There was a short delay before Jonah followed. She could feel his eyes on her body and it made the walk back to the cottage feel like extended foreplay.

Well, extended from the foreplay in the restaurant.

He followed behind her for a few blocks until they turned onto Maple Lane into her neighborhood. The street was empty and dark, the contrast from downtown stark. Now that they were mostly alone, Jonah sidled up beside her and put his body between her and the road, wrapping his arm around her waist. His big hand settled on her ass cheek and squeezed, holding onto her as they walked the rest of the way to her cottage.

He leaned to the side and kissed her right shoulder. "Behave," she mumbled.

Jonah laughed. "That's rich coming from you. Besides,  you said naked, and that's what I want. So unless you tryna let me strip you on your porch, you should tell yourself to behave."

Lorraine refused to look in Jonah's direction, worried  she might see his bright smile and pull her dress up for him on her front lawn. He made her feel reckless in a way no man  had before, so she kept her eyes on the porch light guiding their way home.

The relief she felt as she turned up the walkway toward  her front door, walked up the steps, and pushed her key into the lock was palpable. So was the lust.

"Take your shoes off, please," she whispered, closing the  front door behind him.

"I'ma take off more than that," he laughed.

Lorraine locked the door and pressed her back against  the wood. "Let's see."

She moved her hands behind her butt and trapped them against the wood door, squirming in excitement.

It took Jonah a few seconds before he realized she was  serious and then he started moving. Some men were self-conscious about stripping naked, but not Jonah. His gaze didn't waver from hers while he pulled off one piece of  clothing after another, kicked his shoes from his feet, and then stood in all his naked glory, unselfconscious, dark-skinned, thick, and hard.

"Fuck," she said, drinking him in. Jonah had the

smoothest skin, the kind of even, deep dark brown that made her mouth water. His muscles were hard and strong underneath his flesh — the kind of strong muscles that came from good, honest work.

He was sexy as fuck.

Jonah wrapped a fist around his shaft and stroked. "You like what you see?"

"Obviously," she sighed, rubbing her thighs together.

"Good. Now it's your turn," he said, letting go of his shaft.

Being cute and flirty was well and good, but Lorraine was past that now. She stepped forward and started pulling the hem of her dress up her body, slow enough to heighten the tension but fast enough to get naked as quickly as possible.

When her dress hit her hips, Jonah gasped. "Lorraine, why don't you have any underwear on?"

"I don't wear underwear."

"Ever?" he asked, his palm wrapping around the head of his dick.

"Rarely," she said, pulling her dress over her breasts. She didn't bother with bras often either.

"Fuck, you're wild," he said, stroking himself again.

Her dress dropped onto the floor, a flimsy pile next to his discarded clothes. She stepped out of her heels and batted his hand from his shaft. Lorraine covered the head of his dick and tugged, leading him through the living room.

"Wait," Jonah said, stepping back, pulling the head from her grasp with a groan. Lorraine turned toward him, a frown on her face. He pointed to the bathroom and laughed. "I need to wash my hands before I put my fingers inside you."

She already liked Jonah, but this was the moment Lorraine decided that she liked him a lot more than she realized.

"I have extra toothbrushes too if you want."

"I would, actually," he said. "If that's cool?"

She stepped into the bathroom and flipped the light  switch. "A man who wants to protect the health of my vagina? That's the sexiest part about you, I think. Come on,  we can brush our teeth together because I'm definitely gonna get your entire dick down my throat."

"Goddamn," Jonah breathed, his lips spreading into a  shy smile.

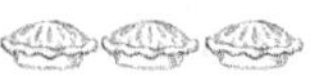

JONAH

A few minutes later, Lorraine pushed Jonah onto the  bed. He moved to the middle of the mattress while she crawled over him.

Lorraine smelled like brown sugar and cocoa butter, and  her skin was soft as fuck. She kissed her way up his chest, over his beard and the corner of his mouth. He turned his head quickly, capturing her lips.

"I've been waiting to kiss you all night," he whispered. 

She laughed softly into his mouth before offering her tongue to him. He sucked it gently between her lips and let her press his shoulders down onto the bed. She straddled his stomach and pressed her pussy into his abs.

She was soaking wet and Jonah was out of patience.

"Oh my god," Lorraine cried as Jonah grabbed her behind her thighs and pulled her up his body. She laughed as he scooted down to get his head between her legs and then laughter turned to moans. The room was dark, but Jonah squinted through the shadows to look up Lorraine's body, watching as she massaged her breasts while his tongue moved through her folds. He didn't give a damn if he didn't sleep at all tonight, so he set a slow, careful pace, letting his tongue move through every soft inch of her flesh. He suckled on her clit until her thighs started to shake and then backed away, licking at her again, keeping her on edge for as long as she'd let him. His orgasm in the restaurant had taken the edge off but it would only hold him off for so long.

She groaned loudly and scratched at his scalp, grinding her pussy onto his mouth, pushing her clit onto the tip of his nose.

He couldn't get enough of Lorraine's taste, the way she moaned, the way she started rolling her hips, using his tongue to get herself off. She leaked her arousal onto his beard as Jonah finally slipped two fingers deep inside her.

Her back bowed, her knees clamped over his ears, and she screamed. Jonah's needy, untouched dick twitched, but he pushed his own desire to the margins of his mind to focus on making Lorraine come again.

He pressed the pads of his fingers against her g-spot and her hips jumped. She was whimpering and her eyes were shut. Jonah couldn't see her face clearly but he could hear her moaning, could feel the delicious bite of her nails against his scalp.

She was leaking around his fingers.

Jonah had never had a sweeter dessert.

He could have stayed between her legs for hours and was on course to do just that until Lorraine fell on her side, pushing his mouth away with shaky hands. "Holy fuck," she panted. 

His fingers were still inside her as he pushed her onto her back so he could dive back in for more. 

"Top drawer," she choked out.

Jonah wiped his mouth. "Huh?"

She moaned before she could find the words, pointing desperately at the dresser across the room. "Condoms. Top drawer," she gasped again. 

Okay, he could eat her again later. Jonah pulled his fingers free and shoved them into his mouth as he hopped  off the bed in search of protection. He pulled the entire box out. They'd need it. Lorraine was flat on her back, her own hand now between her legs, the light bouncing off the thin  sheen of sweat on her body.

"Let me see," he said in a hoarse voice.

Lorraine smiled tiredly and opened her legs so he could  watch her circle her clit while he slid a condom down his shaft. He practically ran back across the bed to get between her legs. She received him happily, moving her hand from  her clit to grasp the head of his dick and lead it toward her opening. There was no awkwardness or hesitation. Lorraine felt as good as Jonah knew she would. 

They groaned together as he bottomed out inside of her. There were so many things he wanted to say in that moment, but they didn't need words. Their gazes locked as he started rocking in and out of her, holding onto one another as if their lives depended on it.

They kissed away one another's moans and sighs and cries.

"I'ma fuck you all night," he breathed into her mouth.

She locked her ankles behind his ass and pulled him deeper. "Faster," was all she said, and he was more than happy to give her everything they both wanted.

WELCOME TO SEA PORT

EIGHTEEN

Lorraine

"You shoulda told me we was gon' be walking. I woulda wore different shoes," Lorraine drawled.

"Where the hell did that accent come from?" Jonah laughed, and the sound of his laughter made Lorraine giggle.

They'd had another dinner at La Bella Rosa. They'd joked about just bouncing back and forth between the town's two restaurants for their dinners and lunches and between Confections and Sully's for their coffee dates. And then they'd laughed louder because that's exactly what they were going to do. There were only so many establishments in Sea Port, so it wasn't like they had any other choice.

Lorraine had laughed with a small note of confusion, surprised to find herself living this kind of life. She'd never been a big city kind of girl — too anonymous — but the first time she'd found herself in a mid-sized city with a young, fun, Black, professional class, she knew she was home. Except Sea Port was nothing like that and she was loving it.

In Sea Port, she had too much notoriety. After a couple months in town, she was pretty sure every resident knew her name at least, if not where she lived and her coffee order at Sully's. Sea Port was also something like ninety percent Black and she guessed there was a professional class, technically, even if it was only nine people — her, Jonah, Mary, Willie, Knox, Sully, Bria, Keith and maybe Charlie — plus Santos, but they were not fun. Well, Mary, Santos, and Knox were fun, and sometimes with other people, but they didn't, like, get together for boozy brunches or have Beyoncé-themed parties.

And still, Lorraine hadn't run away screaming yet. She couldn't put her finger on one thing but everywhere she looked, Lorraine found a new thing to love about the place. The town was quiet and smelled like sugar, every new person she met greeted her with a warm nod at the absolute least, Mary's cookies, and Jonah, of course.

She hadn't put a man on her vision board at the top of the year, but she had added fireworks and that's exactly what she felt when she looked at Jonah. It's why she'd pulled out her sluttiest pair of heels for dinner tonight. Her silk teddy dress was wafer-thin and Jonah's hand was between her legs while they ate. She didn't care that the dress probably cost more than the vinyl booth they sat in or the harsh fluorescent light. If anything, she liked the atmosphere the dying bulb created, and that's when she knew she was sprung.

"They look sexy on you, though," Jonah said, stepping off the curb and turning in the street to face her.

She stepped forward, her toes at the edge of the sidewalk. They still weren't standing quite eye-to-eye, but it was closer.

Lorraine tipped her head back at the same time Jonah tucked his chin. And then they were eye-to-eye.

"You think so?" she asked as if she hadn't used that rationale on herself when she bought these expensive sandals.

Jonah rolled his eyes. "You always fishing for a compliment," he breathed. 

"Fishing in a puddle," she whispered. "You hardly let me open my eyes before you're telling me how beautiful I am." 

"Even with the crust in your eyes," he whispered.

"How good I feel," she sighed.

"That could be about a few things, but they all true." 

"How much you can't wait to get back inside me."

Jonah bent forward. His lips brushed the tip of her nose, his cool icy breath teasing her skin. "I can't tell a lie," he sighed, moving to her mouth. His bottom lip brushed her  top lip and she took a step back.

"See what I mean?" she laughed. "I barely got to breathe  before you're drooling all over me."

Jonah burst into laughter and jogged in a tight circle.

They were just on the edge of Peach Lane, in an alley  behind La Bella Rosa. Lorraine could smell garlic on the night's air. It wasn't the same feeling she had when the air smelled like warm sugar, but Sal's savory contribution to the smell of Sea Port had its own charm.

The street was quiet. There weren't any cars passing by  or even the rumble of engines in the distance. All Lorraine could hear was crickets, Jonah's laughter, and the gentle  scrape of his shoes on asphalt. It all sounded like heaven to her ears.

"Alright, alright," Jonah said, nodding as he turned back toward her. "You got me there."

She lifted her eyebrow with a smirk. "I had you a couple times over here."

His demeanor shifted in degrees with each step he took toward her. The toes of his shoes hit the curb and he waited patiently with a smile on his face until Lorraine stepped forward again. "More than a couple, I think."

"You might be right."

He bent forward and kissed her deeply, opening her mouth with his tongue. She'd been dreaming about a kiss like this all day, from the moment she bumped into Jonah around the corner from Confections. She was picking up mini cupcakes for the kids' story time at the Community Center and his arms were full of boxes of donuts for his crew. They'd stopped to stare at one another for a few heated moments. Jonah told her how excited he was about their date tonight and Lorraine told him how small her dress would be. He'd leaned forward and brushed his mouth against hers, whispering something about coming on her ass, but she couldn't quite hear because his tongue was teasing the seam of her lips. All day, the promise of that kiss had been pulling her forward, from one moment to the next. Knowing Jonah would gently press his mouth against hers, breathing her in while his big, warm hands moved the silk over her skin had kept Lorraine on edge, and finally she got to savor the reward.

A cool night breeze whipped around them as Jonah pulled her body against his. It wouldn't be the first time they'd fucked behind the Italian restaurant.

"Not here," Jonah said.

She frowned against his mouth. "Why not?"

He licked her bottom lip. "Wanna show you something."

"I've seen your dick."

"Ha-ha." He pecked her mouth and then lifted her from the curb, setting her in the street. Lorraine tried not to smile but her cheeks hurt within seconds. "I wanna show you something you haven't seen yet." Their fingers twined together and Jonah led her forward, walking slow enough for her to keep up. "Somewhere new I wanna fuck you," he said.

Lorraine sucked her teeth. "Why didn't you just say that?" she giggled.

JONAH

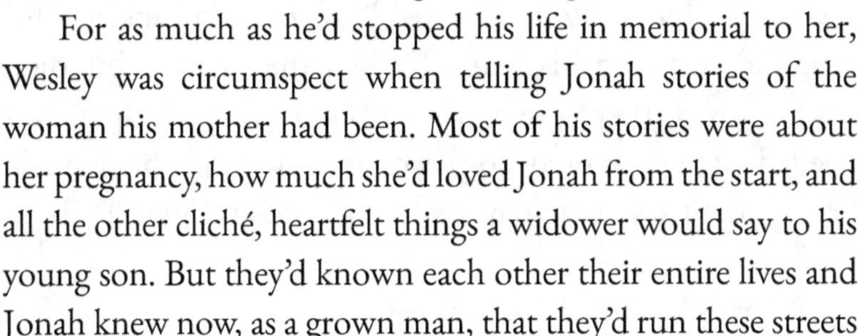

They say a good woman is trouble.

Who 'they' were, Jonah still didn't know, but that's what his father said, so good enough.

For as much as he'd stopped his life in memorial to her, Wesley was circumspect when telling Jonah stories of the woman his mother had been. Most of his stories were about her pregnancy, how much she'd loved Jonah from the start, and all the other cliché, heartfelt things a widower would say to his young son. But they'd known each other their entire lives and Jonah knew now, as a grown man, that they'd run these streets

together. He tried to imagine them walking home from school side-by-side, sneaking out to the outer farms, or marching in the Juneteenth parade — all the things Jonah did when he was young. But one time, when he'd had a beer more than he could handle, Jonah had overheard his father reminiscing about Jonah's mother with Moses. He'd had a look on his face like he was far away. He shook his head and laughed softly.

"A good woman ain't nothing but trouble."

Jonah hadn't known what his father meant then, but he did now.

"Are they gonna build any houses back there?" Lorraine asked.

When Jonah turned to her, she was looking past him at the western woods. "Not unless Willie wants to fight half the town."

"Why? What's back there?"

"Nothing, and they wanna keep it that way. That's why they don't like y'all Transplants."

"What's why?" she asked. Her heels tapped against the concrete as she jogged a few steps to catch up.

"When our people got here, they stopped 'cause they liked the place. Good soil, water nearby, and a beautiful view any which way you looked." Lorraine leaned into his side and squeezed his hand. "When they started building up the town, they agreed not to build up more than they needed. They wanted to keep as much of the natural beauty they saw that day for their kids and grandkids to see."

"That's beautiful," Lorraine sighed.

"It is, but the point I'm making is some people in town think you and Mary and Santos and Knox are more than we need. They're worried y'all will cover up the beauty that used to be here."

"I don't want that," Lorraine whispered.

Jonah shook his head. "Don't matter what you want, it's what people are worried will happen."

"Are you worried?" she asked softly. "Am I distracting you from a tall Portie with a fat ass?"

They laughed together. "That's basically Willie," Jonah said.

"Basically nothing," Lorraine replied. "She can't hide all that in her little pantsuits."

Jonah laughed but he shook his head. "And she's basically like my distant older cousin who may or may not hate me."

"Well, what are your other options?" Lorraine said.

"That's *literally* it," Jonah laughed. "That's exactly why the people who don't want things to change aren't doing too much about y'all being here — because we need you. Better to cut down a few trees to make room for something new than lose the town altogether."

"That's smart. You ever think about running for mayor?"

Jonah laughed louder than he meant to because that was a question only a Transplant would ask. "Absolutely the fuck not. I'ma leave that to the Walthams and maybe the Lincolns."

"Have I met a Lincoln yet?" Jonah laughed louder. "What's so funny?"

"You've met a Lincoln alright," Jonah said, still laughing. "Willie Ann Lincoln Waltham. Lincoln is her mama's maiden name."

"Oh, I see," Lorraine breathed. "Strong name for a little girl."

Jonah laughed. "Perfect name for another Mayor Waltham. Anyway, if I had to go to all those damn meetings and have people who changed my diaper remind me of that in official City Council meetings, I'd quit."

Lorraine ran her hand up his forearm. "I think it's cute how well Porties know each other."

"You mean how well Porties be in each other's business," he corrected, turning into the library parking lot.

"That's one way to look at it."

"Mmhmm," Jonah hummed. "And that's 'cause you don't have as much business for them to be in. Yet."

"Yet," Lorraine laughed, scratching at the inside of his elbow. That soft scratch was like a shot of electricity straight down the length of his dick. "This ain't business?"

There were poles for streetlights out here, but they hadn't been hooked up yet. Moonlight bounced off the tops of Lorraine's cheeks. He bent forward and pressed a kiss on the bridge of her nose. "This ain't the kind of business you want them to be in, but I'm a fan."

She tipped her head back and he brushed his lips against hers. "So am I."

He tasted the air she breathed. He could've lived on that for the rest of his life and if it was up to him, he'd stop right here and fuck her on the ground. He'd happily lay down and scrape up his back so she could ride him on this asphalt, but he'd put a lot of thought into tonight and he didn't want to waste it. Lorraine and those goddamn shoes deserved it.

"Come on," Jonah breathed against her lips. "I need to get in you."

"Get inside," Lorraine corrected.

"I said what I said," Jonah laughed.

"Not you bringing me to work on our little night out."

"I know, I know, but it'll be worth it."

"I'll be the judge of that," she laughed.

He reluctantly let Lorraine's hand go to pull his keyring  from his pocket. It was a cool night for Sea Port, which meant it was in the low seventies, but Lorraine huddled close  at his back, wrapping her arms around his waist.

He pushed the door open and stepped into the library with Lorraine still attached to him. "Seriously?" he sighed. 

He felt her nod against his back. "Seriously."

Jonah thought it was a joke, but when he took the next step, Lorraine stepped with him. "You're so goddamn ridicu-  lous," he laughed.

"You love it."

Jonah chuckled, but he didn't respond because he did  love it. He led Lorraine into the circulation area and stopped just under the skylight. Well, right now it was still a hole in the ceiling, but in a few weeks, it would be covered with a beautiful, steel-enforced glass dome. And tomorrow, they'd  start putting up the scaffolding. Tonight was the last night Lorraine could look up at the sky from the circulation desk with nothing to obscure her view.

He stopped in the center of the room and reached back  with both hands. He grabbed her ass and squeezed, smiling as she shivered against him. "This is where I want you," Jonah said.

Lorraine laughed and finally let go of his waist. "Why, so  you can think about fucking me while y'all are laying down the hardwood?"

She walked around in front of him, looking around. There were tools neatly tucked into corners out of the way — Jonah hated a messy worksite — but this wasn't a fancy hotel room and a bed covered in rose petals.

"Nah," Jonah said as his eyes moved down her body. "I want you to remember me fucking you here when you clock in for a shift."

She turned slowly, a slow smile lifting the corners of her mouth. "Is that right?"

"Yeah."

She licked her lips and looked around again. She was trying to hide her smile, but Jonah could tell how interested she was by the hard points of her nipples, so he focused on them. "That's a few months away," she said seriously.

"It is."

She flattened her hands on her thighs and started pulling her dress up her body slowly. "Then you better fuck me good," Lorraine sighed, pulling her dress over her head. She was bare naked underneath. As usual.

"That's the plan," he whispered. She dropped her dress to the floor and Jonah reached for the button of his pants. "Don't take them shoes off."

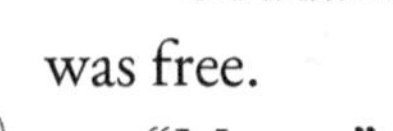

She laughed softly and moved her hand between her legs. "I wasn't. But feel free to try to knock 'em off me."

"Goddamn, Lorraine," Jonah groaned as soon as his dick was free.

"Mmm," she sighed. "That's what I want to hear."

WELCOME TO SEA PORT

NINETEEN

Jonah

Over the last couple of months, Jonah woke up with Lorraine in his arms more mornings than not. Before their little sleepovers started, he'd almost forgotten how it felt to sleep in a bed long enough to accommodate his adult body. Her queen-sized mattress was technically big enough for them to sleep comfortably, but they didn't bother to test its width, preferring instead to wrap their limbs around one another while they slept.

He couldn't have fathomed it from the depth of his grief when they met, but Jonah was getting used to the warmth of waking up just like this. The size of the bed didn't matter so much as the feeling of her skin against his and the smell of her hair when he took his first conscious breath.

"You up?" she whispered, scooting back in his arms.

He ground his hips into her ass and buried his face into the side of her neck. "Obviously."

"What time do you need to leave?" she asked in a voice bright with happiness.

He didn't know how she managed it, but it was not infectious. "Be less excited," he groaned, squeezing his arms around her.

"No," she laughed, pressing her ass into his groin again. "What time do you leave?"

He kissed his way up her neck to her cheek. "I gotta get out of here by five...thirty," he said, already pushing the day's schedule back half an hour in his head.

Lorraine reached for her watch on the nightstand. She checked the time while Jonah rubbed circles over her stomach, his fingers grazing the underside of her breasts. Her skin was hot and so goddamn soft. Her sheets smelled like her body wash. Last night, they'd stumbled around her bedroom to change her sheets and then squeezed their bodies into her small tub-shower combo, trying not to break their necks or get her braids wet while they had sex one more time before bed. His back was a little sore but her braids were bone dry, and he didn't regret a thing.

"We've got an hour," she said quickly, breaking free of his hold.

"I guess that's enough time," Jonah sighed, turning onto his back, reaching for a condom from the nightstand. For ease, there were stacks of condoms all over Lorraine's house, in his work truck, in the library storage room — even her desk in the lending library, but those were only for emergencies. If they could've stashed them in other establishments around town, they would have, but they were already playing fast and loose with their public encounters as is.

Lorraine pushed the covers from their bodies and sat up on her knees, stretching her arms toward the ceiling. Jonah watched her with hungry eyes while he ripped open the condom and pulled it down his shaft.

"How'd you sleep?" she asked casually.

"Good as ever," he said, watching her fingers toy with her nipples, "in a furnace." 

Lorraine rolled his eyes with a smirk. "It wasn't that hot."

"Swear to god it's like you're running a damn marathon  every night but have the nerve to still sleep with this thick ass comforter. Don't make no sense," he laughed, stroking his dick. 

"Whatever. You survived," she said with a saucy roll of her eyes.

Jonah was about to crack another joke, but then  Lorraine leaned over him and pushed one of her breasts directly over his mouth. That shut him up real quick as he licked her nipple until it hardened against his tongue. He  was just about to switch to her other breast when she pulled away, massaging the nipple he'd just sucked with a bemused smile on her lips.

"How'd you sleep?" he asked. 

She squeezed her breast one more time and then opened her palm to show him a small bottle of lubricant. He lifted his eyebrows and stroked his dick with a little more vigor. 

"I slept great," she said, lifting onto her knees. "I had a dream we were fucking in my office in the library." She moved her hand between her legs and started massaging her  pussy.

"Again?" He frantically kicked the cover down to the foot of the bed.

She tossed the bottle to the side, threw her leg over his

body, and straddled his waist. "Mmm, not the temporary site. The new library. When it's done."

She sat her pussy on the back of his hand, gyrating her hips. Jonah grunted softly as she ground her clit into his skin.

"Is that what you want?" he asked.

"You know it is," Lorraine sighed. "You gonna give it to me?" She leaned forward on both hands.

Jonah didn't need direction. As soon as there was enough room to lift his dick, the head was bumping at her opening. They both moaned as she leaned back slowly, taking his entire length in one slow press. She lifted her hips and sat back quickly, pulling the breath Jonah had been holding from his lungs with a grunt.

"Fuck." As usual, Lorraine took that as a sign to push him a little further, bouncing on top of him until he grabbed her by the thighs and moaned. "Slow down. I don't want to come yet. Fuck."

"That's what I like to hear," she moaned, straightening her back and smiling down at him.

He rolled his eyes, but not in annoyance; he couldn't manage that. He was too busy trying to survive the circles she was drawing with her hips. "Jesus."

"That too," she laughed. Lorraine moved her hands back to her breasts and rolled her nipples between her fingers. Her body moved without an ounce of urgency, as if they didn't both have to be to work soon.

But if this was the pace she wanted, Jonah wasn't going to rush her. His crew knew what they were doing and didn't need him to start the day. They'd also gotten used to him being late every now and again. Everyone pretended not to know why.

"That feel good, baby?" she whispered, her own eyelids fluttering closed.

"Yeah. Just like that." He grabbed her hips and started helping her ride him faster. 

She bent forward, pressing her palms against his chest. "You gonna be thinking about me all day?" she asked, bouncing on top of him again. 

"Yeah. Fuck. Yeah."

His stammering words and panting breaths only fed Lorraine's lust. Jonah could feel it in the sharp bite of her  nails on his skin and the way her pussy gushed around him. He didn't know what exactly excited her about breaking him  down like this, but he wasn't complaining.

"You gonna be thinking about me?" he asked.

"Yeah," she moaned.

Jonah pushed his hips up into her. He wanted her to  moan again, and louder this time, and she gave him exactly that. "Not enough," he panted.

Her breasts were bouncing as they fucked into one  another and she couldn't stop smiling while he wrestled a little control from her grasp. "Tell me," she panted.

"I want you to go in your office and fuck yourself," he  whispered, digging his fingers into her soft hips.

"With what?"

"Shit," Jonah hissed as his back tensed. He pressed the  back of his head into the pillow, groaning. "Fingers," he said.

She nodded. "You want me to call you so you can listen? Or watch?"

Their movements were reckless now. The bed was

squeaking, their skin covered in sweat. They'd have to change her sheets again before they left.

Jonah wanted to say yes, but his day was packed and he was absolutely going to be late. "I want to know you're doing it while I work. I want to look at my watch and know you're getting off 'cause I told you to."

She cried out as a full-body shiver moved through her. He gathered her into his arms and held her close while he started flexing his hips to fuck up into her frantically.

He could feel his orgasm coming right on time but knew one wouldn't be enough.

Yeah, he was definitely going to be late today.

For their date the night before, Jonah took Lorraine to the Lincoln farm on the outskirts of town. It was owned by Charlie's paternal family, which was technically connected to the Lincolns, but Jonah couldn't remember how. They weren't as illustrious as the Walthams, but an old Sea Port family, nonetheless. There were Lincolns all over the south, people who'd given themselves the name after slavery's end to honor the president who won the Civil War, just like the Freemans chose the name to denote their change in legal status. Even though Lorraine wasn't related to any of them, she'd wanted to see what her ancestors might have built if they'd lived in a place like Sea Port.

They'd also wanted to have sex under the stars before going back to Lorraine's house to have more sex. A perfect date as far as Jonah was concerned. And it was well worth being late to extend that date into the morning.

He made it back to his house by six to shower and change as quickly as possible. He'd considered stashing a change of work clothes in the back of his truck, but it made  him feel like he was doing something illicit — in the bad way — so he put the thought out of his head as quickly as he put it out of his head to ask Lorraine if he could store some  clothes in her closet. If he asked that, she might ask where he lived, and he just wasn't ready to have a stranger in his dad's home.

Not yet. 

Jonah stomped into the kitchen to make some coffee before leaving for work. While he waited for his coffee to brew, he looked around at the kitchen with a sigh. He origi-  nally stayed in Sea Port without a plan. After his father died, the thought of going back to Atlanta was inconceivable. Besides, there was so much here to do. His dad had contracts  to fulfill and there was an entire house Jonah had inherited that he had no idea what to do with.

The plan had been to clear out his dad's house slowly,  but over the past year, he'd been making little progress. Even before he met Lorraine, there was hardly any evidence that his father had died. If he squinted, it looked more like his  father had left for the day but he'd be back soon. Sure, there were half-empty cupboards and boxes full of plates and cups he kept meaning to give away, but his dad's work boots were  still sitting by the front door. This house was full of decades of memories and Jonah was unprepared to have those memories in his hands, not when his grief still felt fresh as an open wound.

If his phone hadn't started ringing in that moment, he might've started bawling in the middle of the kitchen. He picked up the call without looking at the caller ID. "Yeah," Jonah said, wiping at his dry eyes.

"Hello, is this Jonah Brown?" the woman on the other end asked in a chipper customer service voice.

"Yeah."

"Good morning, Mr. Brown. This is Anna, and I'm calling from Superior Home Mortgage."

It took Jonah a few seconds to realize this was the mortgage company for his condo in Atlanta. He didn't think of Atlanta or his condo there with any regularity. He'd stopped doing so long before Lorraine showed up, but with her in town, his former life had been pushed even further to the margins of his consciousness.

He'd done the bare minimum to keep his life there going. His roommates didn't care if he was there or not so long as the utilities worked, and Jonah got a handyman to cover whatever issues they had; all things he could handle from Sea Port. Their rent covered his mortgage, which was another good thing because he'd left his job at the architecture firm months ago. Technically, he hadn't had more than a month of unemployed bereavement before he'd stepped right into his father's shoes as foreman and owner of Brown & Son, but he didn't really feel like he was employed for real. He hadn't even paid himself a wage in all the months since he'd been home. He knew what his dad paid himself — hardly anything, just enough to keep the bills paid — so Jonah did the same.

"Is something wrong?" Jonah asked in a hoarse voice.

"No, sir, just calling to update your files. Do you have five minutes for that?"

"Sure," he said.

"Wonderful." She read out his address while he rinsed out his travel mug. "Is that still your primary address?"

He'd just been looking for something to distract his mind while he waited for his slow ass coffee machine to work, but the first question was like a punch to the gut. Like almost everything else in his life, the answer was complicated. Yes, no, but also, he wasn't sure. He hadn't been in Atlanta in a year. There was a closet full of clothes he wasn't even sure he could fit anymore. There were three framed pictures on top of the dresser — one of his parents on their wedding day, one of him and his dad at his high school graduation, and one of him and Angie — that he hadn't seen in just as long. He couldn't even remember if he'd made his bed that last day and he hadn't thought about Angie in months.

Confusion and shame felt like fire licking at the back of his neck.

"Sorry, I gotta go," Jonah said, ending the call before he even finished speaking. He shut off the coffee machine, grabbed his keys, and left the house in long, hurried strides, uncaffeinated and emotionally unstable.

The sun was barely in the sky and already, Jonah was wishing he'd never left Lorraine's bed.

WELCOME TO SEA PORT

TWENTY

Lorraine

L orraine was just stepping onto Main Street when her phone rang. "What do you want?" she sang in cheerful greeting.

He sucked his teeth before he answered, and loudly at that. "How you been in the South all these months and haven't picked up any Southern manners?" DeJuan laughed.

"I'm stubborn. You know this," Lorraine said, practically skipping off the curb she was in such a good mood. It was a beautiful day in Sea Port; the sun was shining, the humidity hadn't kicked in yet, and Lorraine's knees were still weak from sex with Jonah. If all her mornings could start like this, Lorraine thought it would be hard to leave Sea Port when her contract ended.

But she didn't want to think of that.

She spotted Sully standing in front of her coffee shop and waved at her as DeJuan's laughter died. "You should come visit me. I think you'd like it here."

"No, ma'am, but I'm calling because I was thinking that you need to get away."

"I'm busy," Lorraine replied, as she had all the other times DeJuan called trying to convince her to plan a little getaway.

"You ain't ever been this busy in your entire life," DeJuan said.

"Well, this little town's little library needs a lot of work."

"Does it have a roof yet?" he asked.

Lorraine rolled her eyes. "Yes. I told you when it went up."

"Oh, that's right. That was your reason for not joining me in Cabo."

Lorraine sighed. "Like I said, I was busy."

"This is the longest you've been in one place without even a damn weekend away. What is going on down there? Is it a cult?"

Lorraine pressed her lips together and patted the heel of her hand at her damp hairline — a little sweat from the heat and a little sweat from frustration. She'd been playing around with Jonah for months but hadn't told DeJuan. She'd meant to tell him dozens of times, maybe even close to a hundred, but the timing never felt right and Lorraine was having too much fun to interrogate why. Keeping secrets was definitely out of the ordinary for her relationship with DeJuan.

They were the kind of besties who told each other everything, including the uncomfortable shit she wouldn't tell the men she dated. But whenever she thought about telling DeJuan about Jonah, she got a strange feeling in her stomach and changed the subject. It should've been nothing for her to tell DeJuan about all the good sex they'd been having, at least — he would've loved that — but the timing still didn't feel right, so she changed the subject again.

"You know, it's entirely possible that I like where I live," Lorraine said, strutting toward the administrative building.  DeJuan scoffed, but Lorraine was undeterred. "Maybe all that running I've been doing was to lead me here."

"Where?" DeJuan cried. "Like girl, where are you even? 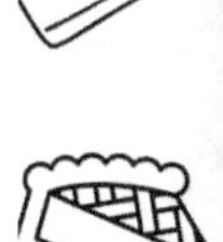 For real."

Lorraine rolled her eyes. "I sent you coordinates."

"And what the hell am I supposed to do with those? Can  you put coordinates in Google Maps?"

"You can, actually," she muttered.

He sucked his teeth again. "Who are you? Where is my  best friend?"

Lorraine laughed softly at DeJuan's distress because he was making a few points, he just didn't know it. Before her  move, Lorraine had coped with her isolation with the promise of weekend trips to nearby towns, but besides a day trip to Parkdale, she hadn't left Sea Port at all. That trip to  Parkdale was in her official capacity as town librarian and she'd been back in Sea Port in time for dinner and a nightcap with Jonah. She was busy, just maybe not *as* busy with work as she'd been leading DeJuan to believe.

"Did you call me just to complain or...?"

"You say that like complaining isn't a core pillar of our friendship," DeJuan joked, but he moved on. "But no, I'm  calling to complain *and* invite you to Scottsdale."

"Do you ever sit still?" she laughed.

"No. I work to afford my next vacation. That's it. And  before you moved to the middle of nowhere, so did you."

"Ouch."

"Capitalism, baby," he sighed.

Lorraine sighed in return. "Well, maybe I like my life here because I have a good work-life balance."

"What's that?"

"*Maybe* if you came to visit me, you'd find out," she teased.

In the back of her head, she realized that if DeJuan ever took her up on her offer, she'd have to tell him about Jonah, but she thought the chances of that were lower than Sea Port's population density.

"*Maybe* you should come to Scottsdale with me and remember the luxurious life of a wellness retreat."

"Sounds expensive," Lorraine laughed as she took the stairs up to the lending library. "Didn't you just go there?"

"A few months ago," DeJuan sighed.

"So why are you going back? Of all places?"

There was a beat of silence on the other end of the phone while she pulled out her keys and unlocked the library's front door. The room smelled like old books and wood polish and it instantly brought a smile to her face. It was the smallest library she'd ever worked in, but this tiny lending library was her favorite office maybe ever.

"I saw a lovely brochure on my last trip," DeJuan said.

"That's it?"

"You know I love a good brochure."

She laughed softly. "You do. When are you going?" she asked, mostly just to move the conversation along.

"Two days."

"Two days?" Lorraine cried. "You couldn't have called me with more notice?"

"If I did, you would've shot me down," he said. "Besides, I just made the decision yesterday during a tornado warning. I gotta get out of here. This is notice."

What he didn't say was that before Lorraine moved to Sea Port, two days was pretty good notice for a little weekend away and she used to be the one to spring these kinds of trips on him. How times had changed. But he didn't need to say all that because she already knew it to be true, and she felt guilty about how long it had been since they'd seen one another.  

"Lemme think about it, okay?"

DeJuan perked up. "Absolutely. I'll email you all the details. I already paid for double occupancy on the room. All you gotta do is show up ready to put a credit card down for your massages and whatnot. Or you can just hang out by the pool while I float in a salt bath. I'll handle the dinner reservations."   

"DeJuan, I said I'll think about it."

"I heard you. See you in Arizona." He hung up before she could tell him that 'thinking about it' wasn't code for yes, but he was gone. 

Lorraine sighed and put her phone away, already anxious at having to call him back later and disappoint him. She wished the invitation was coming from anyone else so she could craft a friendly text message letting him down without a care in the world. But DeJuan was Lorraine's family. Turning him down broke a little piece of her heart and dampened her good mood.  

JONAH

Jonah's day went from great to bad to worse in what felt like a blink of an eye, and he didn't have anyone to blame but himself. He could've forced himself not to dwell on the uncomfortable feelings caused by that phone call. Hell, if he really wanted to forget, he could've dropped by Lorraine's office and given her the orgasm he'd told her to take for herself at lunchtime. But he couldn't get out of his own head.

For months, he'd been drowning his grief in Lorraine, sleeping at her house at night to avoid the uncomfortable loneliness that stalked him around his dad's cluttered house, and that phone call brought all those feelings to the fore. When his crew broke for lunch, Jonah didn't. He barely took a break to hydrate or go to the bathroom. Zeke joked about Jonah using work to punish himself and he wasn't too far off the mark; coping through work was a skill he learned from his father.

When Wesley was stressed, he went out to his shed and didn't come back until he had a bookshelf for Jonah's room or a stool to give away. When he was angry, he went to whatever job site needed demolition and got to work. When he was mad at Jonah, he put him to work hauling trash from his worksites. Wesley didn't yell; he worked. And they didn't talk about their feelings, they worked some more.

It didn't matter how long Jonah had been away, no matter where he was, he'd always be Wesley's son.

"Aye, Jonah. Jonah!"

He didn't know how long Zeke had been yelling his name, but he only heard it when he stopped the orbital sander to check his work. He brushed the wood dust from his safety goggles and pulled one earplug out. "What?"

"Your girlfriend's here."

Jonah's heart started racing and his eyes widened in shock. "What's she doing here?" Angie had stopped calling months ago, in those first few months after his dad's funeral. Jonah hadn't blamed her since he never returned her calls, and when he did pick up, he never had much to say. But why would she be here now?

Zeke shrugged. "I don't know. Probably wondering when we're gonna put windows in so she can start decorating her office."

Lorraine.

Shame burned away the confusion in his chest. "Uh, yeah. Yeah, tell her I'm coming down."

Zeke squinted at Jonah. "You alright? You been quiet today."

Jonah swallowed a lump in his throat and nodded. "Yeah, I'm fine, just tired."

"Then you shoulda let somebody else do these floors." He turned and walked away, muttering something that sounded a lot like, "Just like your daddy," to Jonah's ears.

Jonah stood from the floor and groaned at the ache in his back. He did his best to brush some of the dust from his body but gave up after a while. There was so much glass in the new building that as soon as Jonah stepped into the

hallway, he spotted Lorraine in the entrance chatting with Zeke.

He ducked into the bathroom across the hall, pulled his gloves off, washed his hands, and rinsed his face. They hadn't hung a mirror in the bathroom yet, so Jonah couldn't see what the mess of his emotions had done to his features, and he was thankful for that.

He shoved his gloves in his back pocket and walked to the entrance where Lorraine was still chatting with Zeke. "Hey," Jonah called when he was within earshot.

She turned at the sound of his voice, a smile already forming on his face. "Hey."

"Thanks, Zeke," he said, and the other man rolled his eyes before turning back to Lorraine. "Thanks, Zeke," Jonah said again in a harder tone.

Zeke rolled his eyes again, nodded his head at Lorraine, and walked away without an ounce of urgency.

Jonah shook his head. "Sorry about that."

She looked him up and down. "You alright?"

He looked down at his jeans and knee pads, all covered in dust. "Yeah, yeah, I'm good, just getting those hardwood floors together for you."

Her face lit up. "For the patrons," she said. "They'll be here long after I'm gone." She laughed softly, but Jonah's mouth went dry.

Sure, he understood from the moment he laid eyes on her that Sea Port wasn't really Lorraine's style, but hearing her talk about leaving felt like someone punched him in the gut. This was his home, not hers.

He'd lose her soon.

A sound pulled his attention away from her smiling face.

When he looked over his shoulder, Zeke and Kevin were watching from a few feet away. "Don't y'all got something to do?" he called to his employees.

"We're doing it," Zeke called back.

Jonah sighed loudly.

"You sure you're alright?" Lorraine asked, softly, her fingers landing on his forearm.

Over the last few months, Jonah had spent hours mapping the contours of Lorraine's body with his hands and mouth, but he loved watching her when she slept — he thought it was the only time he got to see her unguarded. He wasn't even sure she realized it, the way she pressed her lips together as if there was something she wanted to say but knew she shouldn't, and the way her eyes shifted around his face as if she was trying to decipher his mood.

All while he was trying to decipher the same for himself.

He realized in the moment how they'd come together while still closing parts of themselves off to one another. He didn't talk about his dad and she didn't talk about her life before Sea Port, and whenever their moods dipped, they took their clothes off until they felt better.

It worked until it didn't.

"My back is killing me," he said, reaching around to squeeze his lower back. He jumped, surprised to find the ache stronger than he thought. "I've been bent over sanding floors all day."

Lorraine's eyes went wide. "Oh no. Is there anything I can do?"

"No, no. But I think I'm gonna stay at mine tonight. To ice my back and rest," he said, because he was too nervous to

be direct and tell her just how sad and broken he felt when he wasn't inside her.

She straightened her back and pressed her lips together for a few seconds. "I don't... We don't—" Lorraine licked her lips. "Got it. I hope you feel better tomorrow," she said, turning and walking away.

"Wait," Jonah called. Lorraine froze, and he watched her take a deep breath before turning around. "Why'd you come by?"

Her mouth lifted into a pained sigh. "The Mayor wants me to do daily check-ins now that y'all are almost done."

He laughed. "Yeah, that sounds like Willie."

"It does. I'll let her know everything's on schedule," she said, forcing a smile on her face.

"Thanks," Jonah said, his chest aching almost as much as his back.

WELCOME TO SEA PORT

TWENTY-ONE

Lorraine

Lorraine hid her insecurities behind mascara and matte lipstick — a trick she first learned from her mother. When a man she wanted didn't want her back, she wiped her tears, put in some eye drops, smeared a fresh coat of lipstick onto her mouth, and went on about her day. Her mother had never seemed to value herself outside of her ability to get and keep a man, so it was fitting that her many breakups had been Lorraine's first school.

Never let a man see you cry.

Leave before he can leave you.

Always have a backup.

Protect your heart and your pocketbook.

It took years of therapy for Lorraine to pry the lessons her mother taught her from deep in her flesh, but they still lingered because they made sense.

She'd practically seen the word 'run' written all over Jonah's face, especially the way he avoided meeting her eyes. Just this morning, he'd been whispering how much he couldn't get enough of her while she was on top of him, but a few hours later, he couldn't even pretend to be excited to see her. The writing was on the wall.

Lorraine left the construction site with a pit in her stomach. She felt the urge to run coursing through her veins and tried not to let it consume her, but it was easier to feel that than admit how sad she felt at Jonah's rejection. Or even the

fact that she saw anything but slavish devotion as rejection.

There weren't any therapists in Sea Port, so she headed toward the place that was as close to therapy as she could get.

"Wanna try my cookies?" Bria asked as soon as Lorraine stepped into Confections.

The question pulled Lorraine from her murky thoughts. She froze just inside the door and looked left and right. "Is

that a proposition?"

Bria's face lit up. "Depends. Is the library willing to commit to purchasing donuts from Confections?"

"For what?" Lorraine asked.

Bria shrugged. "Whatever you want. You can give 'em away for all I care."

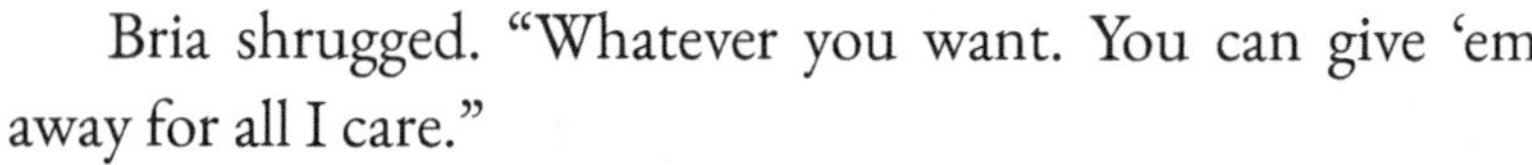

"Alright, Bria, chill," Mary said, waltzing into the storefront with her arms full of the distinctive pink paper bags the bakery used. "We don't need *every* business in Sea Port

ordering from us."

Bria's face screwed up in frustration. "Yeah, we do. Do you know how thin our margins are?"

Mary stopped behind the cash register with a roll of her eyes. "What'd I tell you about looking at the books without me?"

Bria rolled her eyes back. "Do the numbers change when you're not there? No. Besides, if I'm going to be the assistant manager, I need to know these things. And we need the business."

Mary sighed loudly and turned away from Bria to restock the bags in the rack behind the display cases. Lorraine watched Mary's movements through the half-empty shelves of muffins. 

When Mary was done, she stood up straight. "Okay, maybe we do, but you can't bully our potential customers. We need to use a little tact. A little gentleness." 

Bria sucked her teeth. "I'll leave that up to you," she said, placing the tray of cookies on the counter next to the cash register. "Can I take my break, or do you need me?" she asked Mary, already reaching back to untie her apron. 

"Nah, you're good. You can go."

"Just a break," Bria said, hanging her apron on the wall hook. "I told Keith I'd stop by Sully's during his shift." 

"Oh, okay. Tell him I said hey," Mary said.

Bria pushed through the swinging gate. "Will do."

"And Sully."

"Huh?" Bria said, eyes widening. 

Mary was choosing a cookie from the tray with almost her entire concentration. "Say hi to Sully," she said, finally deciding on what looked like a sugar cookie.

"Oh, yeah, sure. Okay," Bria said, scurrying from the front door. 

"Don't worry," Mary said, pushing the tray in Lorraine's direction. "I left the double chocolate for you." 

"Thank god," Lorraine said, rushing forward and snatching the cookie she'd been eyeing since she walked in the door. 

They ate in silence. Lorraine closed her eyes and enjoyed

the rich dark and lighter semi-sweet chocolate melting onto her tongue. She thought she detected a hint of salt. It was perfect, the exact peace she needed in that moment.

"Feel better?" Mary asked as Lorraine popped the last bit of cookie into her mouth.

"No."

"Wanna talk about it?"

"No," Lorraine mumbled, covering her mouth as she spoke. She opened her eyes and immediately turned to the tray of cookies on the counter, as much from a desire to ignore looking Mary in the eye as the fact that she wanted another one.

"Is it Jonah?" Mary asked gently.

"Yeah. But also me," she said. Lorraine hated to acknowledge her own shortcomings and this was as close as she could get right now. "I can't believe I've been here for three months already," she said around another bite of cookie.

"Time flies when you're having as much sex as possible," Mary said.

Lorraine lifted her eyebrows. "Is that your advice?"

"Yes," she trilled. "Not that you need it."

Lorraine's eyes widened. "What's that supposed to mean?"

Mary rolled her eyes. "*Everybody* in town knows about you and Jonah."

Lorraine stopped chewing. "Everybody? Knows?"

Mary pulled an industrial-sized package of napkins from the shelf under the cash register and walked to the little seating area. "Yes. Everybody. Besides the fact that most Porties watch us like hawks, almost everybody in town has known Jonah since he was a baby. They're very invested in you two."

Lorraine walked to the water fountain for a drink and swallowed her little paper cup down in one gulp as images moved through her mind — images of all the places she and Jonah had fucked one another around town. "They do?" 

Mary nodded happily. "I dropped off some pies at the diner and Mrs. Wright told me she hopes you and Jonah's kids don't get his forehead." Lorraine's eyes were wider than ever. "Assuming you have kids, I guess," Mary added hastily. 

Lorraine was mentally frozen, but not speechless; she was never speechless. "I have to get back to work." 

"Oh my god, don't freak out," Mary said.

"I'm not freaking out," Lorraine lied.

"You know how old people are," Mary said. 

Lorraine nodded. She did. This wasn't the first time an older Black woman she barely knew had dedicated time and energy to imagining her fictional future children. What was new was how it made her feel. 

"Jonah and I are just hanging out," Lorraine said.

"And fucking," Mary added with a conspiratorial wink. 

"Yeah. Yes. But we..." Lorraine didn't know how to end that sentence, especially after their brief strange encounter. She sighed sadly, wondering how a day that had started so well was crashing down around her. 

"Here, have another cookie before you go," Mary said, walking to the counter. She picked up the tray and smiled happily as Lorraine took two cookies before she left. 

JONAH

The kitchen smelled like old coffee and bleach. Add cedar and Jonah could've conjured up the scent of his father in one neat ball, and it made the twisting feeling in his stomach worse. He was sweaty, panting, and on the verge of tears, but they wouldn't fall. After months of crying, Jonah had been waiting to cry all day — working while the pressure of tears built behind his eyes — but nothing came of it besides a deepening despair.

"Jonah," Moses Wright called from the front door.

"In here," Jonah yelled back in a hoarse voice. He glanced at the old microwave and blinked. Somehow, it was after six in the evening. He didn't know where the time had gone.

Moses's familiar heavy steps stopped abruptly at the kitchen door. "Boy, what in the hell did you do?"

Jonah flexed his grip on the sledgehammer in his left hand. "The kitchen was old," he said. "Really fucking old."

"Watch your mouth, Jonah Brown."

"Sorry," Jonah said. He spotted a bottle of beer on the only counter he'd yet to demolish. He stepped over the splinters of wood littering the ground, snatched it up, and took a sip. It was warm. He hadn't planned to come home and demolish the kitchen, but he'd walked through the door and seen the old kitchen his dad had always meant to update but never found the time. Or maybe he never had the will.

Either way, this was just one more thing he'd left for Jonah to handle. So he handled it.

"My Lord," Moses whispered as he carefully walked into  the room, surveying the pieces of torn-up wood cabinetry and linoleum tile littering the floor. He reached out to touch a hanging corner of the old floral wallpaper that looked as  out of place in this kitchen as Jonah felt. It wasn't his dad's style — assuming his dad had a style — but no one had ever touched it because Jonah's mother had picked it out well  before he was born. As a kid, Jonah would stare at the wallpaper and think of the mother he couldn't remember. But now, when he saw it, all he could see was his father, the man  who broke his back at work every day in her memory. The man who only cried over the woman he loved in the middle of the night when he thought Jonah was fast asleep.

The father he'd never see again. 

"Did he miss her?" Jonah asked in a voice nearly as broken as he felt.

"What?" Confusion and pain were etched into the deep  lines of Moses's face.

"Did my daddy spend the rest of his life missing my  mom?"

"Every day."

Jonah knew the answer, of course.

In their house, time stopped the day after his mom left  the house one day to go Christmas shopping two towns over and came home in a body bag. A drunk driver fell asleep at the wheel and slammed into her as she crossed the street, shattering two lives and ending one. Long before Black parents were taking their kids to therapy, Wesley spent every penny he had to get Jonah the tools he needed to process his mother's death. He'd never given himself the same gift.

All Jonah's life, his father had lived in a tomb of his own making. There were pictures on nearly every wall of the house capturing small moments in a too-short life shared with the woman he loved. The were pictures of them as babies — because of course, they knew each other all their lives — until they were holding their own baby.

Until this moment, nothing in this house had drastically changed from the way it looked when his mother last saw it; his father had wanted it that way. But now they were both gone, and all Jonah had of them were old pictures, an old house, and a loneliness that would never go away. There was no way this was the life his parents wanted for him.

Jonah took another deep swig of beer, blinking away tears.

"What's this about, boy?"

He took another sip of beer and then set it aside. He couldn't taste it anyway. "Dad's been gone almost a year," Jonah said.

"You think you're the only one who misses him?"

Jonah shook his head. "No. I know everyone misses him, but I'm the one who's stuck."

"Stuck where? Here?" Jonah looked around the half-demolished kitchen, but Moses sucked his teeth. "Not in this house. In Sea Port. You feel stuck here?"

Jonah didn't know how to answer that question. The answer was as much 'yes' as it was 'no.' "I don't know."

"Bullshit," Moses said.

Jonah couldn't help but smile sadly. He looked briefly

into Moses's eyes but was forced to look away before he lost the battle to keep his tears at bay. "I always thought I'd move back to Sea Port eventually."

"That right?" Moses asked, in the same calm voice he used to list the daily specials. It was familiar and comforting, and it hurt because he'd never hear his dad's voice again. 

"I didn't know when," Jonah admitted. "And I know my... I know he probably didn't believe me." 

"He did," Moses said.

Jonah's head whipped back in Moses's direction. There was a gentle, sad smile on his face. 

"You told him you'd be back, and he believed you. I didn't," Moses said, lifting his eyebrows. His smile briefly shifted from sad to playful. "I told him the day you left for  school you wouldn't ever move back here for longer than a visit, and who could blame you? But he always said you'd be back. And here you are."

Jonah shook his head. He needed to swallow the lump of  emotion in his throat before he could speak. "I thought he'd be here when I came back," he admitted finally, a tear falling down his face. The first trickle of the emotional storm to  come. "I thought whenever I was ready to settle down and come back here, my dad would welcome me home. I thought when I was ready to get married, he'd be there.  When I had kids—"

He couldn't finish that sentence and he didn't need to; he was living it. Whenever Jonah had kids, they'd think of  his father the way he thought of his mother — a vague understanding of a person but nothing concrete to hang it on. Jonah's kids would have memories of a man they'd never met, which was worse somehow.

From here on out, Wesley Brown would never be more than a name to the new people in his life — people like Lorraine.

Jonah's shirt and hands were covered in dust, so he let the tears fall down his face. Eventually, the sound of Moses's boots crunched over the kitchen debris. His big, rough hands bracketed Jonah's neck. His thumbs urged Jonah to lift his head. He could hardly see Moses through the tears, but he didn't need to see him for his words to stick.

"The worst lesson any of us ever learn is that we can't go back and change the past. We gotta live with our choices, good and bad." Moses moved a hand to squeeze his shoulder. "But the best lesson your daddy ever taught me was that every day you choose to get up and go on about your life is something to celebrate."

Jonah laughed dryly. "When did my daddy ever celebrate anything? All he did was work, grieve, and sleep until the day he died."

"Now that's not true," Moses said gently. "He raised you. *You* were his celebration, and he'd hate to see you all broken up like this."

WELCOME TO SEA PORT

TWENTY-TWO

Lorraine

Lorraine woke up with the sun and in the worst mood because she was alone.

She didn't believe in getting used to a man's presence, but she'd done that with Jonah. Over the last couple of months, she'd gotten used to watching shadows play across her walls while Jonah moved inside her, but this was the second morning she was waking up alone and she didn't like it.

She reached for her phone and found more unread texts messages than she expected.

A couple from Mary:

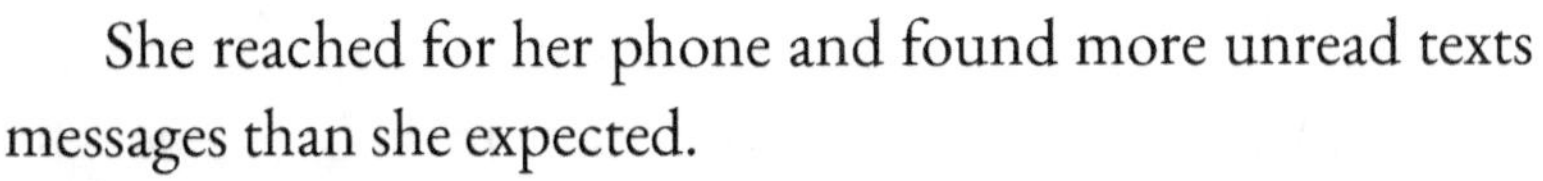

> Red velvet cinnamon rolls.

> Thoughts?

More than a few from Mayor Waltham:

I just found a grant for summer reading programs. We don't have enough kids to qualify, but I sent it to you anyway.

One of the candidates for a teaching position has some plans for the library. I sent their application to you. Send thoughts when you can.

We should set up a meeting for the library reopening event. Construction will be done before we know it.

But nothing from Jonah. His absence made Lorraine's morning feel like a slog before she even climbed out of bed.

They'd never gotten into the habit of texting; they didn't need to. Sea Port was too small and they saw each other every day. Not yesterday, though. For the first time since they started seeing one another, Lorraine hadn't so much as glimpsed Jonah in hours. It felt purposeful, and it hurt.

Thankfully, DeJuan's text message brightened her day.

Not too late to soak up the sun with me!

He included a link to the spa for the third time since the formal invitation. Lorraine had seen the link before, with the beautiful preview of a pool in the desert sun, but she'd never opened it. This morning, she did.

Instead of having slow morning sex with Jonah, Lorraine turned onto her back and scanned through the images of a hotel spa the likes of which Sea Port would never see.

"Well, hello there, Ms. Librarian," Moses called as soon as Lorraine stepped out of her car.

"Morning, Mr. Wright," Lorraine called.

She'd seen Jonah's house before, but only in passing. They'd stopped by once before he drove her out to the Lincoln fields so he could pick up a picnic basket from the garage. He didn't invite her in, and she hadn't thought about it at the time, but now she did. She couldn't help but feel uncomfortable walking up the path to the front of Jonah's house without him.

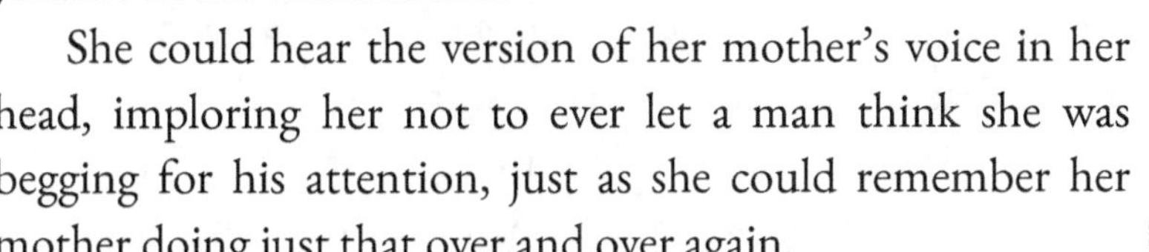

She could hear the version of her mother's voice in her head, imploring her not to ever let a man think she was begging for his attention, just as she could remember her mother doing just that over and over again.

"You don't got to be all formal with me," Mr. Wright said with a warm smile.

Lorraine ripped her gaze from Jonah's front door and smirked. "Ms. Librarian?" she said.

He swatted the air lightly. "Sign of respect."

"Then it's mutual," she said, knowing he couldn't argue with that. "Is Jonah around?" As soon as Jonah's name left her lips, Lorraine could see the bad news written all over Mr. Wright's face.

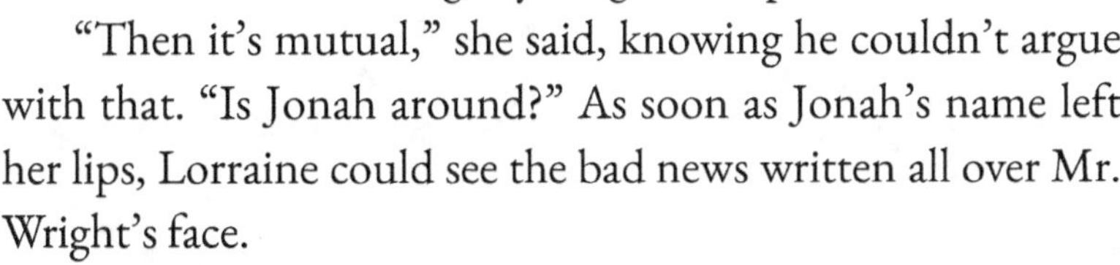

He pulled the worn baseball cap from his head and worried it in his hands. "So, that fool boy didn't call you before he left?"

She felt the ground shift beneath her. "Left?" Her voice was barely a whisper.

Moses took a deep breath and glanced back at the house. He scratched at his bald head. "He left early this morning. I just dropped by to make sure the house was locked up."

"But...where'd he go?"

"Back to Atlanta," Moses said apologetically. "He had some things he needed to handle."

Lorraine's mouth fell open, but none of the hundreds of questions littering her brain made their way onto her tongue. She just couldn't fathom what to say, so she said nothing. It took a few seconds to recover herself, and when she did, she forced a smile onto her face.

She couldn't imagine what she looked like to Mr. Wright, but he smiled gently at her all the same. "I'm sure he'll be back soon," he whispered softly.

Lorraine nodded and waved before turning away, climbing back into her car. She'd already made her decision, but she'd stopped by Jonah's house hoping he'd change her mind.

But he was gone.

And now, so was she.

L orraine drove through the empty Sea Port streets feeling numb. She didn't remember parking her car around the corner from Confections. She didn't know if she passed anyone on the short walk into the bakery. Someone had held open the door for her, but she didn't remember thanking them. She wasn't conscious of anything until Mary's happy face popped up from behind a display case.

"You get my text about the cinnamon rolls?" she asked with a mischievous smile on her face — as if those cinnamon rolls were a new drug about to hit their small-town streets.

Any other day, Lorraine would've been jumping for joy at the chance to get a sneak peek — sneak taste? — of Mary's newest concoction, but today, she burst into tears. Mary's eyes went wide, and she rushed around the counter, ushering her into a chair by the window. Lorraine wasn't really a public crier, but considering all the other things she and Jonah had done in public, crying hardly rated on the scale of appropriateness. And Mary, sweet — literally — saint that she was, sat quietly beside her, shoving fresh napkins into her hands when necessary.

Lorraine's back was to the door and the display cases. She could hear Bria and Charlie serving the late morning crowd. A few months ago, Lorraine could've deluded herself into believing that no one would notice her falling apart in the corner, but Sea Port was too small for her to maintain that lie. Now, she knew everyone — Bria and Charlie, Bria's best friend Keith, Mr. Crawford who drove into town every few days for buttermilk biscuits — had seen her crying; they just had enough tact not to disturb her. In a few hours, half the town would know the new librarian was crying in the bakery, and a few hours later, town gossip would've figured out why. But Lorraine was too sad to worry about that right now; she had tears to shed. And over a man, no less.

DeJuan would be so disappointed.

When Lorraine's tears finally started to dry up, Mary

patted her arm and jumped up from the table. She came back with a cinnamon roll.

Lorraine pressed a wet wad of napkins against her right eye and looked at Mary excitedly with her left.

"It's not the red velvet one. Bria thinks we need to work on our cream cheese frosting, but I put a little nutmeg in the dough and icing on this one. I'm working on a holiday version."

"That's a good idea," Lorraine said, mouth already full of a bite. "I can taste the nutmeg. It's nice."

Mary managed to beam at her while still looking sad. "I'm glad you like it. I have a few new flavor ideas besides the red velvet." Lorraine knew she was spilling Confections secrets to cheer her up, and it was helping. "Bria was thinking of apple. Or maybe a sweet potato filling?"

"I like the sweet potato idea." Lorraine took another bite of her cinnamon roll, her eyes still leaking tears.

"I'll let you know when we have a good version."

"Thanks," Lorraine said around a mouthful of pastry. Her tears made it a little salty, but not bad. "What about a salted caramel one?" she offered.

Mary's mouth fell open. "Fuck, that's a good idea. Bria, salted caramel cinnamon roll!" she yelled across the small shop.

"Fuck, that's a good idea," Bria said.

"Watch your mouth," Mr. Crawford said.

"Sorry," Bria mumbled.

"We can use the salted caramel filling from the donuts as a place to start."

"Y'all have a salted caramel donut?" Mr. Crawford asked.

"Yes, sir." Bria beamed. "You want one?"

Mr. Crawford hummed before nodding. "Just one. I'll try it out."

Lorraine was still chewing on her cinnamon roll, but she turned back to Mary.

Mary nodded, smiling. "I'll get you one."

"Can I get two?" Lorraine asked. "To go?"

Mary sighed. "Fine. But you're paying for the donuts."

Lorraine shrugged. "Then make it three."

JONAH

The drive from Sea Port to Atlanta was just about eight hours. He'd driven the route enough times that by now, he could do it in his sleep. He left Sea Port before dawn, feeling numb. Wherever his head was, it wasn't in his car, or back in his dad's house, or even at his condo in Atlanta. It took him two hours and a pit stop for gas and coffee for his brain to settle, and when it did, all he could think about was Lorraine.

He shoved the gas receipt in the glove compartment, took a long sip of his coffee, and then pulled his cell phone from his pocket. He should've told her he was leaving in person. His father was probably rolling in his grave at Jonah's lapse in judgment — he'd been raised better than that. Although, if his father was having feelings beyond the pale, they'd probably started when Jonah and Lorraine had

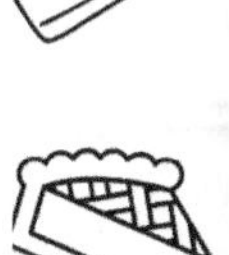

gotten fresh in Sully's that one time. Or the time after. Still, Jonah had been raised with manners and he wasn't using any of them.

The next set of choices he should've made was to call Lorraine and leave her a message explaining himself. He didn't know how long he'd be gone but he needed to check on his life in Atlanta. It wasn't an ideal message to relay and he'd have understood if she dumped him, but it was some-

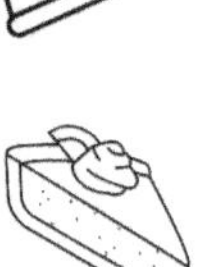

thing. Lorraine deserved that, at the very least.

But he didn't call her. He took his phone out and he pulled up her contact, but he couldn't bring himself to press the button. If he heard her voice, he'd want to turn around.

Even though he'd spent the last three months avoiding talking about his grief, if she asked about it today, there was a chance he might tell her. Jonah didn't want to leave Sea Port,

he wanted to crawl into her bed and lose the threads of his heartbreak inside her.

So, he couldn't call her. He couldn't give himself a

way out.

So instead of calling Lorraine, Jonah pulled up the voice

app on his phone and pretended he was a more courageous man.

"Hey, Lorraine. This is Jonah." His face bunched together in disgust at himself before he continued. "I'm not sure if you know yet, but I had to leave Sea Port. I didn't... I need to go back to Atlanta and my life there. Not for good...I don't think. I just... I wish we'd met before my dad died or after I'd healed a bit, but we didn't. I was running away from the broken pieces of my life before I even met you and being with you made it easier. Being with you made me feel whole when I felt so damn broken. But I don't want to need someone to feel like myself. That's not fair to either of us. So I'm heading back to Atlanta to...figure my shit out. I understand if you hate me. I deserve it."

Jonah poured his heart out while he drove into the morning, certain he'd send the message to her, but not when. If he'd realized it would take him days, he might've just sent the message to Lorraine that morning, but he was far from his right mind that day.

WELCOME TO SEA PORT

TWENTY-THREE

Jonah

"I understand if you hate me and I doubt I'm going to say anything to change your mind, so I won't try. What I will do is tell you about one of my roommates. His name's Avi, and he manages a convenience store downtown. Quiet dude. Weird dude, but he pays his rent on time, so what does it matter, you know? *Except* I just found out that he's this, like, famous cosplayer or something. I don't know all the details, but apparently, one of his fangirls found out where we live and showed up in wedding cosplay. They had to call the cops and put in cameras and I'm just now finding out about it.

Can you believe that?"

"Atlanta smells like smoke and trash — my neighborhood, at least — and I never realized it until right now. I guess I know why my condo was so cheap. I miss walking around downtown Sea Port and smelling sugar and vanilla. I miss smelling fresh turned dirt on the Lincoln farm."

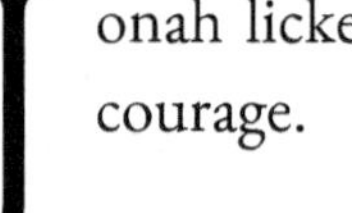
Jonah licked his lips and took a slow, deep breath for courage.

"I miss waking up in the morning and smelling what was left of your perfume on my skin. I just wanted to tell you that."

After sending Lorraine another morning message and staring at her contact photo for a little too long, hoping for a response that never came, Jonah checked the

rest of his text messages, most of which were pictures of the library site with Zeke's unnecessary commentary.

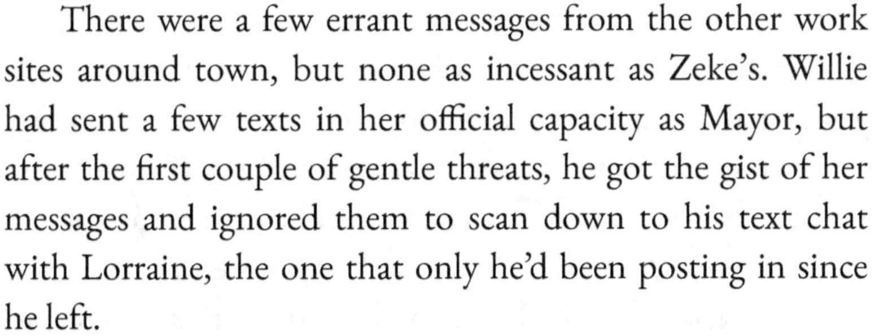

There were a few errant messages from the other work sites around town, but none as incessant as Zeke's. Willie had sent a few texts in her official capacity as Mayor, but after the first couple of gentle threats, he got the gist of her messages and ignored them to scan down to his text chat with Lorraine, the one that only he'd been posting in since he left.

Jonah had been in Atlanta for nearly two weeks, but it felt like months. When he showed up at his old condo, his roommates had looked at him like a stranger, as if they'd forgotten what he looked like, and maybe they had — he had been gone a year. It took a few minutes to get them over the shock of his arrival and then they went on with their lives, which didn't include him.

Jonah walked around his house, surprised at how little he'd thought of this place while he'd been gone. It made sense at first, since losing his father eclipsed everything, but after that — even before Lorraine — this place he'd called home had hardly entered his mind. In fact, it was only once he was back that he realized it had been all too easy to abandon his life here without a second thought. He walked

around his condo, seeing the walls he'd painted, the window treatments he'd chosen, the house he'd decorated for his roommates, not for himself. Because this place had never been his home.

It had always been a difficult choice between Atlanta and Sea Port; there were things Jonah loved about both places. But in those first few days back in Atlanta, he knew his time here had come to an end. *His* place didn't feel like his anymore, so almost as soon as he arrived, he started preparing to leave again, dismantling his life, one packing box at a time.

Jonah had a closet full of clothes he hadn't worn in a year. It took days to sort through what he would keep, what he would donate, and what he should've thrown away years ago. It wasn't the same kind of destruction as wrecking the kitchen back home, but it gave him the same feeling. Whatever life Jonah had lived in this room had come to an end. He didn't know what was next, but it wasn't this, and it wasn't the tomb of his dad's house either.

Jonah's coping methods were the same in Atlanta as in Sea Port. Just like he'd thrown himself into his dad's projects back home, he threw himself into dismantling his old life. After almost a decade, Jonah was surprised at how few strings existed connecting him to the life he'd run away from Sea Port to build. He didn't know how long he'd be home, but he knew it was time to sort out his parents' house and his feelings about their deaths once and for all. Besides, there were still so many loose ends in Sea Port to sort through, a fact Willie refused to let him forget.

His phone rang just as he was about to record another

voice note for Lorraine and he rolled his eyes before answering.

"Mornin', Willie," Jonah trilled.

"Mayor Waltham," she replied, and that was her only greeting.

"Mornin', Mayor Waltham. To what do I owe the pleasure of a phone call" — he stopped here to look at the time on his phone — "before eight in the morning?"

"If I can't count on you, let me know now," Willie said, not even bothering to beat around the bush. She had a politician's inflection — crisp, clear, perfect enunciation — but it was warmer than her father's. All this meant, though, was that it was easier for her to lull people into believing she wasn't angry when she clearly was. Jonah knew better.

"Have my crews been slacking?" Jonah asked. He sat up in his king-sized bed, the only thing in the entire condo he was sure would be making the trip back home.

"No," Willie said. He could just imagine her pacing around her office; she'd never been the kind of person to sit still.

"Have there been any mistakes I'm not aware of?"

Willie exhaled loudly, frustrated. "No," she bit out.

"Then it sounds like you can count on me," Jonah said.

"For how long? How long are you going to be in Atlanta?"

Jonah scrubbed his face. "I'm not sure exactly, but not much longer."

"You sure about that?"

He didn't know if it was because he and Willie had grown up together or if she was just prescient now that she was Mayor, but he didn't like the all-knowing tone in her

voice. Especially because he didn't feel sure about much these days.

"I'll be back before the library's done," Jonah said. His stomach clenched even saying the word 'library' because it made him think of Lorraine. To be honest, so many things made him think of her. When he picked up a jelly donut at the shop in the strip mall a few blocks away, his first thought was that it wasn't nearly as good as Confections. His second thought was that Lorraine would hate it. When he went to bed tired as fuck after a day of hauling boxes and trash bags from his house, he wished he was crawling into Lorraine's bed in Sea Port. He saw a small, slight woman with long braids while on a run to the hardware store for more paint and his heart skipped an actual beat. It wasn't her, and his chest constricted in pain.

For the past two weeks, he'd called her sporadically — when he thought about her, when he hoped she might be awake or free — but she never picked up. Her silence should've curbed his desire to reach out, but it was the opposite. Somehow, in the silence and with all the distance between them, Jonah's affection for Lorraine only grew. He finally called her — and kept calling when she didn't respond — because he missed her and wanted her to know that, even if she hated him.

"And when exactly will the library be done?" Willie asked.

"A few weeks," Jonah said.

Willie grunted at that. "Fine. But there better not be any delays. If I have to find another librarian, I want to be able to offer them a brand-new state-of-the-art...ish library."

"Wait," Jonah said, hopping out of bed. "What's this about a new librarian?"

LORRAINE

Lorraine was a workaholic. That was the only way to explain why she was sitting in a lounge chair next to the most beautiful hotel pool in the bright Arizona sun, squinting at her laptop. DeJuan had invited her to the spa to relax and Lorraine had done a little bit of that, but she'd worked far more than he liked. She'd done most of it by the pool, though, so that had to count for something.

Sure, she'd set up an office in her hotel room, but she made sure she had a view of the spa grounds from her desk. There was just so much work to be done. She dipped her toes into the pool while also coordinating the transfer of books from the depository to the new library. She edited some grant applications and updated the library's staffing requests until happy hour started and she closed her computer. She was also organizing the library opening festivities through a dense email chain between herself, Mayor Waltham, Mary, and Sully, but no one noticed when she dipped from the conversation to get a deep tissue massage. She'd been away from Sea Port for almost a couple of weeks and had managed to stay on top of most of her duties. The only thing she couldn't handle was the lending library's

hours, but Mayor Waltham had convinced Mrs. Jones to come out of retirement for a couple of weeks.

Technically, her contract included three weeks of paid vacation, so she could stay at the spa for another week or follow DeJuan back home if she wanted, but she didn't. Normally, when Lorraine went on vacation, she turned her out-of-office message on and was unreachable until she walked back in the office, but she just couldn't do that to Sea Port. And worst of all, she couldn't share that with DeJuan. They loved each other, but she knew he wouldn't understand how sitting poolside and soaking up the sun in Scottsdale was nice but it didn't make her miss Confections any less.

And none of it could dislodge the part of her brain that was stuck on Jonah.

"Whew, girl, it is hot out here today," DeJuan called down the length of the pool.

"It's been hot every day we've been here," Lorraine called back with a sigh.

He shoved his sunglasses onto his face dramatically, the same way he did everything else. "Take the monotony up with Mother Nature, not me," he said, his long silk floral robe flowing behind him as he walked.

"How was your massage?' she asked when he finally strutted his way to the table where she was working.

He pulled out a chair and sat with a heavy, satisfied sigh. "Heavenly."

"So dramatic," she said.

"And yet true. Ugh, are you working *again*?"

Lorraine pushed her laptop shut for the moment. "Just a little," she said defensively.

He squinted and pursed his lips in judgment. "What magical hooks does that small town have in you?"

He'd asked the question before, and Lorraine gave him the same answer each time. "A legally binding employment contract."

"Mmhmm, that's what you keep saying, but we both know the answer."

Lorraine reached for the glass of water she'd been sipping and drained it. DeJuan laughed softly under his breath. She hadn't mentioned Jonah in all the months they'd been together, and at first, she'd felt guilty about it, but now she was happy she hadn't. If DeJuan knew she'd been seeing someone, he would still be interrogating her about him. Scottsdale was already hot; she didn't need this place to become a literal hell.

But DeJuan was smart and Lorraine thought there was a chance he suspected she'd met someone, but he didn't have any concrete evidence and Lorraine wanted to keep it that way. Especially now. He could fish for information all he wanted, but Lorraine's mouth was a steel trap. At least for now.

"Your year's almost up," he said.

"What? No, it's not. It basically just started."

DeJuan squinted at her. "Really?"

"Yes, really. It's only been a few months."

He sat back in his chair and lifted his sunglasses from his eyes. Lorraine did the same and they stared at one another until he believed her.

"Wow. Anyway, it'll end eventually, and then what're you gonna do?" he asked, pushing his sunglasses back onto his face.

She shrugged, opening her laptop again. "I don't know. Yet. I'm not sure."

"You always know," he said. "You're always three steps ahead of even yourself."

She forced a smile. "Not...always," she lied. Lorraine had a long-term vision for her life, and even a detour like a year in Sea Port was still on the same path she wanted to follow. Nothing in her life was accidental, not if she could help it. Not until Jonah. Actually, not until Jonah, Mary, and Confections. Gaining ten pounds and getting dicked down regularly in Sea Port weren't part of her plan, but she missed Jonah and Confections every day.

"You talked to your mother?" DeJuan asked carefully.

"No," Lorraine spat out in disbelief. "It's not time for our annual check-in. I don't even know where she is."

"I do," he replied, averting his eyes.

Lorraine shut her laptop again and glared a hole into his right cheek. The word 'how' was on the tip of her tongue, but she couldn't ask the question. She wouldn't. After a few long, silent moments, she shook her head and stood from the table. "I need to go to the bathroom," she said. "Watch my computer."

"Lorraine," DeJuan said.

She grabbed her cell phone. "I'll be right back."

She forced herself not to rush away and to wait until she was back in the hotel lobby before she unlocked her phone screen. The list of missed calls from Jonah in her call log was oddly comforting, but it was the sound of his voice that soothed her rapidly beating heart. She found a seat in the lobby and pressed her phone to her ear, listening to his latest message until her pulse eased.

Until she could forget whatever unwanted or unfortunate news DeJuan had about her mother, because that was the only news Inés Freeman ever produced.

JONAH

"My father used to work all day, damn near every day. By the time I was twelve, I used to wake up at home alone 'cause he liked to get to work first thing in the morning. He made sure my book bag was packed and I had my clothes set out. He even left me breakfast warming in the oven. I was fifteen before I realized this wasn't normal — not other people's normal, at least. Just mine. I only had my dad and he had his grief."

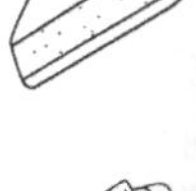

He stopped to laugh softly again, thinking back on all those mornings fondly now. Missing his father from the depth of his soul.

"But no matter how early he got up to leave, he was always right there, leaning against his work

truck, waiting for me to get out of school. Damn near every day of my life, my dad would finish up work just so he could watch my practices — football, track, basketball, whatever I was into — even though I was a horrible athlete. He never missed my games and was always in the bleachers cheering me on. Every race I lost, every missed basket, he saw it all and he was happy for me. It's hitting me now that I'm never going to hear him cheer for me again. That I'm alone in the world. I couldn't talk about my father when we were together 'cause I could hardly admit this to myself."

Jonah stopped here to compose himself. He'd thought long and hard about this message before he called Lorraine's number. She hadn't picked up any of his other calls, but just in case she did, he didn't want to waste time stumbling over his words. But he also wanted to tell Lorraine something that mattered to him. Something he wanted her to know even if she never talked to him again.

"I talked to Willie today. She told me she's worried you won't come back from your vacation. I hope this wasn't 'cause of me. Believe me when I tell you I don't deserve all that. You love Sea Port and everyone loved you. Especially me.

I shouldn't have left the way I did and I'm sorry about that. But if you left town 'cause you thought I didn't care about you, believe me when I tell you that's not the case.

I've just been so goddamn broken since my dad died and I couldn't..."

He had to stop here and breathe for a few moments.

"I couldn't keep running away from my life and my grief. I couldn't hide inside you and be the kind of man that might deserve you. I'm sorry I couldn't tell you that in person. You deserved that. You deserve a lot more than I could give you."

WELCOME TO SEA PORT

TWENTY-FOUR

Jonah

"I used to love living in Atlanta, especially in college. All my friends were here; there was always stuff to do, places to go, new people to meet. It was the opposite of Sea Port and I loved it. Every time I went back home, I couldn't get back to Atlanta fast enough.

Coming back this time wasn't like that.

Most of my friends have moved away. I got fired after I went home to see about my dad. I spent almost a decade building a life here and it disappeared in a few months. And that's the wild part, right? I spent that same decade barely in Sea Port, only going back on holidays, talking to my dad more on the phone than in person, but I went home and stepped right back into a life I used to think I didn't want. Sometimes I still think I don't want it, but I can't lie, now that I'm gone, I miss it.

My back probably can't believe I'm saying this, but I miss waking up at the crack of dawn and getting to work. It makes me feel close to my dad. That's probably not a surprise to anyone else, but it is to me... I— I think... I thought..."

Jonah had to stop here and catch his breath. He was lying on the mattress in his bedroom for probably the last time ever. In a couple of hours, his roommate Luke would help him load the last of his things into the trailer he'd rented. Cleaners would be by tomorrow to get the room together for Luke to take over. He'd already lined up some prospective tenants for the free room. In a couple of months, it would be like Jonah had never even lived here.

He had a few loose ends to tie up and then he'd be back on the road to start whatever new life lay before him in Sea Port.

He'd been leaving Lorraine voicemails for a couple of weeks, and so far, she hadn't picked up his calls, texted him back, or otherwise acknowledged that she was even listening to his messages. It was possible she'd blocked him long ago and was somewhere living her life as if she never met him. He couldn't blame her, but he couldn't stop reaching out either. Somehow, all the distance between them — and he wasn't even sure how many miles at this point — made him miss her more each day. And missing Lorraine somehow heightened his longing for Sea Port, but this longing wasn't the same as the homesickness he'd felt before. Sea Port wasn't just his tiny hometown or the place his dad died, it had become the place he met Lorraine. In all those months with her, Sea Port had become a place where he could see a future again.

"A year ago, I thought I'd never be able to feel close to my dad again. I spent months living in my childhood bedroom, in the home where he raised me, looking at things he touched every day, and I still felt lost. But every time I hopped in his work truck and put on his tool belt, it was like I could feel him standing over me, probably telling me to move the nail gun just a little bit to the right."

He laughed for the first time in days. He hoped wherever Lorraine was, she was smiling and laughing too, even if it was at his expense.

"I'm heading back home tomorrow. To Sea Port," he clarified. "I don't know where you are or what you're planning, but I want to tell you I'm going back, just in case it might change your mind. As soon as I get home, I'm stopping by the Sunnyside for a slice of pie, but all I really want is to see you."

Wesley didn't raise Jonah to be a coward or treat women poorly, but everyone can be the villain in someone else's story. And Jonah was absolutely the villain in Angie's.

"Where the fuck have you been?" Angie said before she'd even opened her front door fully.

They stared at one another through her screen door. "I know you're mad at me," he said.

She rolled her eyes. "I stopped being mad at you six months ago. Ain't no reason being mad at someone who doesn't give a shit about you. Waste of energy."

Jonah took a deep breath. "I deserve that."

"I know," she shot back.

"Look, can I... Can I come in?"

Angie stared at him for a minute, considering her options. There was a time in his life when he thought he was going to marry her. Maybe if their relationship had been on its last leg, he could've left town without this pit stop, but things had been good between them until his father died. They'd been talking about moving in together. He'd even been looking at rings in the weeks before his world fell apart. In an alternate timeline, Jonah and Angie should've been deep in wedding planning, but in this timeline, they felt almost like strangers. He left Angie and Atlanta with little explanation and he deserved her scorn just like she deserved some answers.

"I want to explain and apologize, Angie. That's all," he said gently.

She pursed her lips together, glaring at him for a few seconds more. "Fine," she said, flipping the lock on her screen door and turning away. 

It had been a year since he'd been in Angie's apartment and much had changed. She'd been talking about painting the living room for as long as she'd lived here, hinting at  Jonah to help, but he never seemed to have enough time. In his absence, she'd finally done it. He wondered what else she'd done now that she wasn't wasting time waiting on him,  but he knew Angie well enough to stay on task.

"Have a seat," she said, sitting in the middle of the couch. She gestured toward the hard-backed chair across  from her, a sign that he wouldn't be welcome for long.

He sat across from Angie for the last time and inter-  twined his fingers together. "I came here to apologize."

"You said that already," she cut in.

Jonah rolled his eyes. "You gonna let me finish?"

"Depends," she said. "You gonna get to the point?"

"I *just* started," Jonah said. Angie smiled. "Seriously?" 

She crossed her legs and smiled harder. "Yep. I'm not gonna make this easy for you."

Jonah exhaled loudly through his nose. "I deserve that  too."

"I know."

Jonah was ashamed to admit this to himself, but he  hadn't thought about Angie in months. At first, he was consumed with his own grief, and then there was work, and then there was Lorraine. He'd forgotten about her and all the things he'd once loved about her, like the way she liked to bust his balls. Remembering all this made him feel even worse about how he'd let their relationship fizzle out without a word of closure.

"My dad died," he said, realizing the last she'd heard, it was just a heart attack.

The smile fell away. "I'm sorry. I know how much you loved him."

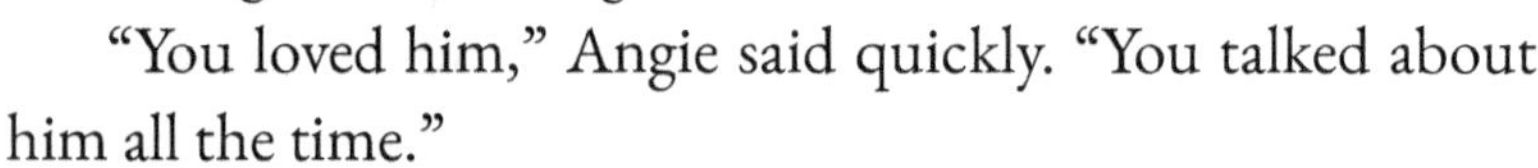

Jonah started blinking, the pressure of tears coming on full force in an instant. "I wasn't a good son to him," he said. "I didn't go home enough. I—"

"You loved him," Angie said quickly. "You talked about him all the time."

Jonah's eyebrows bunched together. "I did?"

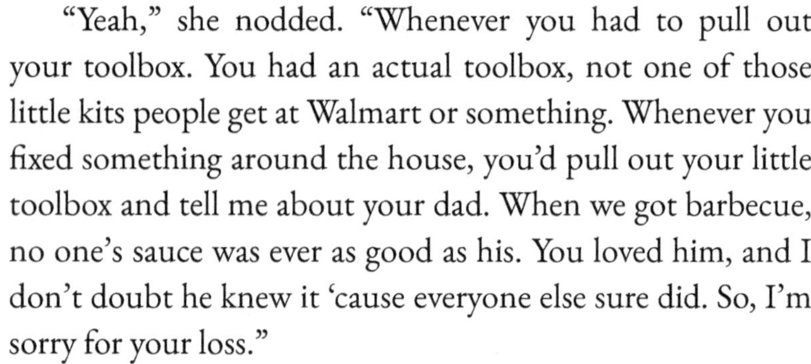

"Yeah," she nodded. "Whenever you had to pull out your toolbox. You had an actual toolbox, not one of those little kits people get at Walmart or something. Whenever you fixed something around the house, you'd pull out your little toolbox and tell me about your dad. When we got barbecue, no one's sauce was ever as good as his. You loved him, and I don't doubt he knew it 'cause everyone else sure did. So, I'm sorry for your loss."

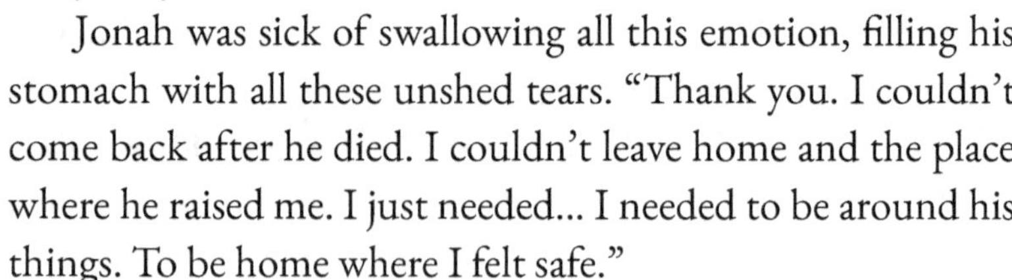

Jonah was sick of swallowing all this emotion, filling his stomach with all these unshed tears. "Thank you. I couldn't come back after he died. I couldn't leave home and the place where he raised me. I just needed... I needed to be around his things. To be home where I felt safe."

Angie nodded but didn't interrupt.

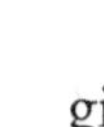

"I got caught up in my own pain and I'm not apologizing for that, but you deserved to at least hear that from me. Months ago," he added quickly. "You deserved for me to have the guts to break up with you, if not face-to-face then at least over the phone."

"I did."

"I'm sorry I didn't give that to you." He wiped at his wet eyes before meeting her gaze again.

"Thank you," Angie replied in a soft voice.

Jonah smiled. "That's it?"

She shrugged with the easy smile that first caught his attention. "I told you, I forgave you months ago. And I understood long before that. But I appreciate the apology. Are you better now?" she asked gently.

He smiled but shook his head. "Not even close. I should definitely look into getting a therapist, but I don't think there are too many of them back home."

"Home?"

He rubbed the back of his neck. "Yeah, I'm moving back to Sea Port. Atlanta's not really where I see myself ending up now." He could feel the smile on his face as a picture of Lorraine appeared in a corner of his mind.

"There's a woman, isn't there?"

Jonah froze as if he'd been caught red-handed because he had.

She rolled her eyes. "Don't worry, I'm over you. But I know what you look like when you're sprung. You deserve to be happy again. I won't begrudge you that." Her smile widened. "Not now that you apologized, at least."

"Thank you. I hope the next guy treats you better than I did."

Angie was full-on beaming now. "Don't worry, he does. And I hope you treat this woman better than you treated me."

"I'll try."

WELCOME TO SEA PORT

Lorraine

Lorraine was having a lazy day in bed with her phone, listening to Jonah's voicemails while she touched herself.

She wasn't proud of it, but he started it.

> "I was up all night packing. I swear I didn't know I had all this shit."

This was Lorraine's favorite message. Jonah sent it the day after she arrived in Scottsdale. She'd watched her phone ring while doing her makeup for dinner with DeJuan, glancing down at his name on her lockscreen but refusing to pick up. The time for him to call was before he left Sea Port, not when he was in a whole different state, so she'd decided not to pick up his calls. She'd moved the mascara wand through her eyelashes while her phone rang out; she didn't even silence the ringer.

She was dipping her ring finger into a pot of lip balm when her phone finally chimed with a new message. She smoothed her finger over her lips, back and forth, staring at her phone in the mirror. She slowly twisted the cap back onto her lip balm and then finally caved, pressing play on the message.

She hadn't talked to him in almost a week, which was nothing in the grand scheme of life, but as soon as she heard Jonah's deep voice, Lorraine's stomach tightened.

She reached for her blush, but her fingers hesitated.

"I'ma sleep all day maybe. Don't really have anything to do but pack unless somebody wants to buy some stuff."

She didn't know what it was about Jonah's voice that triggered the response, that made her neaten the clutter of her overturned makeup bag rather than finish her makeup. Maybe it was the gentle, tired rumble that made her heart flutter. She remembered that voice viscerally, the way he'd whisper to her before they fell asleep at night. While he was still inside her. Yeah, it was probably that, so it was no surprise that instead of finishing her makeup, Lorraine had stood from the chair at the vanity in her hotel room and walked to the door. She grabbed the *do not disturb* sign and hung it from the door handle in the hallway before turning the deadbolt into place. She pulled the blackout curtains closed and grabbed her cell phone. She resumed playing the message while she finished setting the mood — pulling her silk robe from her body and rummaging through the cosmetic bag of toys she'd made sure to pack, letting Jonah's deep, sleepy voice lull her back into bed.

"I ordered pizza from my favorite place in town and it just made me realize that Sal ain't got pizza on the menu. Never even thought about it until right now. Isn't that crazy?"

Lorraine fell into bed and lay on her back. "That is," she said in whispered response even though Jonah would never hear.

"Willie better have a new restaurant or two on her list of essential businesses. The town needs more than burgers and pasta. Pizza and Mexican food, that's top of my list. Maybe I'll—"

He stopped here to yawn and Lorraine lifted her butt from the mattress and pulled her panties up her thighs and over her knees. She pulled her left leg from the underwear and spread her legs, reaching between her thighs. She wasn't wet yet, but she was well on the way.

"Maybe I'll send in a formal request."

He stopped to laugh here and it sent a shiver down her spine, arching her back from the mattress. She moved her fingers to her clit and sighed.

"If you'd picked up, I woulda made a request for you."

The first time she'd listened to this voice message, it had been through earbuds, and it had sounded like the rumble of laughter bounced around in her brain. And it made her wet — then and now.

"You probably somewhere looking all pretty and drawing on that mole I know ain't real."

Lorraine always laughed at that part, but this morning it came out on a moan as her fingers caressed her lips.

"But if you'd picked up, I'd have asked if you wanted to breathe with me for a minute."

His voice had gone husky as he spoke and it made her wetter. Hornier. Needier.

She didn't have to wonder if he remembered that night because she could hear it in his voice. Her fingers were no substitute for his, but when she closed her eyes and listened to Jonah's soft voice, she could imagine that they were the ones she wanted.

Lorraine listened closely as his breath grew ragged. She closed her mouth and swallowed a moan, imagining him tired, laid out in his bed, stroking his dick, talking to her in his sad whiskey voice.

Her ass flexed and her hips lifted from the bed as she fucked up into her hand.

Lorraine knew when she ran away from Sea Port that she was sprung on Jonah, but it was how easily she was gut clenching, heart racing, ragged breath falling apart just thinking about him that had her stressed.

Those were the signs that she was in trouble.

Lorraine was relaxed, freshly showered, and back at the dressing table, reapplying the makeup she'd smeared while masturbating. It wasn't an early start to her day anymore, but she was on vacation. She'd just swiped a fresh coat of mascara on when there was a knock on the door. She recapped the tube and shuffled to let DeJuan in. 

"Girl, did you even look through the peephole?" DeJuan said. 

"No. I knew it was you."

"Bullshit. You eat breakfast?"

"No, I just woke up," she said. It was kinda true. She took a little nap after her last orgasm and that counted. "Come in. I'm almost done with my makeup." 

"How can you bear makeup with this heat?" he said, fanning himself even though the hotel was perfectly cool. 

"It's just a little mascara and lipstick," Lorraine said, turning back into the room. "Just wanna make my face presentable." 

The words fell from her lips without thinking — she didn't even trip over them, they were so ingrained in her brain. 

"I ain't heard you drop any of Inés's advice in a long while," DeJuan said.

Lorraine fell into her seat at the mention of her mother's name. Her fingers hovered over the tube of mascara but she  didn't pick it up. For a second, she couldn't even remember what it was used for. "I... I don't think I've had any use for  her advice in a while," she admitted carefully; something she could only admit to DeJuan.

His reflection moved behind her in the room. He pushed the blackout curtains open, flooding the room in light. "Not since you moved to Sea Breeze," he replied casually.

"Sea *Port*," she said with more force than was necessary.

He stopped behind her in the mirror and they stared at one another. "You really like it there, don't you?"

She licked her lips and looked away. "Yeah," she said, even though the last couple weeks had dimmed her feelings about the town a bit. She liked Sea Port, but it was hard to extricate her fondness for the town from her feelings for Jonah, as unsettled as they were.

"And that's why you've been ducking and dodging coming on vacation with me?" he asked.

She couldn't look him in the eyes. "It's a lot of work to get done."

He didn't respond immediately and Lorraine lifted her eyes to his. "Does that mean you're gonna stay there?"

"No," she replied quickly, but the word tasted like ash on her tongue. "I don't know."

"Why not?" She quirked her eyebrow at him and he clarified. "If you like that tiny speck of a town, why wouldn't you stay there?"

She forced a soft laugh from her lips. "You'd hate that. Gonna need more than two transfers to get to me."

"I would," he conceded, "but this ain't about me. If you like that tiny town so much, why wouldn't you stay?"

Lorraine swallowed an uncomfortable lump in her throat. She grabbed the mascara tube and started untwisting the top slowly. "You know me," she said casually, even though she felt like her heart was trying to punch its way out of her chest. "I can't ever stay in one place for too long."

"'Cause of Inés."

Her hand slipped at her mother's name again and she accidentally smeared some mascara on her index finger. She dropped the tube and reached for a napkin. "Can you stop saying her name?"

"No," DeJuan said.

Lorraine glared at him in the mirror. "What the fuck is going on with you?"

"I could ask you the same thing, but I'm not petty."

"Since when?" she scoffed.

He rolled his eyes with a grin. "I think," DeJuan said carefully, "that you've been hiding something from me." Lorraine's heart froze for at least a full beat. "But that's okay."

"Since when?" she asked again.

"For now," he corrected himself. "Because I didn't bring you here to interrogate you."

"Coulda fooled me."

"I brought you here 'cause I think the thing holding you back is your mother."

"Is that news to you? I'm pretty sure that was my ice breaker the day we met. 'Hi, I'm Lorraine, and my mother is desperate for male affection. I need therapy.'"

DeJuan tried to fight it but he broke out in laughter. "I still can't believe you said that."

Lorraine's shoulders relaxed. "I was young and angry. You're the one who made a beeline in my direction, desperate to be my friend."

"Desperate is two steps too far," he warned warmly. "But that was so long ago, Lorraine. You've dropped a small fortune on therapy since then and still can't admit that maybe the reason you don't want to stay in

little Sea—" She squinted her eyes at him. "Port. Sea Port?"

"Sea Port."

"Anyway, we both know the reason you won't admit to wanting to settle in the middle of nowhere is because you don't know how to do that."

"How to do what?"

"How to put down roots."

Lorraine shifted her eyes away and wiped at the mascara on her skin. "So what if I don't?"

"No skin off my back if job hopping gets you the job you want eventually. Especially if it keeps your vacation fund full. But if you want to settle down, seems like the goal should be to deal with your past."

"I've *been* dealing with my past," she said, rolling her eyes.

"No, you haven't," DeJuan said gently. "I love you, but no, you haven't. You are smart and funny and kind, but the minute life gets too comfortable, you wanna tear it apart and start over. Just like your mother taught you."

Lorraine forced a hollow smile onto her face. "Some women teach their children how to bake, mine taught me how to flirt my way into a small discount on a moving van. It takes all kinds."

"It does, and maybe if you said any of this to her face, it would set you free."

Lorraine laughed. "I doubt it. Talking to my mother is like talking to a brick wall unless I'm saying exactly what she wants to hear."

"You sure about that?"

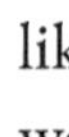

"Very. I have a whole life of trying to get through to her. A whole life of failing."

DeJuan stepped forward until he could rest his hand on her shoulder. "When's the last time you tried getting through to her? When's the last time you did more than make sure she was alive?" 

Lorraine shook her head. "I don't know." 

He nodded. "I figured. That's why I brought you here."

It took a few seconds for his words to register. "What?"

WELCOME TO SEA PORT

TWENTY-SIX

Lorraine

They skipped breakfast. Lorraine wouldn't have been able to taste it anyway. She was sitting in the passenger seat of DeJuan's rental car, worrying her fingers as he drove through Phoenix.

"Did she put you up to this?" she finally asked, raising her voice over the music he was playing.

He turned the volume down before he replied. "Not in the way you're thinking."

"You don't know what I'm thinking."

He sighed gently. "I know it's easier to be mad at me than admit you're nervous and afraid, but girl, be real. No one knows you better than me."

That took the fight right out of her and she sighed before she replied. "Fine. Tell me."

Lorraine and DeJuan had built their relationship on their mother wounds, but it had grown into so much more. In all their years together, however, this was the first time

Lorraine had ever worried about the words that might fall from his mouth.

"I got a call a few months ago, right after you left for Sea Port. I guess your mother noticed when your old job announced that you were gone and she was worried. She wanted to know where you were going."

Lorraine rolled her eyes. "Why'd she call you?"

"I asked her the same question."

"You did?"

"I did. She said she was worried you wouldn't tell her and she didn't want to intrude."

Lorraine shifted in her seat. "*My* mother said that."

"Yes, ma'am. I told her you moved to a new job but I didn't give her any details. She said she just wanted to know if you were safe and happy. She didn't want to intrude on your life."

Lorraine scoffed. "Surprised she even realizes I have a life."

"She said she's texted you while you've been in Sea Port but hadn't heard much back."

Lorraine turned back to the front windshield and shrugged. "I guess."

"Did she or did she not text you?"

Lorraine had to rack her brain. "I think I have her blocked."

DeJuan nodded. "I figured. Any particular reason?"

She shrugged again. "I blocked her when I started packing. I didn't want her to derail me with one of her life crises again. Her timing is always perfect when it comes to fucking up my plans. I *meant* to unblock her after I settled in, I just... forgot."

"You forgot to unblock your mother."

Lorraine smiled sadly. "I was having too much fun," she whispered.

DeJuan turned to her, glancing at her for a few seconds before setting his eyes back on the road. "Hmm."

"What's that mean?" she asked.

"Nothing. Anyway, I told her you probably just needed some space. She knows what y'all's relationship is like."

"Relationship feels like the wrong word."

"That's about what she said."

"She did?"

"She also asked me to tell you she was thinking about you."

"You never did that," Lorraine said, sucking her teeth.

"'Cause you were all the way out there in the middle of nowhere. If you were gonna fall apart about your mother, I didn't want it to happen when you were out there by yourself. I was going to do it in person, but you kept rejecting all my vacation plans."

"Damn," Lorraine breathed.

"Exactly."

It was small moments like this that made it hard for Lorraine to stay mad at DeJuan. She couldn't say if she would've spiraled at the news that her mother, of all people, was worried about her, but she knew his caution had been the right choice. She also knew that hearing about her mother might've ruined the bliss that had been her first few months in Sea Port. Thinking about her mother might have eaten away at all the time she'd spent basking in that Southern sun and melting into Jonah's arms.

Thinking about him brought an image of Jonah smiling

down at her from tall scaffolding and then another of him kissing his way down her body. She remembered the sound of his laughter echoing in her ears and she felt something as close to homesick as she'd ever experienced.

"So did y'all concoct the plan to lure me out here together or was that your meddling ass alone?"

"All mine," he trilled proudly. "I told her we were in the area, no specifics. I didn't want her ruining your vacation just in case she's back on her shit. But I did promise her we'd stop by before we left *if* you were interested. You can talk to her or not; that's totally up to you. I'm driving you there, but when you say go, we go."

"You're right on the edge of making me cut you out of my life," Lorraine said.

DeJuan laughed. "That's how I know I'm doing my job."

Lorraine reached over the center console and placed her hand on DeJuan's wrist and squeezed. "If you see some man's shoes by the front door, don't even ask, just grab me and go."

"Obviously," DeJuan laughed. And even though Lorraine's chest felt tight from fear, she laughed with him.

They drove for another half an hour into a small suburb that didn't fit any of Lorraine's memories of Inés. Her mother had loved big cities with endless things to do every night of the week. She'd moved Lorraine all across the country in a desperate search for an ever-wider pool of men to date; men who would give her life purpose.

"If I want a man, I need to be where the men are."

Lorraine had gotten that advice from women over the years, always unsolicited, and she disregarded it every time. She knew what it looked like to live that life, to reorient your daily decisions around catching some man's eye. And even worse, she knew the havoc it could wreak on a life to do so without an ounce of consideration about the quality of that man outside of his bank account.

Lorraine had never met her father; sometimes she couldn't even remember his name. He'd left her mother long before Lorraine was born, so she never got the chance to miss him — maybe the idea of him, but not the man himself. But she had a brain full of memories of Inés and a soul torn to shreds from wanting her mother to love her more than she loved the idea of some man. It had always struck Lorraine as cruel that her mother wanted to be loved unconditionally, but Lorraine's love was never enough.

She held out hope that Inés could change right up until she left for college and then she gave up. She didn't cut her mother out of her life; she simply put her in a room all to herself and opened the door once a month or so, just to make sure the woman was still alive and still chasing after something she couldn't seem to find. Every now and then, they managed to have a conversation that seemed normal — whatever that meant — but mostly, Lorraine moved through the world as if she had no family because it was easy. That type of loneliness stung, but not nearly as bad anymore. And it explained how she'd flown into the city

where her mother lived but never once thought about contacting her.

"I forgot she lived in Arizona," Lorraine whispered as DeJuan's foot eased off the gas.

"I figured," he said gently. "And that's okay."

He pulled his car in front of a small blue Spanish bungalow with a neatly manicured front garden full of desert plants.

"This is cute," Lorraine said.

"It is. We can just—"

Lorraine didn't give him time to finish that sentence. She hated stewing in her own discomfort, especially when it had never been her burden to carry. The dry desert heat hit her in the face, but she didn't let that stop her. Instead, she set her sights on the path that wound to the white front door and walked toward it. She could hear DeJuan strolling behind her as she stepped onto the small concrete porch and rapped her knuckles against the hard wood three times.

DeJuan came to stand at her side and she was grateful for that, even if her tongue felt too heavy to express it. They waited for a few quiet moments before the door swung open and she came face-to-face with her mother for the first time in... Actually, she couldn't remember.

"Lorraine?" Her mother had said her name in so many ways throughout her childhood — exasperated, annoyed, careless — but this was the first time she'd ever heard the woman who birthed her sigh her name in happiness. She shook her head in disbelief, a faint smile lifting the corners of her mouth. "I honestly didn't think you'd show up."

"That makes two of us then, I guess."

Inés laughed softly while Lorraine looked her up and

down. She tried to see her mother with fresh eyes, noting for the first time in far too many years that her mother looked like *her* mother, Lorraine's grandmother. In the chaos of Inés's own making, Lorraine's constant for the first six years  of her life, at least, had been her grandmother. She went months without thinking of her mother but hadn't gone more than a couple weeks without remembering her grand-  mother with fondness. In her young mind, the two women couldn't have been more unalike — one warm where the other was cold, one round and soft where the other was thin and brittle, one loving where the other was...absent. But  time had done a number on them all because in that moment, all Lorraine could see in her mother's face were the soft, faint wrinkles of the woman she'd loved uncondition-  ally and been loved unconditionally by in return.

"I'm sorry," Inés said.

Lorraine reared back in confusion. Inés didn't apologize.  "Come again?"

Inés opened her mouth to speak when a raised voice called from inside the house.

Lorraine's back tensed and she took a half-step back.  She'd been so shocked and surprised at the turn this day had taken that she'd somehow forgotten the reason she avoided her mother like the plague. She'd spent her childhood  coming in second to some random man; she was too old for that.

"Looks like you have company," Lorraine said. "I'll let you—"

"Oh no, no," Inés said quickly. "It's just my support group."

"Your what?" she and DeJuan said at the same time.

Inés nodded seriously. "I'm part of a support group for Black women over sixty. Not therapy technically, just a way for some old women to help each other be better versions of ourselves."

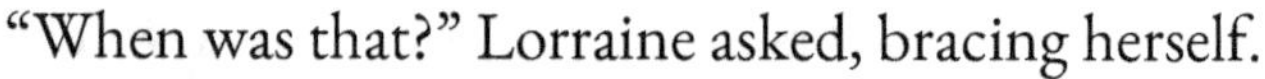

"For...what?" Lorraine asked, still waiting for the other shoe to drop.

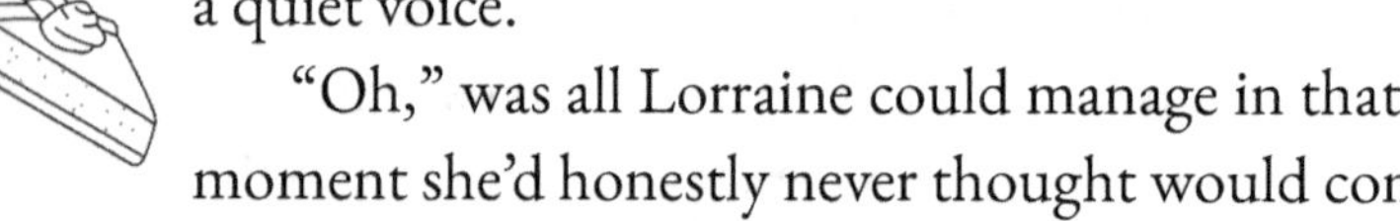

Inés frowned at her. "For ourselves," she said. "That's why I'm sorry. I wish I'd learned all that when it mattered."

"When was that?" Lorraine asked, bracing herself.

"When you were little and needed me," Inés admitted in a quiet voice.

"Oh," was all Lorraine could manage in that moment. A moment she'd honestly never thought would come.

WELCOME TO SEA PORT

TWENTY-SEVEN

Lorraine

Inés ushered Lorraine and DeJuan into her house and introduced them to her friends. Lorraine didn't catch all their names because she was too busy looking around Inés's living room in shock.

The cottage was cute, neat, and clearly built for one. Everywhere Lorraine looked, she saw signs of her mother's life alone, and it was...surprisingly adorable, not the lonely hell Inés had been trying to outrun when Lorraine was a child.

Her living room was small but cozy, especially with every available chair and seat occupied by an older Black woman. Her mother's comfortable recliner was set in a corner near a window, with a small console table next to it and a lamp at the back. There was a small basket at the bottom of the table stuffed with yarn and needles. She didn't even know her mother could knit, but apparently, she could do that and more. Inés's house was littered with hobbies — a puzzle covering her dining room table, a book

of crosswords open on a side table, a kit for pressing flowers on the coffee table — activities Lorraine couldn't imagine her mother doing, just in case some man might disapprove.

As soon as introductions were done, Lorraine excused herself to the bathroom to catch her breath, but once she walked into the bathroom and saw the matching mustard yellow bathmat and shower curtain with a knitted cozy over the toilet seat and tissue holder, she realized what had her shocked about what she was seeing. She'd spent her entire life with bags half-packed, waiting for her mother to once again uproot their lives for some man who'd leave her in a year or so. Their apartments had always been blank and under furnished because Inés didn't know how long they planned to stay. But this house looked like Inés didn't just plan to stay, she'd finally let herself get comfortable.

Lorraine washed her hands and stared at her reflection in the mirror, looking for signs of what was happening on her face, but she found nothing.

By the time she made it back into the living room, DeJuan was sitting in her mother's chair, telling Inés's support group all about the facial massage he'd gotten the day before.

Her mother was waiting at the mouth of the hallway, clearly waiting for Lorraine to return. "Do you want something to drink?" Inés asked.

"Um...no. I'm okay. Do you play that?" Lorraine asked, pointing at a small piano behind her.

Her mother beamed before nodding. "I used to play when I was a kid, but I haven't in a while. I've been using YouTube videos to jog my memory."

"I never knew that," Lorraine said in a small, biting tone. She hadn't meant it as an accusation, but she hadn't lied.

Shame crept into her mother's face as she nodded softly. "I guess you wouldn't. I was too focused on other things when you were little. Things that didn't really matter in the long run." She smiled sadly. "I found it at a secondhand shop in Phoenix. It was in bad shape, but it still worked mostly, so I bought it and spent a few months fixing it up." 

"Yourself?"

Inés nodded. "Mostly. There's a music store in town and the owner helped me with some tricky parts when I needed another pair of hands, then once it was back together, she helped me tune it." 

"She?" Lorraine asked and then pressed her lips shut.

"She," Inés confirmed gently. "Come on. Let's get you something to drink and then we can go outside and talk." 

"Outside?" Lorraine said.

"In the shade," her mother laughed. 

"Oh, okay. Good."

In the backyard, Inés led Lorraine to a covered porch. It was hot as fuck and she started sweating as soon as she  stepped through the screen door. They sat in silence on a small wicker couch for a few moments. Lorraine pressed her palms around an ice-cold glass of lemonade, sipping it every  now and again as she stared at the neatly manicured yard covered in more desert landscaping.

"This is nice," she said, watching her mother in her  peripheral vision.

Inés was watching Lorraine with a small sad smile on her face. "Thank you. The previous owner did most of it. Now I just have to maintain it, which doesn't take much time or energy. A little water every now and again, but that's it. It's peaceful out here, though."

"It is," Lorraine said. "But I don't know how you're living in all this dry heat?"

Her mother shrugged, sipping at her own glass of lemonade. "You get used to it," she said.

"*You* got used to this?" Lorraine laughed. "You used to tell me to stay out the sun before I got wrinkles."

Inés hummed in frustration. "And I got wrinkles anyway," she said, swatting her hand at the air. A droplet of water landed on Lorraine's arm. "I used to say a lot of things I wouldn't say now."

Lorraine turned toward her mother. Their knees bumped together. "Like what?" she asked hungrily.

The question seemed to catch her mother off-guard, but it caught Lorraine off-guard as well. She'd never actually imagined she'd have the opportunity to ask it. She expected her mother to shut down, to press her mouth shut and bunch her eyebrows in frustration like she did the few times Lorraine asked questions she clearly didn't want to answer, but she didn't.

Instead, Inés set her glass of lemonade on the glass table in front of them and wiped her wet fingers on her bare legs. "I could keep you here all day going through my regrets, but I..." Her voice trailed off here. She licked her lips and swiped her fingers over her forehead. They were in the shade, but the heat was relentless all the same. "You were six the first time you told me you didn't like whatever man I was dating. I don't even remember his name."

"Neil," Lorraine said. She didn't remember all her mother's boyfriends, but some of them had stuck in her mind.

Inés flinched at his name. "Neil," she said sadly, which was a far cry from the swooning Lorraine remembered clear as day. "I asked if you liked him. If you wanted him to be your new daddy."

"I don't remember that," Lorraine said, shaking her head. "But I believe I said no."

"You did. You said he smelled like smoke and wouldn't play with you."

"Don't remember that either."

"You said you wanted it to just be the two of us."

Lorraine frowned at her mother. She didn't remember this conversation, but it sounded familiar enough. She could probably count on one hand how often she'd told her mother this same sentiment, but the number of times she'd wished for that were innumerable.

"That's what you regret? Asking me if I wanted him to be my new father?"

"No," Inés said, shaking her head. "I regret telling you for the first time that we couldn't be a real family without a daddy. I regret making you think that we weren't a family, just the two of us. I regret thinking that myself."

"And how long have you had those regrets?" Lorraine asked, looking for any reason not to get her hopes up.

Inés carefully plucked Lorraine's lemonade from her hands and set it next to her glass. She grabbed Lorraine's wet hands and held them in hers. "Not nearly as long as I should have. That's why I didn't press too hard when you blocked me this time. I wanted to apologize and start to maybe, if you wanted, work on rebuilding our relationship, but how could I blame you if the answer was no? How could I blame you for wanting nothing to do with me considering..."

"Considering?" Lorraine pressed.

"Considering how I raised you. Not to rely on me or anyone really, especially if relying on someone got in the way of a man."

Lorraine let out a hard breath, surprised as hell to hear her mother echoing things she'd thought for damn near her entire life. "Yeah," was all she could say.

Inés did have wrinkles, but they were soft and made her look almost elegant, and they perfectly expressed the pain written on her face. "I know I don't deserve this, but if you're interested, I still would like us to get to know each other as we are now. We can go as slow as you want. I'll respect whatever boundaries you put in place. If you just want to text, we can do that. And maybe if you're open to it, I can come visit you in Sea Breeze one day."

"Sea Port," Lorraine corrected.

"Huh?"

She rolled her eyes. "The town I live in is called Sea Port."

"DeJuan said it was Sea Breeze," Inés said. "I don't know where that is."

Lorraine shrugged. "Don't worry about it, I hardly know where it is either. And maybe..." she said. "We can see how things go and maybe you can come visit later." She stressed the last word, unwilling to get either of their hopes up.

Inés nodded quickly. "Later sounds good."

"Okay," Lorraine said, blinking back the pressure of unexpected tears. "Okay."

WELCOME TO SEA PORT

TWENTY-EIGHT

Jonah

Jonah's return to Sea Port was bittersweet. Willie was happy — in her own way — that he was finally back to handle the last of the library renovation and the other projects around town. They'd finished Willie's basement and moved on to the condos in Knox's old building. He'd left Zeke in charge of the library project, which had moved along at a steady pace, a little faster even than Jonah had expected. And based on Zeke's eagerness to give foreman responsibilities back to Jonah, he guessed Willie was probably behind their accelerated pace and the fear in the other man's eyes. But his crews had done a damn good job without him. The library was so close to done, Jonah could practically see Lorraine at the circulation desk in his mind, a testament to his father's ability to hire good workers.

That was the sweet part; the bitter was that wherever Lorraine was, it wasn't Sea Port. As soon as he towed his car and the trailer hitched to the back into town, his eyes bounced around the familiar streets, looking for her around every corner, but to no avail. He parked his car in front of his father's house and hopped in his dad's truck to ride around town, ostensibly to let everyone know he was back but mostly in search of her. He didn't find her at the lending library or the Sunnyside, not in line at Sully's or hogging the tasting tray in Confections. And when he finally drove by her house, the cottage was closed and dark.

That was the moment he accepted that he'd probably lost her for good and he had no one to blame but himself.

Jonah started searching for a telehealth therapist that wouldn't cost him an arm and a leg, but in the meantime, he soothed his mind the same way he always did. He got to work.

Jonah hadn't brought much back to Sea Port, but there wasn't room for most of it in his father's house so he threw himself into packing up his parents' lives, for real this time, giving a sharp edge to the bitter in his bittersweet return. He didn't rush himself, tackling one thing at a time — his dad's work clothes, family photo albums, small things he could bear, crying in small bouts when he needed to.

And through it all, he kept calling Lorraine because his life in Sea Port didn't feel the same without her.

"I've been back in Sea Port for a few days and I thought I'd give you the rundown on the town gossip. Looks like we missed a lot. First, Mary made a banana pudding that has the senior Zumba class in a tizzy. Most of them thought it was decent, but was it better than Grandma Pearl's? Oh, you don't know who Grandma Pearl is? Don't worry, no one else does either, but everyone remembers Bria's mom's banana pudding, which wasn't *her* banana pudding or her grandmother's, but it was apparently the best banana pudding they've ever had. How many times can I say banana pudding? One more time."

J onah laughed softly to himself, putting his arm behind his head as he relaxed in his twin bed after a hard day polishing hardwood floors. His feet hung off the foot of the bed like always and he was surprised at how comfortable he felt being home. He didn't know where he'd put his king-sized bed yet, but he'd figure it out eventually. His messages to Lorraine were more important.

"Mary's not liking the mixed reviews, so she's currently investigating Grandma Pearl. She's trying to get Bria's mom to give up the recipe. I don't see it for her, but I commend her for trying at least.

Planning for the fall apple festival just started. I say festival, but you know, scale down for Sea Port. It's fun, but I once drank so much damn apple cider that I threw up, so it's not my

favorite event. You might like it though, I think. Are you..."

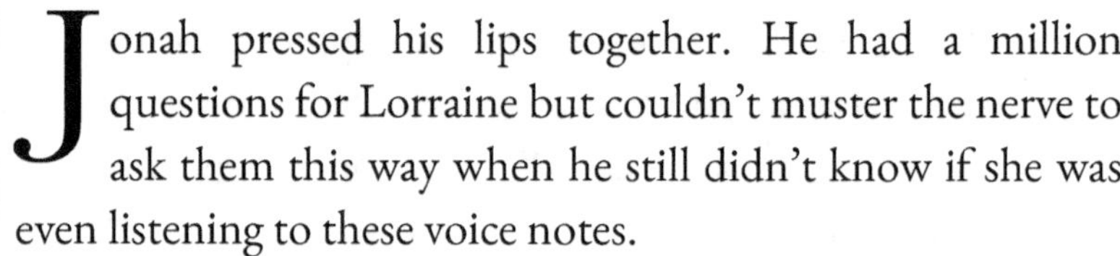

Jonah pressed his lips together. He had a million questions for Lorraine but couldn't muster the nerve to ask them this way when he still didn't know if she was even listening to these voice notes.

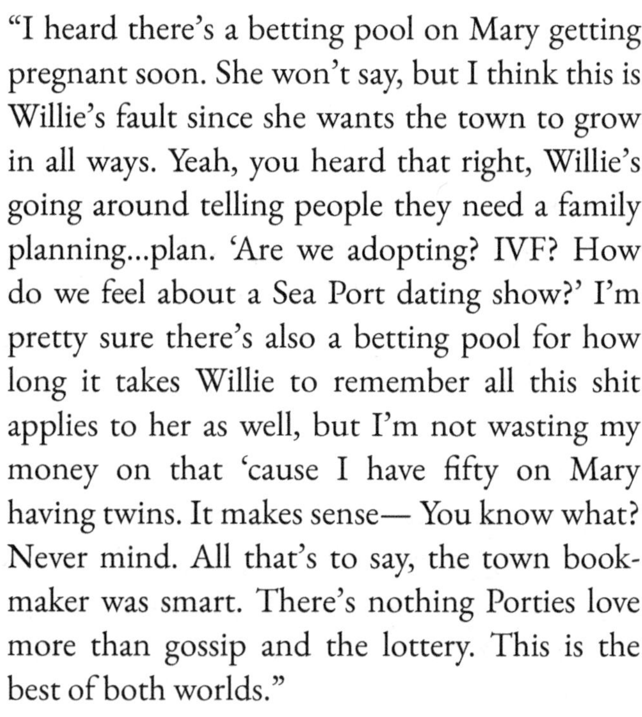

"I heard there's a betting pool on Mary getting pregnant soon. She won't say, but I think this is Willie's fault since she wants the town to grow in all ways. Yeah, you heard that right, Willie's going around telling people they need a family planning...plan. 'Are we adopting? IVF? How do we feel about a Sea Port dating show?' I'm pretty sure there's also a betting pool for how long it takes Willie to remember all this shit applies to her as well, but I'm not wasting my money on that 'cause I have fifty on Mary having twins. It makes sense— You know what? Never mind. All that's to say, the town bookmaker was smart. There's nothing Porties love more than gossip and the lottery. This is the best of both worlds."

Jonah stopped here for a few seconds, racking his brain for more gossip, but he came up short because there was only one thing he really wanted to say, so he did.

"I miss you," he breathed softly before hanging up. He stared at the ceiling of his childhood bedroom for a few more seconds before climbing to his feet and starting his day.

"Well, damn, this looks better than I thought it would," Knox called as he stepped into the main circulation area.

Jonah was squatting behind the circulation desk, testing the outlets one last time. Their electrician would be back in a couple weeks to finish the job and Jonah wanted to make sure he checked everything beforehand. The library renovation wasn't entirely complete, but the project was quickly winding down. There was paint to touch up, squeaky hinges to oil, and other small details, which was why Knox was here again, preparing for his final inspection.

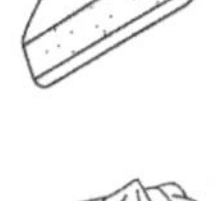

"I'm gonna take that as a compliment," Jonah said.

Knox laughed softly. "I didn't know you were back there."

"You wanna take what you said back?" Jonah asked.

"Not particularly," Knox shrugged. "It's beautiful, though. I bet the Mayor's happy."

Jonah rolled his eyes and walked around the counter. "Who can tell? She was here this morning, making sure the

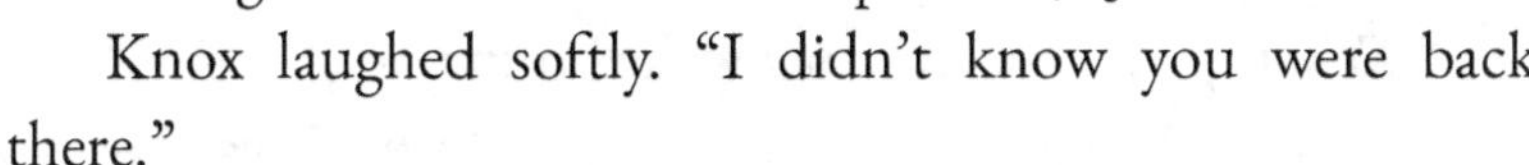

building will be presentable for the welcome reception tonight."

"Will it?" Knox asked.

"Well, that's up to you," Jonah offered with a smile.

Knox beamed at him. "I bet your crew's happy as hell that you're back to take the brunt of her pressure."

"You have no idea."

Knox sighed. "I wish someone would take the pressure off me. You know she wants to put us on the website?"

"What do you mean?"

Knox crossed his arms. "She wants to get a photographer from the big city to take professional photographs of me, Mary, and Santos. Something about hitting up the single, over-thirty crowd as a target demographic."

Jonah was trying to hold in a laugh, but he was failing fast.

"Where the hell'd she get that idea from?" Knox asked, shaking his head in confusion.

"No idea," Jonah laughed, but he could guess. "So, you gonna do it?"

Knox shrugged and dropped his arms. "Don't think I have a choice if Mary and Santos say yes, but we're talking about it."

"Well, if you want to know what I think—"

"I don't," Knox said, holding his hand up. "I want to do my job and go home without this whole town in my business."

"Good luck with that," Jonah chuckled.

"Yeah," Knox sighed. "In lieu of that, I want to be free of Willie breathing down my back about this renovation. So, I guess I'm happy you're back too."

"My crew knows what they're doing," Jonah said testily.

"That's what I told her. I also told her I don't know how to do half this shit, I'm just here to make sure this place won't fall apart the first time it rains. Not that she listens to me. But now that you're back," he said, a serene smile on his face, "she can hound you about all that." 

"Thanks," Jonah mumbled.

"No, thank you," he laughed, offering Jonah his hand. 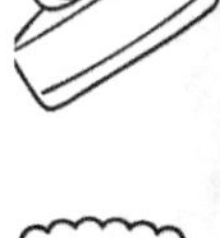 "Welcome back, by the way."

"Thanks," Jonah said again as they shook hands quickly.

"So you...back for good or...?"

"Is that Willie asking?" Jonah asked. 

"No, Mary. She's also nosy, but I love her, so it's fine."

Jonah laughed. "Yeah, I am."

"Good, we missed you and—" Knox pressed his lips shut  and looked away. "This was a big project. What are y'all up to next?"

Jonah's gut clenched. He knew what Knox was about to  say, and the silence affected him almost as much as if he'd just said her name. He wanted to ask if Mary had heard from her, but he couldn't bring himself to do that, so he followed  Knox's lead. "We're doing the condos in your old building now," Jonah said. "That'll keep us occupied for a minute while Willie works on a grant to expand the clinic into a  hospital."

"Ah, I forgot about that," Knox said, rubbing at his eyes tiredly. "Me and Santos have been working on part of that  grant for a couple weeks. If I never have to write another statement of purpose again... Never mind, I will."

Jonah laughed. "Well, she's already got me working on plans for the hospital. I'd complain, but I liked being an architect in Atlanta. I thought I'd have to give that up if I moved back here, but I guess I was wrong about that too. But actually, before we really get started on the condos, most of this crew will be working on one of my projects for a couple months."

"That right?"

Jonah nodded, avoiding Knox's eyes as he answered. "I'm, uh...gonna renovate my dad's place. Top to bottom."

"That makes sense. You gotta have somewhere to live."

Jonah shook his head. "I'm not...gonna live there, actually. I don't— I love Sea Port and I love that house, but I don't think I can handle living there. Not without my dad."

Knox was kind enough to let the silence settle between them before he spoke. "That makes sense too. So where are you gonna stay?"

Jonah shrugged. "Not sure yet, but I'll figure it out."

Knox's eyebrows lifted in excitement. "The cottage next to us is for sale as-is. Needs a lot of work too, if you're looking to keep your crew busy."

Jonah frowned. "It is?"

Knox smiled. "It is. Think about it." He sighed and then looked at his watch. "Lord, lemme get out of here. City Council is having a meeting right before the party tonight. About what? Don't know, don't care, but I need to go home and change. See you back here tonight?"

Jonah nodded. "Yeah. Yeah, I just need to check a few more outlets and head home to change myself."

"Alright. See ya."

"Good luck with the Council," Jonah called at Knox's back.

Knox groaned and waved a hand over his head as he walked from the building.

When he was alone in the circulation area again, he looked around the wide-open room before tipping his head back. His gaze moved up to the glass skylight. It was exactly as he'd designed it, exactly as his father had wanted. He'd taken over this project in tribute to the man who'd raised him, but when he looked up to the sky or around at the empty bookshelves Lorraine had picked out and the paint she'd special ordered, all he could see was her.

WELCOME TO SEA PORT

TWENTY-NINE

Lorraine

Lorraine drove the speed limit until she was close to Sea Port. Somehow, she'd managed to keep her anxiety in check on the flight from Phoenix to Atlanta and then to the small regional airport on a rickety plane that made her blood pressure spike. She picked up her car from the airport's long-term lot and drove toward Sea Port. She set her GPS toward the coordinates for town but was surprised at how much of the route she remembered. As if she was coming home. She drove fifteen miles above the speed limit for the last twenty miles because there wasn't nothing out here but farmland and asphalt.

She made it to Main Street at dusk. There was no welcome crew waiting for her this time because the whole town was at the library's soft opening. She checked her watch knowing she'd be late, but she needed to pee and take a hot shower something fierce. Besides, most things in Sea Port started late anyway, so she had time to freshen up before she saw Jonah for the first time in nearly a month. Lorraine

didn't want to be in a worn pair of leggings and an oversized t-shirt with her braids pulled into a messy bun the first time they came face-to-face again.

"You have arrived home," her GPS announced as she pulled along the curb in front of her cottage.

She was always going to come back to Sea Port — she didn't have the money to break her employment contract even if she wanted to — but the warm safety she felt as she let herself into her cottage was when she really decided to stay, not just until her contract was over but longer, maybe indefinitely, maybe forever. Even if Jonah had left again. Even if his feelings had changed.

For the first time in Lorraine's life, she thought she was ready to put down a root or two.

JONAH

Jonah slipped out the library's back door during Willie's speech. It wasn't that he didn't want to hear what she had to say, it was just that he'd been hearing a version of this speech ever since he took over the project after his dad's death. Besides, he needed some fresh air and quiet to collect his feelings.

He'd been so sure Lorraine would be here.

He was normally tactfully late to most events, but he showed up early for this one, looking for Lorraine in the crowd as people filtered in. He'd mapped out the library garden in his plans, but his crew had handled the renovations without him and he closed his eyes, smelling the fresh flowers, wishing he'd shown Lorraine the plans before he left.

"This is beautiful," Lorraine gasped.

Jonah wrenched his eyes open and turned toward the sound of her voice. Lorraine stood at the mouth of a paved path, the glow from the library's warm lights washing over her. She was wearing the same red dress she'd worn to that first dinner at Mary's — same shoes, same deep red lipstick — but she looked different. Her deep brown skin was a little darker and richer, shining with a hint of gold shimmer on her bare skin. She was as beautiful as the last time he saw her, but she looked happy in a way he'd never known before.

Seeing Lorraine for the first time in so long made him smile in a way he hadn't since their last morning together. "Lorraine?"

"Jonah?" she said seriously, even as her mouth lifted into a soft smile.

"What are you doing here?'

She ran her pink tongue over her lips and took a slow step forward. "Well, it'd probably set a bad example if the librarian missed the library opening."

"Welcome reception," Jonah corrected.

She rolled her eyes and smiled. "Same thing. What are you doing out here?"

"Willie's giving a speech."

"Even more reason to be inside," she said.

"I disagree. When'd you get back?"

She lifted her arm to glance at a slender gold watch

wrapped around her delicate wrist. "One hour and twenty-two minutes ago."

The wind shifted and Jonah caught a whiff of her perfume in the air. He licked his lips. "You stopped by the cottage?"

"I needed to change. I looked a mess."

"I doubt that," he said, looking her up and down. He loved the way she smiled when he complimented her. All he could do was hope he'd have time to do that again and again and again. "Did you get—"

"Your messages?" she asked, already nodding.

"But you didn't respond to them? Or pick up?"

She was close enough to reach out and touch now. "No," she admitted. "But I listened to them all. A few times, actually." She kept walking toward him. "I loved hearing your voice on demand."

He grabbed her around the waist and pulled her into him. She yelped out a laugh but wrapped her arms around his shoulders. "Did you?"

She nodded. They were close enough for her perfume to fill his nostrils. It was a cool fall evening, but Lorraine's perfume made Jonah think of spring.

"You came back," he whispered.

"I did," she sighed.

"Because of...me?" he asked, as nervous to ask the question as he was to hear her answer.

She licked her lips.

"Because I came back for you," he added quickly, just in case it might change her mind.

"Is that right?" she asked in a smug tone.

He nodded gently, brushing the tip of his nose against

hers. "I came back for a lot of reasons," he said, wanting to be totally honest. "But you were always at the top of the list."

Lorraine's fingers shook as she covered his warm cheeks. "I'm glad we're on the same page."

Jonah had been thinking about kissing Lorraine every day they'd been apart, and when her tongue slid into his mouth, he had a visceral response, groaning into her mouth like a starved man. She kissed him back just as desperately, moaning onto his tongue.

He'd had dreams of pushing her against one of the stacks and fucking her right in the middle of the brand-new library he'd built for her, but since that room was full of people, the new garden would have to do.

She whined softly when he pulled away. "Not here," Jonah said.

The fire in her eyes made his dick jump in his pants. He bent forward and brushed his lips against hers quickly while his right hand slid from her waist to her ass. Her cheek was soft and hard and she ground her front against his dick.

"Lemme show you the garden," he said, grabbing her hand and pulling her into the brushes.

"I saw. On the walk here. I thought this was going to be just a patch of grass," she laughed.

"It probably should be. This whole area is one of the *worst* plots of land in town."

She frowned as her eyes scanned around them. There was a paved area close to the library that would have a nice little courtyard for sitting in a few months and a little flower garden with more seating just ahead of them. Jonah led Lorraine through a small leafy arch into the little maze he'd

planned from flowering shrubs and twisting vines grown over wooden fences. He'd meant to bring her here at some point and tonight was as good a time as any.

"Why would you build a garden on bad land?" she asked.

Jonah smiled. "When the Firsts settled what's now Sea Port, all this was bad land. But this plot used to be owned by Old Man Keith's great-great-grandfather. He donated it to the city for a garden to honor his late wife."

"Okay?"

"Apparently, his wife was barren and he was a huge fucking dick." Lorraine's jaw dropped, and Jonah squeezed her hand. "Yeah. Fucked up."

"Supremely fucked up. Who does that?"

"Like I said, some old rich white dude who also knocked up his maid like two years before he died. He was seventy, she was twenty-five."

"Ew," Lorraine shrieked, looking around in horror.

"Don't worry, we pulled that old garden up. *I* pulled it up." He stressed that word as he turned toward her. "But my mother loved flowers and every time we passed this little patch of sad soil, my dad would tell me how she'd wanted to make this place bloom. She just never got the chance, and neither did he."

"Oh," Lorraine breathed.

"Yeah," he whispered. Jonah led her into a bend in the maze. This section was full of gardenias and the scent lingered in the air. He looked around with a smile on his face. "This probably ain't what she woulda planted or how my dad mighta designed it, but I think they'd like it nonetheless."

"Jonah."

It had been too long since he heard her whisper his name like that. He turned and pulled her back into his arms, wrapping one arm around her waist while the other moved to her thigh. He fisted the hem of her dress the same way he had  that night on her front porch. She gasped out a smile and inched her feet apart, making way for his hand between her thighs.

"Did you leave because of me?" he asked gently, his  fingers brushing her inner thigh.

She gulped. "Yes. And no. You asked me months ago how I ended up here and I didn't tell you the full truth." 

"It's okay," he whispered, but she shook her head.

"It wasn't, but we didn't know each other yet. We do now, I think." 

"We do," he sighed, brushing his fingers over her mound. "No panties. Again."

"Always," she sighed as he touched her opening. "I have  a habit of running away when life gets hard," she said, swallowing a moan. He smoothed his fingers down her wet lips. "I was hurt you left without telling me. And then I was  surprised I was hurt, so I left."

His fingers stilled. "I'm sorry. I didn't mean to hurt you. I had my own shit to deal with." 

Lorraine grabbed his face again. "I figured. Maybe we should've talked about some of that instead of fucking all the time." 

"We probably coulda done both. No need to choose just one," he said, laughing nervously.

She nodded. "Smart."

"Did you handle your baggage?" he asked just as his fingers found her clit.

"Fuck," she breathed. "I think I started. And I think I want to tell you about it."

"I want to hear it," he said quickly. "And I want to tell you about my baggage. Well, the things I haven't already told your voicemail."

Her left hand moved down his chest. "Good, 'cause I want to hear it, but not *right* now," she clarified.

Jonah's body was hot like it was the middle of summer. He bent forward to kiss her while his fingers went in search of her opening. "But we will," he promised in a heartfelt whisper against her lips.

"We will," she moaned as he pushed his fingers deep inside her. "We've got all the time in the world."

"God, I was hoping you'd say that," Jonah moaned as he slipped his tongue between her lips and her hand caressed the outline of his dick.

WELCOME TO SEA PORT

Epilogue

LORRAINE

FOUR MONTHS LATER

Lorraine had never lived with a man, not even DeJuan, but living with Jonah was better than she'd expected.

Sure, he left his work boots and tool belt in a jumbled mess by the front door and his toolbox took up too much space in the laundry room, but he gave her more than half their closet and he always put the toilet seat down. The biggest issue about living together was that her cottage wasn't really built for two, so they bought the house next to Mary, Knox, and Santos, and things went from better than she expected to downright amazing.

Their house needed all new electrical, a new roof, and some other work Lorraine didn't understand, but she was dating a contractor and he did it all with a skeleton crew, and now they had a house designed specifically for them. Each room had a colorful accent wall and as many bookshelves as

Jonah could build. Finally, her favorite books had a permanent home. They covered the walls in art and framed pictures of Jonah's family. He built a shed out back, and every morning, Lorraine got to wake up naked in bed with Jonah's big, rough hands caressing her skin, his hard dick pressing against the small of her back. This last move was the easiest of Lorraine's life.

They even had friendly neighbors who didn't ask questions when she and Jonah got naked in their backyard and appreciated that they looked the other way when they got naked in theirs. Lorraine had been so happy in the last four months that even DeJuan had stopped asking when she was leaving Sea Port. She wasn't, case closed, but they had a spare room with his name on it. She'd even started negotiating her new contract as the head librarian, which made Willie happier than everyone else involved.

"What time you gotta get to work?" Jonah asked. His voice was thick with sleep and lust.

Lorraine lifted her right leg immediately. "Who cares?" she whispered.

His deep rumble of laughter made her pussy shiver. "I don't wanna make you late," he groaned, the soft head of his dick already bumping at her opening.

"I have an IUD. We're good."

His laughter came out in a choked breath as he pushed inside her.

He tried to go slow, but Lorraine wasn't interested in that. She bore down on him, clenching her muscles, hungrily taking his full length.

"You think you're funny," he whispered, pulling back slowly and then pushing in again.

"I'm hilarious," she moaned.

"And beautiful," he said, quickly losing track of their banter.

She loved knowing he was so weak for her.

She loved feeling safe enough to be weak for him in return even more.

DeJuan thought they were moving too fast, and truth be told, Lorraine thought the same. But she'd never felt safer than when she was in Jonah's arms and never been happier than she was in Sea Port.

Maybe there was something in the water. Maybe Mary put something in her teacakes. Or maybe, after all her time wandering, Lorraine had finally found the place where she belonged.

Yeah, she thought, as the sound of their skin slapping together filled the room, it was the latter. Sea Port was where she was always meant to be.

And Jonah was the love she deserved.

Also by Katrina Jackson

Welcome to Sea Port

From Scratch

Inheritance

Small Town Secrets

Her Christmas Cookie

The Spies Who Loved Her

Pink Slip

Private Eye

Bang & Burn

New Year, New We

His Only Valentine

Bright Lights

Honey Pot

Erotic Accommodations

Room for Three?

Neighborly

Love At Last

Every New Year

One More Valentine

<u>Heist Holidays</u>

Grand Theft N.Y.E.

<u>The Family</u>

Beautiful and Dirty

The Hitman

The Enforcer

Dolci

The Don

Dolore

<u>Bay Area Blues</u>

Layover

Back in the Day

<u>Curriculum Vitae</u>

Office Hours

Sabbatical

<u>Mosley Coven</u>

The Night Gate (website exclusive)

A Flicker to a Flame

Invocation

-

<u>Standalone stories</u>

Encore

The Tenant

Sex Toy Soldier

Looking

And When You Leave Me

Small Mercies